JULIA QUINN

The Sum of All Kisses

piatkus

PIATKUS

First published in the US in 2013 by Avon Books,
An imprint of HarperCollins, New York
First published in Great Britain in 2013 by Piatkus
by arrangement with Avon

A CIP catalogue record for this book
is available from the British Library.

ISBN 978-0-7499-5634-9

Printed and bound in Great Britain by
Clays Ltd, Elcograf S.p.A.

Papers used by Piatkus are from well-managed forests
and other responsible sources.

MIX
Paper from
responsible sources
FSC
www.fsc.org   FSC® C104740

Piatkus
An imprint of
Little, Brown Book Group
100 Victoria Embankment
London EC4Y 0DY

An Hachette UK Company
www.hachette.co.uk

www.piatkus.co.uk

This one is for me.

And also for Paul.

But mostly for me.

Prologue

London
Quite late at night
Spring 1821

"PIQUET FAVORS THOSE with a vivid memory," the Earl of Chatteris said, to no one in particular.

Lord Hugh Prentice didn't hear him; he was too far away, over at the table by the window, and more pertinently, he was somewhat drunk. But had Hugh heard Chatteris's remark—and had he not been intoxicated—he would have thought:

That is why I play piquet.

He would not have said it out loud. Hugh had never been the sort to speak merely for the sake of making his voice heard. But he would have thought it. And his expression would have changed. One corner of his lips would have twitched, and his right eyebrow might have arched—just the barest hint of a movement, but still, enough for a careful observer to think him smug.

Although the truth was, London society was quite devoid of careful observers.

Except for Hugh.

Hugh Prentice noticed everything. And he remembered it all, too. He could, if he wished, recite all of *Romeo and Juliet*, word for word. *Hamlet*, too. *Julius Caesar* he could not do, but that was only because he had never taken the time to read it.

It was a rare enough talent that Hugh had been disciplined for cheating six times during his first two months at Eton. He soon realized that his life was made infinitely easier if he purposefully flubbed a question or two on his examinations. It wasn't that he minded the accusations of cheating so much—*he* knew he hadn't cheated, and he didn't much care what anyone else thought of it— but it was such a bother, getting hauled up before his teachers and being forced to stand there and regurgitate information until they were satisfied of his innocence.

Where his memory really came in handy, though, was cards. As the younger son of the Marquess of Ramsgate, Hugh knew that he was due to inherit precisely nothing. Younger sons were expected to join the army, the clergy, or the ranks of fortune hunters. As Hugh lacked the temperament for any of these pursuits, he would have to find some other means of support. And gambling was so very easy when one had the ability to recall every card played—in order—for an entire evening.

What had become difficult was finding gentlemen willing to play—Hugh's remarkable skill at piquet had become the stuff of legend—but if young men were drunk enough, they always tried their hand. Everyone wanted to be the man to beat Hugh Prentice at cards.

The problem was that this evening, Hugh had also drunk "enough." It wasn't a common occurrence; he'd never been comfortable with the loss of control that flowed from a bottle of wine. But he'd been out and about with friends, and they'd gone to a somewhat salty tavern, where the pints were large, the crowd was loud, and the women uncommonly buxom.

By the time they'd reached their club and pulled out a deck of cards, Daniel Smythe-Smith, who had recently come into his title as the Earl of Winstead, was well in his cups. He was offering vivid descriptions of the maid he'd just tupped, Charles Dunwoody was vowing to go back to the tavern to improve upon Daniel's performance, and even Marcus Holroyd—the young Earl of Chatteris, who had always been a bit more serious than the others—was laughing so hard he nearly tipped over his chair.

Hugh had preferred his barmaid to Daniel's—a little less fleshy; a little more lithe—but he just grinned when pressed for the details. He remembered every inch of her, of course, but he never kissed and told.

"Going to beat you this time, Prentice!" Daniel

boasted. He leaned sloppily against the table, his signature grin nearly blinding the rest of them. He'd always been the charmer of the group.

"For the love of God, Daniel," Marcus groaned, "not again."

"No, no, I can do it." Daniel wagged a finger in the air, laughing when the motion made him lose his balance. "I can do it this time."

"He can!" Charles Dunwoody exclaimed. "I know he can!"

No one bothered to comment. Even sober, Charles Dunwoody seemed to know a lot of things that were untrue.

"No, no, I can," Daniel insisted, "because you"—he wagged a finger in Hugh's general direction—"have had a lot to drink."

"Not as much as you have," Marcus pointed out, but he hiccupped when he said it.

"I counted," Daniel said triumphantly. "He had more."

"I had the most," Dunwoody boasted.

"Then you *definitely* should play," Daniel said.

A game was struck, and wine was served, and everyone was having a grand time until—

Daniel won.

Hugh blinked, staring at the cards on the table.

"I won," Daniel said, with not inconsiderable awe. "Will you look at that?"

Hugh ran through the deck in his mind, ignoring the fact that some of the cards were uncharacteristically fuzzy.

"I won," Daniel said again, this time to Marcus, his longtime closest friend.

"No," Hugh said, mostly to himself. It wasn't possible. It just wasn't possible. He never lost at cards. At night, when he was trying to sleep, when he was trying not to listen, his mind could bring up every card he'd played that day. That week, even.

"I'm not even sure how I did it," Daniel said. "It was the king, but then it was the seven, and I . . ."

"It was the ace," Hugh snapped, unable to listen to another moment of his idiocy.

"Hmmm." Daniel blinked. "Maybe it was."

"God," Hugh cried out. "Somebody shut him up." He needed quiet. He needed to focus and remember the cards. If he could just do that, this would all go away. It was like the time he'd come home late with Freddie, and their father had already been waiting with—

No no no. That was something different. This was cards. Piquet. He never lost. It was the one thing, the only thing, he could count on.

Dunwoody scratched his head and looked at the cards, counting out loud. "I think he—"

"Winstead, you bloody cheat!" Hugh yelled, the words pouring unbidden from his throat. He didn't know where they'd come from, or what had prompted him to say them, but once out, they filled the air, sizzling violently above the table.

Hugh began to shake.

"No," Daniel said. Just that. Just *no*, with an unsteady hand and a confused expression. Baffled, like—

But Hugh wouldn't think of that. He couldn't think of that, so instead he lurched to his feet,

upending the table as he clung to the one thing
he knew was true, which was that he *never* lost at
cards.

"I didn't cheat," Daniel said, blinking rapidly.
He turned to Marcus. "I don't cheat."

But he had to have cheated. Hugh flipped
through the cards in his mind again, ignoring the
fact that the jack of clubs was wielding an actual
club, and he was chasing after the ten, which was
drinking wine out of a glass much like the one
currently shattered at his feet. . . .

Hugh started yelling. He had no idea what he
was saying, just that Daniel had cheated, and
the queen of hearts had stumbled, and 42 times
306 was always 12,852, not that he had any idea
what that had to do with anything, but there
was wine all over the floor now, and the cards
were everywhere, and Daniel was just standing there, shaking his head, saying, "What is he
talking about?"

"There is no way you could have had the ace,"
Hugh hissed. The ace had been after the jack,
which had been next to the ten . . .

"But I did," Daniel said with a shrug. And a
burp.

"You couldn't," Hugh shot back, stumbling for
balance. "I know every card in the deck."

Daniel looked down at the cards. Hugh did,
too, at the queen of diamonds, madeira dripping
from her neck like blood.

"Remarkable," Daniel murmured. He looked
straight at Hugh. "I won. Fancy that."

Was he mocking him? Was Daniel Smythe-

Smith, the oh-so venerable Earl of Winstead, *mocking* him?

"I will have satisfaction," Hugh growled.

Daniel's head snapped up in surprise. "What?"

"Name your seconds."

"Are you challenging me to a duel?" Daniel turned incredulously to Marcus. "I think he's challenging me to a duel."

"Daniel, shut up." Marcus groaned—Marcus, who suddenly looked far more sober than the rest of them.

But Daniel waved him off, then said, "Hugh, don't be an ass."

Hugh didn't think. He lunged. Daniel jumped to the side, but not fast enough, and both men went down. One of the table legs jammed into Hugh's hip, but he barely felt it. He pounded Daniel—one, two, three, four—until two sets of hands pulled him back, up and off, barely restraining him as he spat, "You're a bloody cheat."

Because he knew this. And Winstead had *mocked* him.

"You're an idiot," Daniel replied, shaking blood from his face.

"I will have my satisfaction."

"Oh, no, you won't," Daniel hissed. "*I* will have satisfaction."

"The Patch of Green?" Hugh said coolly.

"At dawn."

There was a hushed silence as everyone waited for either man to come to his senses.

But they didn't. Of course they didn't.

Hugh smiled. He couldn't imagine why he had

anything to smile about, but he felt it slinking along his face nonetheless. And when he looked at Daniel Smythe-Smith, he saw another man's face.

"So be it."

"You don't have to do this," Charles Dunwoody said, grimacing as he finished his inspection of Hugh's gun.

Hugh didn't bother to reply. His head hurt too much.

"I mean, I believe you that he was cheating. He'd have to be, because, well, it's you, and you always win. Don't know how you manage it, but you do."

Hugh barely moved his head, but his eyes traveled a slow arc toward Dunwoody's face. Was Dunwoody accusing *him* of cheating now?

"I think it's the maths," Dunwoody went on, oblivious to Hugh's sardonic expression. "You always were freakishly good at it . . ."

Pleasant. Always so very pleasant to be called a freak.

" . . . and I *know* you never cheated at maths. Heaven knows we quizzed you enough at school." Dunwoody looked up with a frown. "How *do* you do that?"

Hugh gave him a flat stare. "You're asking me *now*?"

"Oh. No. No, of course not." Dunwoody cleared his throat and backed up a step. Marcus Holroyd was heading their way, presumably in an attempt to put a halt to the duel. Hugh watched as Marcus's boots ate up the damp grass. His left stride was longer than his right, although not by much. It would probably take him fifteen more steps to reach them, sixteen if he was feeling ornery and wanted to butt up into their space.

But this was Marcus. He'd stop at fifteen.

Marcus and Dunwoody exchanged guns for inspection. Hugh stood by next to the surgeon, who was just *full* of useful information.

"Right here," the surgeon said, smacking his upper thigh. "I've seen it happen. Femoral artery. You bleed like a pig."

Hugh said nothing. He wasn't going to actually *shoot* Daniel. He'd had a few hours to calm down, and while he was still livid, he saw no reason to try to kill him.

"But if you just want something really painful," the surgeon continued, "you can't go wrong with the hand or foot. The bones are easy to break, and there are a hell of a lot of nerves. Plus you won't kill him. Too far from anything important."

Hugh was very good at ignoring people, but even he couldn't hold out against this. "The hand's not important?"

The surgeon rolled his tongue over his teeth, then made a sucking noise, presumably to dislodge some rancid piece of food. He shrugged. "It's not the heart."

He had a point, which needled. Hugh hated when annoying people had valid points. Still, if the surgeon had any sense, he'd shut the bloody hell up.

"Just don't go for the head," the surgeon said with a shudder. "No one wants that, and I'm not just talking about the poor sod who's taken the bullet. There'll be brains everywhere, faces shot open. Shoots the funeral straight to hell."

"This is your choice of surgeon?" Marcus asked.

Hugh jerked his head toward Dunwoody. "He found him."

"I'm a barber," the surgeon said defensively.

Marcus shook his head and walked back to Daniel.

"Gentlemen at your ready!"

Hugh wasn't sure who had called out the order. Someone who'd found out about the duel and wanted bragging rights, most probably. There weren't many sentences in London more coveted than "I saw it myself."

"Take aim!"

Hugh lifted his arm and aimed. Three inches to the right of Daniel's shoulder.

"One!"

Good God, he'd forgot about the counting.

"Two!"

His chest clenched. The counting. The yelling. It was the one time that numbers became the enemy. His father's voice, hoarse in his triumph, and Hugh, trying not to hear . . .

"Three!"

Hugh flinched.

And he pulled the trigger.

"Yaaaaooooowwwwww!"

Hugh looked at Daniel in surprise.

"Bloody hell, you shot me!" Daniel yelled. He clutched his shoulder, his rumpled white shirt already oozing with red.

"What?" Hugh said to himself. "No." He'd aimed to the side. Not far to the side, but he was a good shot, an excellent shot.

"Oh, Christ," the surgeon muttered, and he took off along the side of the field at a run.

"You shot him," Dunwoody gasped. "Why'd you do that?"

Hugh had no words. Daniel was hurt, perhaps even mortally, and he'd done it. *He* had done it. No one had forced him. And even now, as Daniel raised his bloody arm—his *literally* bloody arm—

Hugh screamed as he felt his leg tearing into pieces.

Why had he thought he'd hear the shot before he felt it? He knew how it worked. If Sir Isaac Newton was correct, sound traveled at a rate of 979 feet per second. Hugh was standing about twenty yards from Daniel, which meant that the bullet would have had to travel . . .

He thought. And thought.

He couldn't work out the answer.

"Hugh! Hugh!" came Dunwoody's frantic voice. "Hugh, are you all right?"

Hugh looked up at Charles Dunwoody's blurry face. If he was looking up, then he must be on the ground. He blinked, trying to set his world back into focus. Was he still drunk? He'd had a staggering amount of alcohol the night before, both before and after the altercation with Daniel.

No, he wasn't drunk. At least not very much. He had been shot. Or at least, he thought he'd been shot. It had felt as if he'd taken a bullet, but it didn't really hurt so much any longer. Still, it would explain why he was lying on the ground.

He swallowed, trying to breathe. Why was it so hard to breathe? Hadn't he been shot in the leg? *If* he'd been shot. He still wasn't sure that was what had happened.

"Oh, dear God," came a new voice. Marcus Holroyd, breathing hard. His face was ashen.

"Put pressure on it!" the surgeon barked. "And watch out for that bone."

Hugh tried to speak.

"A tourniquet," someone said. "Should we tie a tourniquet?"

"Bring me my bag!" the surgeon yelled.

Hugh tried to speak again.

"Don't spend your energy," Marcus said, taking his hand.

"But don't fall asleep!" Dunwoody added frantically. "Keep your eyes open."

"The thigh," Hugh croaked.

"What?"

"Tell the surgeon . . ." Hugh paused, gasping for breath. "The thigh. Bleeding like a pig."

"What is he talking about?" Marcus asked.

"I— I—" Dunwoody was trying to say something, but it kept catching in his throat.

"What?" Marcus demanded.

Hugh looked over at Dunwoody. He looked ill.

"I believe he's trying to make a joke," Dunwoody said.

"God," Marcus swore harshly, turning back to Hugh with an expression that Hugh found difficult to interpret. "You stupid, contrary . . . A joke. You're making a joke."

"Don't cry," Hugh said, because it looked like he might.

"Tie it tighter," someone said, and Hugh felt something yanking on his leg, then squeezing it, hard, and then Marcus was saying, "You'd best stay baaaaaaack . . ."

And that was it.

WHEN HUGH OPENED his eyes, it was dark. And he was in a bed. Had an entire day passed? Or more? The duel had been at dawn. The sky had still been pink.

"Hugh?"

Freddie? What was Freddie doing here? He couldn't remember the last time his brother had stepped foot in their father's house. Hugh wanted to say his name, wanted to tell him how happy he was to see him, but his throat was unbelievably dry.

"Don't try to talk," Freddie said. He leaned forward, his familiar blond head coming into the arc of the candlelight. They'd always looked alike, more than most brothers. Freddie was a little shorter, a little slighter, and a little blonder, but they had the same green eyes set in the same angular face. And the same smile.

When they smiled.

"Let me get you some water," Freddie said. Carefully, he put a spoon to Hugh's lips, dribbling the liquid into his mouth.

"More," Hugh croaked. There had been nothing left to swallow. Every drop had just soaked into his parched tongue.

Freddie gave him a few more spoonfuls, then said, "Let's wait a bit. I don't want to give you too much at once."

Hugh nodded. He didn't know why, but he nodded.

"Does it hurt?"

It did, but Hugh had the strange sensation that it hadn't hurt quite so much until Freddie asked about it.

"It's still there, you know," Freddie said, motioning toward the foot of the bed. "Your leg."

Of course it was still there. It hurt like bloody hell. Where else would it be?

"Sometimes men feel pain even after they lose a limb," Freddie said in a nervous rush. "Phantom pain, it's called. I read about it, I don't know when. Some time ago."

Then it was probably true. Freddie's memory was almost as good as Hugh's, and his tastes had always run toward the biological sciences. When they were children, Freddie had practically lived outside, digging in the dirt, collecting his specimens. Hugh had tagged along after him a few times, but he'd been bored out of his skull.

Hugh had quickly discovered that one's interest in beetles did not increase with the number of beetles located. The same went for frogs.

"Father's downstairs," Freddie said.

Hugh closed his eyes. It was the closest he could manage to a nod.

"I should get him." Said without conviction.

"Don't."

A minute or so went by, and Freddie said,

"Here, have a bit more water. You lost a great deal of blood. It will be why you feel so weak."

Hugh took a few more spoonfuls. It hurt to swallow.

"Your leg is broken, too. The femur. The doctor set it, but he said the bone was splintered." Freddie cleared his throat. "You're going to be stuck here for quite some time, I'm afraid. The femur is the largest bone in the human body. It's going to take several months to heal."

Freddie was lying. Hugh could hear it in his voice. Which meant that it was going to take quite a bit longer than a few months to heal. Or maybe it wouldn't heal at all. Maybe he was crippled.

Wouldn't that be funny.

"What day is it?" Hugh rasped.

"You've been unconscious for three days," Freddie answered, correctly interpreting the question.

"Three days," Hugh echoed. Good Lord.

"I arrived yesterday. Corville notified me."

Hugh nodded. It figured their butler would be the one to let Freddie know his brother had nearly died. "What about Daniel?" Hugh asked.

"Lord Winstead?" Freddie swallowed. "He's gone."

Hugh's eyes flew open.

"No, no, not dead gone," Freddie quickly said. "His shoulder was injured, but he'll be fine. He's just left England is all. Father tried to have him arrested, but you weren't dead yet—"

Yet. Funny.

"—and then, well, I don't know what Father said to him. He came to see you the day after it happened. I wasn't here, but Corville told me Winstead tried to apologize. Father wasn't having . . . well, you know Father." Freddie swallowed and cleared his throat. "I think Lord Winstead went to France."

"He should come back," Hugh said hoarsely. It wasn't Daniel's fault. He hadn't been the one to call for the duel.

"Yes, well, you can take that up with Father," Freddie said uncomfortably. "He's been talking about hunting him down."

"In *France*?"

"I didn't try to reason with him."

"No, of course not." Because who reasoned with a madman?

"They thought you might die," Freddie explained.

"I see." And that was the awful part. Hugh did see.

The Marquess of Ramsgate did not get to choose his heir; primogeniture would force him to give Freddie the title, the lands, the fortune, pretty much anything that wasn't nailed down by entail. But if Lord Ramsgate could have chosen, they all knew he would have chosen Hugh.

Freddie was twenty-seven and had not yet married. Hugh was holding out hope that he might yet do so, but he knew there was no woman in the world who would catch Freddie's eye. He accepted this about his brother. He didn't understand it, but he accepted it. He just wished Freddie would understand that he could still get married and do his duty and take all this bloody pressure off Hugh.

Surely there were plenty of women who would be thrilled to have their husbands out of their beds once the nursery was sufficiently populated.

Hugh's father, however, was so disgusted he'd told Freddie not to bother with a bride. The title might have to reside with Freddie for a few years, but as far as Lord Ramsgate was planning, it ought to end up with Hugh or his children.

Not that he ever seemed to hold Hugh in much affection, either.

Lord Ramsgate was not the only nobleman who saw no reason to care for his children equally. Hugh would be better for Ramsgate, and thus Hugh was better, period.

Because they all knew that the marquess loved Ramsgate, Hugh, and Freddie in precisely that order.

And probably Freddie not at all.

"Would you like laudanum?" Freddie asked abruptly. "The doctor said we could give you some if you woke up."

If. Even less funny than the *yet.*

Hugh gave a nod and allowed his older brother to help him into something approaching a sitting position. "God, that's foul," he said, handing the cup back to Freddie once he'd downed the contents.

Freddie sniffed the dregs. "Alcohol," he confirmed. "The morphine is dissolved in it."

"Just what I need," Hugh muttered. "More alcohol."

"I beg your pardon?"

Hugh just shook his head.

"I'm glad you're awake," Freddie said in a tone that forced Hugh to notice that he had not sat back down after pouring the laudanum. "I'll ask Corville to tell Father. I'd rather not, you know, if I don't have to . . ."

"Of course," Hugh said. The world was a better place when Freddie avoided their father. The world was a better place when Hugh avoided him as well, but someone had to interact with the old bastard on occasion, and they both knew it had to be he. That Freddie had come here, to their old home in St. James's, was a testament of his love for Hugh.

"I will see you tomorrow," Freddie said, pausing at the door.

"You don't have to," Hugh told him.

Freddie swallowed, and he looked away. "Perhaps the next day, then."

Or the next. Hugh wouldn't blame him if he never came back.

FREDDIE MUST HAVE instructed the butler to wait before notifying their father of the change in Hugh's condition, because nearly a full day went by before Lord Ramsgate blustered into the room.

"You're awake," he barked.

It was remarkable how much that sounded like an accusation.

"You bloody stupid idiot," Ramsgate hissed. "Nearly getting yourself killed. And for what? For what?"

"I'm delighted to see you, too, Father," Hugh replied. He was sitting up now, his splinted leg thrust forward like a log. He was quite certain he sounded better than he felt, but with the Marquess of Ramsgate, one must never show weakness.

He'd learned that early on.

His father gave him a disgusted look but otherwise ignored the sarcasm. "You could have died."

"So I understand."

"Do you think this is funny?" the marquess snapped.

"As a matter of fact," Hugh replied, "I do not."

"You *know* what would have happened if you died."

Hugh smiled blandly. "I've pondered it, to be sure, but does anyone really know what happens after we die?"

God, but it was enjoyable to watch his father's face bulge and turn red. Just so long as he didn't start to spit.

"Do you take nothing seriously?" the marquess demanded.

"I take many things seriously, but not this."

Lord Ramsgate sucked in his breath, his entire body shaking with rage. "We both know your brother will never marry."

"Oh, is *that* what this is all about?" Hugh did his best imitation of surprise.

"I will not have Ramsgate pass from this family!"

Hugh followed this outburst with a perfectly timed pause, then said, "Oh come now, Cousin Robert isn't so bad. They even let him back into Oxford. Well, the first time."

"Is that what this is?" the marquess spat. "You're trying to kill yourself just to vex me?"

"I would imagine I could vex you with significantly less effort than that. And with a far more pleasant outcome for myself."

"If you want to be rid of me, you know what you have to do," Lord Ramsgate said.

"Kill you?"

"You damned—"

"If I'd known it would be so easy, I really would have—"

"Just marry some fool girl and give me an heir!" his father roared.

"All things being equal," Hugh said with devastating calm, "I'd rather she not be a fool."

His father shook with fury, and a full minute passed before he was able to speak. "I need to know that Ramsgate will remain in the family."

"I never said I wouldn't marry," Hugh said, although why he felt the need to say even this much he had no idea. "But I'm not going to do so on your schedule. Besides, I'm not your heir."

"Frederick—"

"Might still marry," Hugh cut in, each syllable hard and clipped.

But his father just snorted and headed for the door.

"Oh, Father," Hugh called out before he could leave. "Will you send word to Lord Winstead's family that he may safely return to Britain?"

"Of course not. He can rot in hell for all I care. Or France." The marquess gave a grim chuckle. "It's much the same place, in my opinion."

"There is no reason why he should not be allowed to return," Hugh said with more patience than he would have thought himself capable. "As we have both noted, he did not kill me."

"He shot you."

"I shot him first."

"In the *shoulder*."

Hugh clenched his teeth. Arguing with his father had always been exhausting, and he was far overdue for his laudanum. "It was my fault," he bit out.

"I don't care," the marquess said. "He left on his own two feet. You're a cripple who may not even be able to sire children now."

Hugh felt his eyes grow wide with alarm. He had been shot in the leg. The *leg*.

"Didn't think of that, did you?" his father taunted. "That bullet hit an artery. It's a miracle you didn't bleed to death. The doctor thinks your leg got enough blood to survive, but God only knows about the rest of you." He yanked the door open and tossed his last statement over his shoulder. "Winstead has ruined my life. I can bloody well ruin his."

THE FULL EXTENT of Hugh's injuries would not become known for several months. His femur healed. Somewhat.

His muscle slowly knit back together. What was left of it.

On the bright side, all signs pointed toward his still being able to father a child.

Not that he wanted to. Or perhaps more to the point, not that he'd been presented with an opportunity.

But when his father inquired . . . or, rather, demanded . . . or, rather, yanked off the bedsheets in the presence of some German doctor Hugh would not have wanted to come across in a dark alley . . .

Hugh pulled the covers right back up, feigned mortal embarrassment, and let his father think he'd been irreparably damaged.

And the whole time, throughout the entire excruciating recuperation, Hugh was confined to his father's house, trapped in bed, and forced to endure daily ministrations from a nurse whose special brand of care brought to mind Attila the Hun.

She looked like him, too. Or at least she had a face that Hugh imagined would be at home on Attila. The truth was, the comparison wasn't very complimentary.

To Attila.

But Attila the nurse, however rough and crude she might be, was still preferable to Hugh's father, who came by every day at four in the afternoon, brandy in hand (just one; none for Hugh), with the latest news on his hunt for Daniel Smythe-Smith.

And every day, at four-oh-one in the afternoon, Hugh asked his father to stop.

Just stop.

But of course he didn't. Lord Ramsgate vowed to hunt Daniel until one of them was dead.

Eventually Hugh was well enough to leave Ramsgate House. He didn't have much money— just his gambling winnings from back when he gambled—but he had enough to hire a valet and take a small apartment in The Albany, which was well known as the premier building in London for gentlemen of exceptional birth and unexceptional fortune.

He taught himself to walk again. He needed a cane for any real distance, but he could make it the length of a ballroom on his own two feet.

Not that he visited ballrooms.

He learned to live with pain, the constant ache of a badly set bone, the pulsing throb of a twisted muscle.

And he forced himself to visit his father, to try to reason with him, to tell him to stop hunting Daniel Smythe-Smith. But nothing worked. His father clung to his fury with pinched white fingers. He would never have a grandson now, he fumed, and it was all the fault of the Earl of Winstead.

It did not matter when Hugh pointed out that Freddie was healthy and could still surprise them and get married. Lots of men who would rather have remained unwed took wives. The marquess just spat. He literally spat on the floor and said that even if Freddie took a bride, he would never manage to sire a son. And if he did—if by some miracle he did—it wouldn't be any child worthy of their name.

No, it was Winstead's fault. Hugh was supposed to have provided the Ramsgate heir, and now look at him. He was a useless cripple. Who probably couldn't sire a son, either.

Lord Ramsgate would never forgive Daniel Smythe-Smith, the once dashing and popular Earl of Winstead. Never.

And Hugh, whose one constant in life had been his ability to look at a problem from all angles and sort out the most logical solution, had no idea what to do. More than once he'd thought about getting married himself, but despite the fact that he *seemed* to be in working order, there was always the chance that the bullet had indeed done him some damage. Plus, he thought as he looked down at the ruin of his leg, what woman would have him?

And then one day, something sparked in his memory—a fleeting moment from that conversation with Freddie, right after the duel.

Freddie had said that he hadn't tried to reason with the marquess, and Hugh had said, "Of course not," and then he'd thought, *Because who reasons with a madman?*

He finally knew the answer.

Only another madman.

Chapter One

Fensmore
nr. Chatteris
Cambridgeshire
Autumn 1824

LADY SARAH PLEINSWORTH, veteran of three unsuccessful seasons in London, looked about her soon-to-be cousin's drawing room and announced, "I am plagued by weddings."

Her companions were her younger sisters, Harriet, Elizabeth, and Frances, who—at sixteen, fourteen, and eleven—were not of an age to worry about matrimonial prospects. Still, one might think they would offer a bit of sympathy.

One might, if one was not familiar with the Pleinsworth girls.

"You're being melodramatic," Harriet replied,

sparing Sarah a fleeting glance before dipping her pen in ink and resuming her scribbles at the writing desk.

Sarah turned slowly in her direction. "You're writing a play about Henry VIII and a unicorn and you're calling *me* melodramatic?"

"It's a satire," Harriet replied.

"What's a satire?" Frances cut in. "Is it the same as a satyr?"

Elizabeth's eyes widened with wicked delight. "Yes!" she exclaimed.

"Elizabeth!" Harriet scolded.

Frances narrowed her eyes at Elizabeth. "It's not, is it?"

"It ought to be," Elizabeth retorted, "given that you've made her put a bloody unicorn in the story."

"Elizabeth!" Sarah didn't really care that her sister had cursed, but as the oldest in the family, she knew she ought to care. Or at the very least, make a pretense of caring.

"I wasn't cursing," Elizabeth protested. "It was wishful thinking."

This was met with confused silence.

"If the unicorn is bleeding," Elizabeth explained, "then the play has at least a chance of being interesting."

Frances gasped. "Oh, Harriet! You're not going to injure the unicorn, are you?"

Harriet slid a hand over her writing. "Well, not very much."

Frances's gasp whooshed into a choke of terror. "Harriet!"

"Is it even possible to *have* a plague of weddings?" Harriet said loudly, turning back to Sarah. "And if so, would two qualify?"

"They would," Sarah replied darkly, "*if* they were occurring just one week apart, *and* if one happened to be related to one of the brides and one of the grooms, and *especially* if one was forced to be the maid of honor at a wedding in which—"

"You only have to be maid of honor once," Elizabeth cut in.

"Once is enough," Sarah muttered. No one should have to walk down a church aisle with a bouquet of flowers unless she was the bride, already had been the bride, or was too young to be the bride. Otherwise, it was just cruel.

"I think it's divine that Honoria asked you to be the maid of honor," Frances gushed. "It's so romantic. Maybe you can write a scene like this in your play, Harriet."

"That's a good idea," Harriet replied. "I could introduce a new character. I'll have her look just like Sarah."

Sarah didn't even bother to turn in her direction. "Please don't."

"No, it will be great fun," Harriet insisted. "A special little tidbit just for the three of us."

"There are four of us," Elizabeth said.

"Oh, right. Sorry, I think I was forgetting Sarah, actually."

Sarah deemed this unworthy of comment, but she did curl her lip.

"My point," Harriet continued, "is that we will

always remember that we were right here together when we thought of it."

"You could make her look like me," Frances said hopefully.

"No, no," Harriet said, waving her off. "It's too late to change now. I've already got it fixed in my head. The new character must look like Sarah. Let me see . . ." She started scribbling madly. "Thick, dark hair with just the slightest tendency to curl."

"Dark, bottomless eyes," Frances put in breathlessly. "They must be bottomless."

"With a hint of madness," Elizabeth said.

Sarah whipped around to face her.

"I'm just doing my part," Elizabeth demurred. "And I certainly see that hint of madness now."

"I should think so," Sarah retorted.

"Not too tall, not too short," Harriet said, still writing.

Elizabeth grinned and joined in the singsong. "Not too thin, not too fat."

"Oh oh oh, I have one!" Frances exclaimed, practically bouncing along the sofa. "Not too pink, not too green."

That stopped the conversation cold. "I beg your pardon?" Sarah finally managed.

"You don't embarrass easily," Frances explained, "so you very rarely blush. And I've only ever seen you cast up your accounts once, and that was when we all had that bad fish in Brighton."

"Hence the green," Harriet said approvingly. "Well done, Frances. That's very clever. People really do turn greenish when they are queasy. I wonder why that is."

"Bile," Elizabeth said.

"Must we have this conversation?" Sarah wondered.

"I don't see why you're in such a bad mood," Harriet said.

"I'm not in a bad mood."

"You're not in a *good* mood."

Sarah did not bother to contradict.

"If I were you," Harriet said, "I would be walking on air. You get to walk down the aisle."

"I *know*." Sarah flopped back onto the sofa, the wail of her final syllable apparently too strong for her to remain upright.

Frances stood and came over to her side, peering down over the sofa back. "Don't you want to walk down the aisle?" She looked a bit like a concerned little sparrow, her head tilting to one side and then the other with sharp little birdlike movements.

"Not particularly," Sarah replied. At least, not unless it was at her own wedding. But it was difficult to talk to her sisters about this; there was such a gap in their ages, and there were some things one could not share with an eleven-year-old.

Their mother had lost three babies between Sarah and Harriet—two as miscarriages and one when Sarah's younger brother, the only boy to have been born to Lord and Lady Pleinsworth, died in his cradle before he was three months old. Sarah was sure that her parents were disappointed not to have a living son, but to their credit, they never complained. When they mentioned the title going to Sarah's cousin William, they did not grumble. They just seemed to accept it as the way it was. There had been some talk of Sarah marrying William, to keep things "neat and tidy and all in the family" (as her mother had put it), but William was three years younger than Sarah. At eighteen, he'd only just started at Oxford, and he surely wasn't going to marry within the next five years.

And there was not a chance that Sarah was going to wait five years. Not an inch of a chance. Not a fraction of a fraction of an inch of a—

"Sarah!"

She looked up. And just in time. Elizabeth appeared to be aiming a volume of poetry in her direction.

"Don't," Sarah warned.

Elizabeth gave a little frown of disappointment and lowered the book. "I was asking," she (apparently) repeated, "if you knew if all of the guests had arrived."

"I think so," Sarah replied, although truthfully she had no idea. "I really couldn't say about the ones who are staying in the village." Their cousin Honoria Smythe-Smith was marrying the Earl of Chatteris the following morning. The ceremony was to be held here at Fensmore, the ancestral Chatteris home in northern Cambridgeshire. But even Lord Chatteris's grand home could not hold all of the guests who were coming up from London; quite a few had been forced to take rooms at the local inns.

As family, the Pleinsworths had been the first to be allotted rooms at Fensmore, and they had arrived nearly a week ahead of time to help with the preparations. Or perhaps more accurately, their mother was helping with the preparations. Sarah had been tasked with the job of keeping her sisters out of trouble.

Which wasn't easy.

Normally, the girls would have been watched over by their governess, allowing Sarah to attend to her duties as Honoria's maid of honor, but as it happened, their (now former) governess was getting married the next fortnight.

To Honoria's brother.

Which meant that once the Chatteris-Smythe-Smith nuptials were completed, Sarah (along with half of London, it seemed) would take to the roads and travel from Fensmore down to Whipple Hill, in Berkshire, to attend the wedding of Daniel Smythe-Smith and Miss Anne Wynter. As Daniel was also an earl, it was going to be a huge affair.

Much as Honoria's wedding was going to be a huge affair.

Two huge affairs. Two grand opportunities for Sarah to dance and frolic and be made painfully aware that *she* was not one of the brides.

She just wanted to get married. Was that so pathetic?

No, she thought, straightening her spine (but not so much that she had to actually sit up), it wasn't. Finding a husband and being a wife was all she'd been trained to do, aside from playing the pianoforte in the infamous Smythe-Smith Quartet.

Which, come to think of it, was part of the reason she was so desperate to be married.

Every year, like clockwork, the four eldest unmarried Smythe-Smith cousins were forced to gather their nonexistent musical talents and play together in a quartet.

And perform.

In front of actual people. Who were not deaf.

It was hell. Sarah couldn't think of a better word to describe it. She was fairly certain the appropriate word had not yet been invented.

The noise that came forth from the Smythe-Smith instruments could also be described only by words yet to be invented. But for some reason, all of the Smythe-Smith mothers (including Sarah's, who had been born a Smythe-Smith, even if she was now a Pleinsworth) sat in the front row with beatific smiles on their faces, secure in their mad knowledge that their daughters were musical prodigies. And the rest of the audience . . .

That was the mystery.

Why *was* there a "rest of the audience"? Sarah never could figure that out. Surely one had to attend only once to realize that nothing good could ever come of a Smythe-Smith musicale. But Sarah had examined the guest lists; there were people who came every single year. What were they thinking? They had to know that they were subjecting themselves to what could only be termed auditory torture.

Apparently there *had* been a word invented for that.

The only way for a Smythe-Smith cousin to be released from the Smythe-Smith Quartet was marriage. Well, that and feigning a desperate illness, but Sarah had already done that once, and she didn't think it would work a second time.

Or one could have been born a boy. *They* didn't have to learn to play instruments and sacrifice their dignity upon an altar of public humiliation.

It was really quite unfair.

But back to marriage. Her three seasons in London had not been complete failures. Just this past summer, two gentlemen had asked for her hand in marriage. And even though she'd known she was probably consigning herself to another year at the sacrificial pianoforte, she'd refused them both.

She didn't need a mad, bad passion. She was far too practical to believe that everyone found her true love—or even that everyone *had* a true love. But a lady of one-and-twenty shouldn't have to marry a man of sixty-three.

As for the other proposal . . . Sarah sighed. The gentleman had been an uncommonly affable fellow, but every time he counted to twenty (and he seemed to do so with strange frequency), he skipped the number twelve.

Sarah didn't need to wed a genius, but was it really too much to hope for a husband who could count?

"Marriage," she said to herself.

"What was that?" Frances asked, still peering at her from above the back of the sofa. Harriet and Elizabeth were busy with their own pursuits, which was just as well, because Sarah didn't really need an audience beyond an eleven-year-old when she announced:

"I have *got* to get married this year. If I don't, I do believe I will simply die."

HUGH PRENTICE PAUSED briefly at the doorway to the drawing room, then shook his head and moved on. Sarah Pleinsworth, if his ears were correct, and they usually were.

Yet another reason he hadn't wanted to attend this wedding.

Hugh had always been a solitary soul, and there were very few people whose company he deliberately sought. But at the same time, there weren't many people he avoided, either.

His father, of course.

Convicted murderers.

And Lady Sarah Pleinsworth.

Even if their first meeting hadn't been a mind-numbingly mad disaster, they would never have been friends. Sarah Pleinsworth was one of those dramatic females given to hyperbole and grand announcements. Hugh did not normally study the speech patterns of others, but when Lady Sarah spoke, it was difficult to ignore her.

She used far too many adverbs. And exclamation points.

Plus, she despised him. This was not conjecture on his part. He had heard her utter the words. Not that this bothered him; he didn't much care for her, either. He just wished she'd learn to be quiet.

Like right now. She was going to die if she did not get married this year. Really.

Hugh gave his head a little shake. At least he would not have to attend *that* wedding.

He'd almost got out of this one, too. But Daniel Smythe-Smith had insisted, and when Hugh had pointed out that this wasn't even his wedding, Daniel had leaned back in his chair and said that this was his sister's wedding, and if they were to convince the rest of society that they had put their differences behind them, Hugh had better bloody well show up with a smile on his face.

It hadn't been the most gracious of invitations, but Hugh didn't care. He much preferred when people said what they meant and left it at that. But Daniel was right about one thing. In this case, appearances were important.

It had been a scandal of unimaginable proportions when the two men had dueled three and a half years earlier. Daniel had been forced to flee the country, and Hugh had spent a full year learning to walk again. Then there was another year of Hugh's trying to convince his father to leave Daniel alone, and then another of trying to actually *find* Daniel once Hugh had finally figured out how to get his father to call off his spies and assassins and leave bloody well alone.

Spies and assassins. Had his existence truly descended that far into melodrama? That he could ponder the words *spies and assassins* and actually find them relevant?

Hugh let out a long sigh. He had subdued his father, and he had located Daniel Smythe-Smith and brought him back to Britain. Now Daniel was getting married and would live happily ever after, and all would be just as it should have been.

For everyone except Hugh.

He looked down at his leg. It was only fair. He'd been the one to start it all. He should be the one with the permanent repercussions.

But damn, it hurt today. He'd spent eleven hours in a coach the day prior, and he was still feeling the aftereffects.

He really did not understand why he needed to put in an appearance at *this* wedding. Surely his attendance at Daniel's nuptials later in the month would be enough to convince society that the battle between Hugh and Daniel was old news.

Hugh was not too proud to admit that in this case, at least, he cared what society thought. It had not bothered him when people labeled him an eccentric, with more aptitude at cards than he had with people. Nor had he minded when he'd overheard one society matron say to another that she found him very strange, and she would not allow her daughter to consider him as a potential suitor—if her daughter were to become interested, which, the matron said emphatically, she never would.

Hugh had not minded that, but he did remember it. Word for word.

What did bother him, however, was being thought a villain. That someone might think he'd wanted to kill Daniel Smythe-Smith, or that he'd rejoiced when he'd been forced to leave the country . . . This, Hugh could not bear. And if the only way to redeem his reputation was to make sure that society knew that Daniel had forgiven him, then Hugh would attend this wedding, and whatever else Daniel deemed appropriate.

"Oh, Lord Hugh!"

Hugh paused at the sound of a familiar feminine voice. It was the bride herself, Lady Honoria Smythe-Smith, soon to be Lady Chatteris. In twenty-three hours, actually, if the ceremony began on time, which Hugh had little confidence it would. He was surprised she was out and about. Weren't brides meant to be surrounded by their female friends and relatives, fussing about last-minute details?

"Lady Honoria," he said, shifting his grip on his cane so that he could offer her a bow of greeting.

"I am so glad you are able to attend the wedding," she said.

Hugh stared into her light blue eyes for a moment longer than other people might have thought necessary. He was fairly certain she was being truthful.

"Thank you," he said. Then he lied. "I am delighted to be here."

She smiled broadly, and it lit up her face in the way only true happiness could. Hugh did not delude himself that *he* was responsible for her joy. All he had done was utter a nicety and thus avoid doing anything to take away from her current wedding-induced bliss.

Simple maths.

"Did you enjoy your breakfast?" she asked.

He had a feeling she had not flagged him down to inquire about his morning meal, but as it must have been obvious that he had just partaken, he replied, "Very much so. I commend Lord Chatteris on his kitchens."

"Thank you very much. This is quite the largest event to be held at Fensmore for decades; the servants are quite frantic with apprehension. And delight." Honoria pressed her lips together sheepishly. "But mostly apprehension."

He did not have anything to add to that, so he waited for her to continue.

She did not disappoint. "I was hoping I might ask you a favor."

Hugh could not imagine what, but she was the bride, and if she wanted to ask him to stand on his head, it was his understanding that he was obligated to try.

"My cousin Arthur has taken ill," she said, "and he was to sit at the head table at the wedding breakfast."

Oh, no. No, she wasn't asking—

"We need another gentleman, and—"

Apparently she was.

"—I was hoping it could be you. It would go a long way toward making everything, well . . ." She swallowed and her eyes flicked toward the ceiling for a moment as she tried to find the correct words. "Toward making everything right. Or at least appear to be right."

He stared at her for a moment. It wasn't that his heart was sinking; hearts didn't sink so much as they did a tight panicky squeeze, and the truth was, his did neither. There was no reason to fear being forced to sit at the head table, but there was every reason to dread it.

"Not that's it not *right*," she said hastily. "As far as I am concerned—and my mother, too, I can say quite reliably—we hold you in great esteem. We know . . . That is to say, Daniel told us what you did."

He stared at her intently. What, exactly, had Daniel told her?

"I know that he would not be here in England if you had not sought him out, and I am most grateful."

Hugh thought it uncommonly gracious that she did not point out that he was the reason her brother had had to leave England in the first place.

She smiled serenely. "A very wise person once told me that it is not the mistakes we make that reveal our character but what we do to rectify them."

"A very wise person?" he murmured.

"Very well, it was my mother," she said with a sheepish smile, "and I will have you know that she said it to Daniel far more than to me, but I've come to realize—and I hope he has, too—that it is true."

"I believe he has," Hugh said softly.

"Well, then," Honoria said, briskly changing both subject and mood, "what do you say? Will you join me at the main table? You will be doing me a tremendous favor."

"I would be honored to take your cousin's place," he said, and he supposed it was the truth. He'd rather go swimming in snow than sit up on a dais in front of all the wedding guests, but it was an honor.

Her face lit up again, her happiness practically a beacon. Was this what weddings did to people?

"Thank you so much," she said, with obvious relief. "If you had refused, I would have had to ask my other cousin, Rupert, and—"

"You have another cousin? One you're passing over in favor of me?" Hugh might not have cared overmuch for the myriad rules and regulations that bound their society, but that did not mean he didn't know what they were.

"He's awful," she said in a loud whisper. "Honestly, he's just terrible, and he eats far too many onions."

"Well, if that's the case," Hugh murmured.

"*And*," Honoria continued, "he and Sarah do not get on."

Hugh always considered his words before he spoke, but even he wasn't able to stop himself from blurting half of "*I* don't get on with Lady Sarah" before clamping his mouth firmly shut.

"I beg your pardon?" Honoria inquired.

Hugh forced his jaw to unlock. "I don't see why that would be a problem," he said tightly. Dear God, he was going to have to sit with Lady Sarah Pleinsworth. How was it possible Honoria Smythe-Smith didn't realize what a stupendously bad idea that would be?

"Oh, thank you, Lord Hugh," Honoria said effusively. "I do appreciate your flexibility in this matter. If I sit them together—and there would be no other place to put him at the head table, trust me, I looked—heaven only knows what rows they'll get into."

"Lady Sarah?" Hugh murmured. "Rows?"

"I know," Honoria agreed, completely misinterpreting his words. "It's difficult to imagine. We never have a cross word. She has the most marvelous sense of humor."

Hugh made no comment.

Honoria smiled grandly at him. "Thank you again. You are doing me a tremendous favor."

"How could I possibly refuse?"

Her eyes narrowed for a hint of a moment, but she seemed not to detect sarcasm, which made sense, since Hugh himself didn't know if he was being sarcastic.

"Well," Honoria said, "thank you. I'll just tell Sarah."

"She's in the drawing room," he said. Honoria looked at him curiously, so he added, "I heard her speaking as I walked by."

Honoria continued to frown, so he added, "She has a most distinctive voice."

"I had not noticed," Honoria murmured.

Hugh decided that this would be an excellent time for him to shut up and leave.

The bride, however, had other plans. "Well," she declared, "if she's right there, why don't you come with me, and we will tell her the good news."

It was the last thing he wanted, but then she smiled at him, and he remembered, *She's the bride.* And he followed.

IN FANCIFUL NOVELS—the sort Sarah read by the dozen and refused to apologize for— foreshadowing was painted by the bucket, not the brushstroke. The heroine clasped her hand to her forehead and said something like, "Oh, if only I could find a gentleman who will look past my illegitimate birth and vestigial toe!"

Very well, she'd yet to find an author willing to include an extra toe. But it would certainly make for a good story. There was no denying that.

But back to the foreshadowing. The heroine would make her impassioned plea, and then, as if called forth from some ancient talisman, a gentleman would appear.

Oh, if only I could find a gentleman. And there he was.

Which was why, after Sarah had made her (admittedly ridiculous) statement about dying if she did not marry this year, she looked up to the doorway. Because really, wouldn't that have been funny?

Unsurprisingly, no one appeared.

"Hmmph," she hmmphed. "Even the gods of literature have despaired of me."

"Did you say something?" Harriet asked.

"Oh, if only I could find a gentleman," she muttered to herself, "who will make me miserable and vex me to the end of my days."

And then.

Of course.

Lord Hugh Prentice.

God above, was there to be no end to her travails?

"Sarah!" came Honoria's cheerful voice as the bride herself stepped into the doorway beside him. "I have good news."

Sarah came to her feet and looked at her cousin. Then she looked at Hugh Prentice, who, it had to be said, she'd *never* liked. Then she looked back to her cousin. Honoria, her very best friend in the entire world. And she knew that Honoria (her very best friend in the entire world who really should have known better) did *not* have good news. At least not what Sarah would consider good news.

Or Hugh Prentice, if his expression was any indication.

But Honoria was still glowing like a cheerful, nearly wed lantern, and she practically floated right off her toes when she announced, "Cousin Arthur has taken ill."

Elizabeth came immediately to attention. "That *is* good news."

"Oh, come now," Harriet said. "He's not half as bad as Rupert."

"Well, that part's not the good news," Honoria said quickly, with a nervous glance toward Hugh, lest he think them a completely bloodthirsty lot. "The good news is that Sarah was going to have to sit with Rupert tomorrow, but now she doesn't."

Frances gasped and leapt across the room. "Does that mean I might sit at the head table? Oh, please say I may take his place! I would love that above all things. Especially since you're putting it up on a dais, aren't you? I would actually *be* above all things."

"Oh, Frances," Honoria said, smiling warmly down at her, "I wish it could be so, but you know there are to be no children at the main table, and also, we need it to be a gentleman."

"Hence Lord Hugh," Elizabeth said.

"I am pleased to be of service," Hugh said, even though it was clear to Sarah that he was not.

"I cannot begin to tell you how grateful we are," Honoria said. "Especially Sarah."

Hugh looked at Sarah.

Sarah looked at Hugh. It seemed imperative that he realize that she was not, in fact, grateful.

And then he smiled, the lout. Well, not really a smile. It wouldn't have been called a smile on anyone else's face, but his mien was so normally stony that the slightest twitch at the corner of his lips was the equivalent of anyone else's jumping for joy.

"I am certain I shall be delighted to sit next to you instead of Cousin Rupert," Sarah said. Delighted was an overstatement, but Rupert had terrible breath, so at least she'd avoid *that* with Lord Hugh at her side.

"Certain," Lord Hugh repeated, his voice that odd mix of flatness and drawl that made Sarah feel as if her mind were about to explode. Was he mocking her? Or was he merely repeating a word for emphasis? She couldn't tell.

Yet another trait that rendered Lord Hugh Prentice the most aggravating man in Britain. If one were being made fun of, didn't one have the right to *know*?

"You don't take raw onions with your tea, do you?" Sarah asked coolly.

He smiled. Or maybe he didn't. "No."

"Then I am certain," she said.

"Sarah?" Honoria said hesitantly.

Sarah turned to her cousin with a brilliant smile. She'd never forgotten that mad moment the year before when she'd first met Lord Hugh.

He had turned from hot to cold in a blink of an eye. And damn it all, if he could do it, so could she. "Your wedding is going to be perfect," she declared. "Lord Hugh and I will get on famously, I'm sure."

Honoria didn't buy Sarah's act for a second, not that Sarah really thought she would. Her eyes flicked from Sarah to Hugh and back again about six times in the space of a second. "Ahhhhh," she hedged, clearly confused about the sudden awkwardness. "Well."

Sarah kept her smile pasted placidly on her face. For Honoria she would attempt civility with Hugh Prentice. For Honoria she would even smile at him, and laugh at his jokes, assuming he made jokes. But still, how was it possible that Honoria didn't realize how very much Sarah hated Hugh? Oh very well, not hate. Hate she would reserve for the truly evil. Napoleon, for example. Or that flower seller at Covent Garden who'd tried to cheat her the week before.

But Hugh Prentice was beyond vexing, beyond annoying. He was the only person (aside from her sisters) who had managed to infuriate her so much that she'd had to literally hold her hands down to keep from smacking him.

She had never been so angry as she had that night. . . .

Chapter Two

How They Met
(the way *she* remembers it)

*A London ballroom, celebrating the engagement of
Mr. Charles Dunwoody to Miss Nerissa Berbrooke
Sixteen months earlier*

"Do you think Mr. St. Clair is handsome?"

Sarah didn't bother to turn toward Honoria as she asked the question. She was too busy watching Mr. St. Clair, trying to decide what she thought of him. She'd always favored men with tawny hair, but she wasn't so sure she liked the queue he wore in the back. Did it make him look like a pirate, or did it make him look as if he was *trying* to look like a pirate?

There was an enormous difference.

"*Gareth* St. Clair?" Honoria queried. "Do you mean Lady Danbury's grandson?"

That yanked Sarah's eyes right back to Honoria's. "He's not!" she said with a gasp.

"Oh, he is. I'm quite sure of it."

"Well, that takes him right off my list," Sarah said with no hesitation whatsoever.

"Do you know, I admire Lady Danbury," Honoria said. "She says exactly what she means."

"Which is precisely why no woman in her right mind would want to marry a member of her family. Good heavens, Honoria, what if one had to live with her?"

"You have been known to be somewhat forthright yourself," Honoria pointed out.

"Be that as it may," Sarah said, which was as far as she would go toward agreement, "I am no match for Lady Danbury." She glanced back at Mr. St. Clair. Pirate or aspiring pirate? She supposed it didn't matter, not if he was related to Lady Danbury.

Honoria patted her arm. "Give yourself time."

Sarah turned toward her cousin with a flat, sarcastic stare. "How much time? She's eighty if she's a day."

"We all need something to which to aspire," Honoria demurred.

Sarah could not forestall a roll of her eyes. "Has my life become so pathetic that my aspirations must be measured in decades rather than years?"

"No, of course not, but . . ."

"But what?" Sarah asked suspiciously when Honoria did not complete her thought.

Honoria sighed. "Will we find husbands this year, do you think?"

Sarah couldn't bring herself to form a verbal answer. A doleful look was all she could manage.

Honoria returned the expression in kind, and in unison, they sighed. Tired, worn-out, when-will-this-be-over sighs.

"We *are* pathetic," Sarah said.

"We are," Honoria agreed.

They watched the ballroom for a few more moments, and then Sarah said, "I don't mind it tonight, though."

"Being pathetic?"

Sarah glanced over at her cousin with a cheeky smile. "Tonight I have you."

"Misery loves company?"

"That's the funny thing," Sarah said, feeling her brow knit into a quizzical expression. "Tonight I'm not even miserable."

"Why, Sarah Pleinsworth," Honoria said with barely suppressed humor, "that might be the nicest thing you've ever said to me."

Sarah chuckled, but still she asked, "Shall we be spinsters together, old and wobbly at the annual musicale?"

Honoria shuddered. "I am fairly certain that is *not* the nicest thing you've ever said to me. I do love the musicale, but—"

"You don't!" Sarah just barely resisted the urge to clap her hands over her ears. *No one* could love that musicale.

"I said I loved the musicale," Honoria clarified, "not the music."

"How, pray tell, are they different? I thought I might *perish*—"

"Oh, Sarah," Honoria scolded. "Don't exaggerate."

"I *wish* it were an exaggeration," Sarah muttered.

"I thought it was great fun practicing with you and Viola and Marigold. And next year will be even better. We shall have Iris with us to play the cello. Aunt Maria told me that Mr. Wedgecombe is mere weeks away from proposing to Marigold." Honoria furrowed her brow in thought. "Although I'm not quite sure how she knows that."

"That's not the point," Sarah said with great gravity, "and even if it were, it's not worth the public humiliation. If you want to spend time with your cousins, invite us all out for a picnic. Or a game of Pall Mall."

"It's not the same."

"Thank *God*." Sarah shuddered, trying to *not* recollect a single moment of her Smythe-Smith Quartet debut. Thus far it was proving a difficult memory to repress. Every awful chord, every pitying stare . . .

It was why she needed to consider *every* gentleman as a possible spouse. If she had to perform with her discordant cousins one more time, she *would* perish.

And that was not an exaggeration.

"Very well," Sarah said briskly, then straightened her shoulders to punctuate the tone. It was time to get back to business. "Mr. St. Clair is off my list. Who else is here tonight?"

"No one," Honoria said morosely.

"No one? How is that possible? What about Mr. Travers? I thought you and he— Oh." Sarah gulped at the pained expression on Honoria's face. "I'm sorry. What happened?"

"I don't know. I thought everything was going so well. And then . . . nothing."

"That's very odd," Sarah said. Mr. Travers wouldn't have been her first choice for a husband, but he seemed steadfast enough. Certainly not the sort to drop a lady with no explanation. "Are you sure?"

"At Mrs. Wemberley's soirée last week I smiled at him and he ran from the room."

"Oh, but surely you're imagining—"

"He tripped on a table on the way out."

"Oh." Sarah grimaced. There was no putting a cheerful face on that. "I'm sorry," she said sympathetically, and she was. As comforting as it was to have Honoria by her side as fellow failure on the marriage mart, she did want her cousin to be happy.

"It's probably for the best," Honoria said, ever the optimist. "We share very few interests. He's actually quite musical, and I don't know how he would ever— Oh!"

"What is it?" Sarah asked. If they had been closer to the candelabra, Honoria's gasp would have sucked the flame right out.

"Why is he here?" Honoria whispered.

"Who?" Sarah's eyes swept across the room. "Mr. Travers?"

"No. *Hugh Prentice.*"

Sarah's entire body went rigid with rage. "How dare he show his face?" she hissed. "Surely he knew we would be in attendance."

But Honoria was shaking her head. "He has just as much right to be here—"

"No, he does not," Sarah cut in. Trust Honoria to be kind and forgiving when neither was deserved. "What Lord Hugh Prentice needs," Sarah ground out, "is a public flogging."

"Sarah!"

"There is a time and a place for Christian charity, and Lord Hugh Prentice intersects with neither." Sarah's eyes narrowed dangerously as she spied the gentleman she thought was Lord Hugh. They had never been formally introduced; the duel had occurred before Sarah had entered society, and of course no one had dared to make them known to each other after that. But still, she knew what he looked like.

She had made it her business to know what he looked like.

She could only see the gentleman from the back, but the hair was the correct color—light brown. Or maybe dark blond, depending on how charitable one was feeling. She could not see if he held a cane. Had his walking improved? The last time she had spied him, several months earlier, his limp had been quite pronounced.

"He is friends with Mr. Dunwoody," Honoria said, her voice still small and fragile. "He will have wanted to congratulate his friend."

"I don't care if he wanted to give the happy couple their own private Indian island," Sarah spat. "*You* are also friends with Mr. Dunwoody. You have known him for years. Surely Lord Hugh is aware of this."

"Yes, but—"

"Don't make excuses for him. I don't care what Lord Hugh thinks of Daniel—"

"Well, I do. I care what everyone thinks of Daniel."

"That's not the point," Sarah railed. "*You* are innocent of any wrongdoing, and *you* have been wronged beyond all measure. If Lord Hugh has a decent bone in his body, he would stay away from any gathering at which there is even a chance that you might be present."

"You're right." Honoria closed her eyes for a moment, looking unbearably weary. "But right now I don't care. I just want to leave. I want to go home."

Sarah continued to stare at the man in question, or rather at his back. "He should know better," she said, mostly to herself. And then she felt herself step forward. "I'm going to—"

"Don't you dare," Honoria warned, yanking Sarah back with a swift tug at her arm. "If you cause a scene . . ."

"I would never cause a scene." But of course they both knew she would. For Hugh Prentice, or rather, *because* of Hugh Prentice, Sarah would create a scene that would be the stuff of legend.

Two years ago, Hugh Prentice had ripped her family to shreds. Daniel's absence was still a gaping hole at family gatherings. One couldn't even mention his name in front of his mother;

Aunt Virginia would simply pretend she hadn't heard, and then (according to Honoria), she'd lock herself in her room and cry.

The rest of the family had not gone untouched, either. The scandal following the duel had been so great that both Honoria and Sarah had been forced to forgo what would have been their first season in London. It had not escaped Sarah's notice (nor Honoria's, once Sarah had pointed it out, repeated it, raged about it, then flopped on her bed with despair), that 1821 had been an uncommonly productive season as judged by the matchmaking mothers of London. Fourteen eligible gentlemen had become engaged to be married that season. Fourteen! And that wasn't even counting the ones who were too old, too strange, or too fond of their drink.

Who knows what might have happened if Sarah and Honoria had been out and about in town during that matrimonially spectacular season. Call her shallow, but as far as Sarah was concerned, Hugh Prentice was directly responsible for their rapidly approaching spinsterhood.

Sarah had never met the man, but she hated him.

"I'm sorry," Honoria said abruptly. Her voice caught, and she sounded as if she was fighting a sob. "I must leave. Now. And we must find my mother. If she sees him . . ."

Aunt Virginia. Sarah's heart plummeted. She would be a wreck. Honoria's mother had never recovered from her only son's disgrace. To come face-to-face with the man who'd caused it all . . .

Sarah grabbed her cousin's hand. "Come with me," she urged. "I'll help you find her."

Honoria nodded limply, letting Sarah lead the way. They snaked through the crowds, trying to balance speed with discretion. Sarah did not want her cousin to be forced to speak with Hugh Prentice, but she would die before she allowed anyone to think that they were running from his presence.

Which meant that *she* was going to have to stay. Perhaps even speak with him. Sarah would have to save face on behalf of the entire family.

"There she is," Honoria said as they approached the grand ballroom doors. Lady Winstead was standing in a small clutch of matrons, chatting amiably with Mrs. Dunwoody, their hostess.

"She must not have seen him," Sarah whispered. She wouldn't have been smiling otherwise.

"What shall I feign?" Honoria asked.

"Fatigue," Sarah said immediately. No one would doubt it. Honoria had turned ashen the moment she'd spied Hugh Prentice, setting the grayish smudges under her eyes into stark relief.

Honoria gave a quick nod and dashed off, politely pulling her mother aside before whispering a few words in her ear. Sarah watched as the two of them made their excuses, then slipped out the door to the waiting line of carriages.

Sarah let out a pent-up breath, relieved that her aunt and cousin would not have to come into contact with Lord Hugh. But every rainbow had a black and grimy lining, it seemed, and Honoria's departure meant that Sarah was stuck here for at least an hour. It would not be long before the gossips realized that Lord Hugh Prentice was in the same room as a Smythe-Smith cousin. First there would be stares, and then whispers, and then everyone would be watching to see if they crossed paths, and did they speak, and even if they didn't, which one would leave the party first?

Sarah judged that she needed to remain in the Dunwoody ballroom for at least an hour before it no longer mattered who left first. But before any of that, she needed to be seen having a lovely time, which meant she couldn't stand at the edge of the front hall by herself. She needed to find a friend with whom to chatter, and she needed someone to dance with her, and she needed to laugh and smile as if she hadn't a care in the world.

And she had to do all of that while making it perfectly plain that she did indeed know that Lord Hugh Prentice had wormed his way into the party and that she found him utterly beneath her notice.

Keeping up appearances could be so exhausting.

Luckily, within seconds of reentering the ballroom, she spied her cousin Arthur. He was dull as a stick, but he was dashingly handsome and always seemed to attract attention. More importantly, if she yanked on his sleeve and told him she needed him to dance with her immediately, he would do it, no questions asked.

Upon completing her dance with Arthur, she directed him to steer her toward one of his friends, who then had no choice but to request her company in the ensuing minuet, and before she knew it, Sarah had danced four times in rapid succession, three of which with men of the sort who made a young lady look very popular. The fourth was with Sir Felix Farnsworth, who, sadly, had never made any lady look popular.

But by that point, Sarah was becoming the sort of young lady who made the *gentlemen* look popular, and she was glad to lend a glow to Sir Felix, whom she had always been rather fond of, despite his unfortunate interest in taxidermy.

She did not see Lord Hugh, but she did not know how he could have failed to see *her*. By the time she finished drinking a glass of lemonade with Sir Felix, she decided she had put on a good enough show, even if it hadn't been a full hour since Honoria had departed.

Let's see, if each dance lasted about five minutes, with a bit of time in between, plus the brief chat with Arthur and two glasses of lemonade . . .

Surely that equaled one family name restored. At least for this evening.

"Thank you again for a lovely dance, Sir Felix," Sarah said as she handed her empty glass to a footman. "I wish you the best of luck with that vulture."

"Yes, they're great fun to pose," he replied with an animated nod. "It's all in the beak, you know."

"The beak," she echoed. "Right."

"Are you leaving, then?" he asked. "I was hoping to tell you about my other new project. The shrew."

Sarah felt her lips move in an attempt to form words. Yet when she spoke, all that came out was "My mother."

"Your mother is a shrew?"

"No! I mean, not ordinarily." Oh, good heavens, it was a good thing Sir Felix was not a gossip, because if this got back to her mother . . . "What I meant to say is that she is not a shrew. Ever. But I need to find her. She specifically told me she wanted to leave before . . . ehrm . . . well . . . now."

"It is near to eleven," Sir Felix supplied helpfully.

She gave an emphatic nod. "Precisely."

Sarah said her farewells, leaving Sir Felix with Cousin Arthur, who, if he wasn't interested in shrews, at least put on a good show of it. Then she set off in search of her mother to let her know that she wished to depart earlier than planned. They didn't live far from the Dunwoodys; if Lady Pleinsworth was not ready to leave, it should not prove difficult for the Pleinsworth carriage to transport Sarah home and then return for her mother.

Five minutes of searching did not reveal Lady Pleinsworth's whereabouts, however, and soon enough Sarah was muttering to herself as she tromped down the corridor to where she thought the Dunwoodys had a gaming room.

"If Mama is playing cards . . ." Not that Lady Pleinsworth couldn't afford to lose a guinea or two in whatever it was that matrons played these days, but still, it seemed rather unfair that she'd be gambling away while Sarah was saving the family from utter embarrassment.

Caused by her cousin, while he'd been gambling.

"Ah, irony," she murmured. "Thy name is . . ."

Thy name was . . .

Thy name could be . . .

She actually stopped walking as she frowned. Apparently irony's name was some word she couldn't think of.

"I *am* pathetic," she muttered, resuming her search. And she wanted to go home. Where the devil was her mother?

Soft light shone from a partially open doorway just a few feet ahead. It was rather quiet for a card game, but on the other hand, the open doorway would seem to indicate that whatever Sarah walked in on, it would not be *too* inappropriate.

"Mama," she said, walking into the room. But it wasn't her mother.

Irony's new name was apparently Hugh Prentice.

She froze in the doorway, unable to do anything but stare at the man sitting by the window. Later, when she was reliving every awful moment of the encounter, it would occur to her that she could have left. He wasn't facing her, and he didn't see her; he wouldn't see her unless she spoke again.

Which of course she did.

"I hope you're satisfied," she said coldly.

Lord Hugh stood at the sound of her voice. His movements were stiff, and he leaned heavily on the arm of the chair as he rose. "I beg your pardon?" he said politely, regarding her with an expression that was completely devoid of emotion.

He did not even have the decency to appear uncomfortable in her presence? Sarah felt her hands turn to rocky little fists. "Have you no shame?"

This elicited a blink, but little else. "It really depends on the situation," he finally murmured.

Sarah searched her repertoire for suitable exclamations of feminine outrage, finally settling on "You, sir, are no gentleman."

At that, she finally gained his full attention. His grass-green eyes met hers, narrowing ever-so-slightly in thought, and it was then that Sarah realized—

He did not know who she was.

She gasped.

"Now what?" he muttered.

He didn't know who she was. He had bloody well ruined her life, and he didn't know who she *was*?

Irony, thy name was about to be cursed.

Chapter Three

How They Met
(the way *he* remembers it)

In retrospect, Hugh thought, he should have realized that the young woman standing before him was unhinged when she declared him no gentleman. Not that it wasn't the truth; for all that he tried to behave as a civilized adult, he knew that his soul had been black as soot for years.

But really . . . *"You, sir, are no gentleman"* directly following *"I hope you're satisfied"* and *"Have you no shame?"*

Surely no adult of reasonable intelligence and sanity would be so redundant. Not to mention trite. Either the poor woman had been spending too much time at the theater, or she'd convinced herself she was a character in one of those awful melodramas everyone was reading lately.

His inclination was to turn on his good heel and depart, but judging by the wild look in her eyes she'd probably follow, and he wasn't exactly the speediest fox in the hunt these days. Best to tackle the problem head-on, so to speak.

"Are you unwell?" he asked carefully. "Would you like me to fetch someone for you?"

She sputtered and fumed, her cheeks turning so pink he could see the deepening color even in the dim light cast by the sconces. "You . . . You . . ."

He took a discreet step away. He did not think she was literally spitting her words, but with the way her lips were pressing together, he really could not be too careful.

"Perhaps you should sit down?" he suggested. He motioned to a nearby settee, hoping she would not expect him to help her get there. His balance was not what it once was.

"Fourteen men," she hissed.

He could not even begin to wonder what she was about.

"Did you know that?" she asked, and he realized she was shaking. "Fourteen."

He cleared his throat. "And only one of me."

There was a moment of silence. A moment of blessed silence. Then she spoke.

"You don't know who I am, do you?" she demanded.

Hugh regarded her more closely. She looked vaguely familiar, but logically speaking, this meant nothing. Hugh did not socialize very often, but there were only so many members of the ton. Eventually every face would look familiar.

If he had remained at this evening's gathering for more than a few moments, he might have learned her identity, but he had left the ballroom almost as quickly as he'd found it. Charles Dunwoody's expression had turned ashen when Hugh had offered his felicitations, leaving Hugh to wonder if he had lost his last friend in London. Finally Charles pulled him aside and informed him that Daniel Smythe-Smith's mother and sister were present.

He had not asked Hugh to leave, but then again, they'd both known he'd not needed to. Hugh had immediately bowed and retreated. He'd caused those two women enough pain. To remain at the ball would have been nothing short of spiteful.

Especially since he couldn't bloody well dance.

But his leg had hurt, and he hadn't felt like pushing through the line of carriages outside to find a hired hack, at least not right away. So he'd made his way to a quiet salon, where he'd been hoping to sit and rest in solitude.

Or not.

The woman who had intruded upon his refuge was still standing just inside the doorway, her fury so palpable that Hugh was almost prepared to reexamine his beliefs on the possibility of spontaneous combustion of the human form.

"You have ruined my life," she hissed.

That he knew to be untrue. He had ruined Daniel Smythe-Smith's life, and by extension possibly that of his unmarried younger sister, but this darkly brunette woman in front of him was not Honoria Smythe-Smith. Lady Honoria had much lighter hair, and her face wasn't nearly as expressive, although the deep emotion on this woman could easily have been brought on by insanity. Or, now that he thought on it, drink.

Yes, that was far more likely. Hugh was not sure how many glasses of ratafia were required to intoxicate a woman of approximately nine stone, but clearly she'd managed it.

"I regret that I have distressed you," he said, "but I'm afraid you have confused me with someone else." Then he added—not because he wanted to but rather because he had to; she was bloody well blocking the corridor and clearly needed some sort of verbal nudge to be on her way—"If I may be of any further assistance . . ."

"You may assist me," she spat, "by removing your presence from London."

He tried not to groan. This was getting tedious.

"Or from this world," she said venomously.

"Oh, for the love of Christ," he swore. Whoever this woman was, she'd long since sacrificed any obligation he had to speak as a gentleman in her presence. "*Please*" —he bowed, with flair and sarcasm in equal measure—"allow me to kill myself at your tender request, O unnamed woman whose life I have destroyed."

Her mouth fell open. Good. She was speechless. Finally.

"I would be happy to fulfill your bidding," he continued, "once you get out of my *WAY*." His voice rose to a roar, or rather, his version of a roar, which was more of a malevolent growl. He thrust his cane into the empty space at her left, hoping its jabbing presence would be enough to convince her to step to the side.

Her breath sucked the air from the room in a loud gasp worthy of Drury Lane. "Are you attacking me?"

"Not yet," he muttered.

She snarled. "Because I wouldn't be surprised if you attempted it."

"Neither," he said, eyes slitting, "would I."

She gasped again, this one a short little puff far more in keeping with her role as an offended young lady. "You, sir, are no gentleman."

"So we have established," he bit off. "Now then, I am hungry, I am tired, and I want to go home. You, however, are blocking my sole means of egress."

She crossed her arms and widened her stance.

He tilted his head and considered the situation. "We appear to have two choices," he finally said. "You can move, or I can push you out of the way."

Her head bobbed to the side in what could only be described as a swagger. "I'd like to see you try."

"Remember, I'm no gentleman."

She smirked. "But I have two good legs."

He patted his cane with some affection. "I have a weapon."

"Which I'm fast enough to avoid."

He smiled blandly. "Ah, but once you move, there will be no obstruction." He indulged himself with a midair twirl of his free hand. "Then I may be on my way, and if there is any God in our heaven, I shall never lay eyes upon you again."

She didn't exactly step out of the way, but she did seem to lean slightly to one side, so Hugh took the opportunity to thrust his cane out as a barrier and shove his way past her. He made it out, too, and in retrospect he really should have kept going, but then she yelled, "I know exactly who you are, Lord Hugh Prentice."

He stopped. Exhaled slowly. But he did not turn around.

"I am Lady Sarah Pleinsworth," she announced, and not for the first time he wished he knew how to better interpret ladies' voices. There was something in her tone he didn't quite understand, a little catch where her throat might have closed, just for a millisecond.

He didn't know what that meant.

But he did know—he certainly did not need to see her face to know it—that she expected him to recognize her name. And as much as he wished he did not recognize it, he did.

Lady Sarah Pleinsworth, first cousin to Daniel Smythe-Smith. According to Charles Dunwoody, she had been quite vocal in her fury over the outcome of the duel. Much more so than Daniel's mother and sister, who, in Hugh's opinion, had a far more valid claim to anger.

Hugh turned. Lady Sarah was standing just a few feet away, her posture tight and furious. Her hands were fisted at her sides, and her chin was jutting forward in a manner that reminded him of an angry child, trapped in an absurd argument and determined to stand her ground.

"Lady Sarah," he said with all due politeness.

She was Daniel's cousin, and despite what had transpired in the last few minutes, he was determined to treat her with respect. "We have not formally met."

"We hardly need—"

"But nonetheless," he cut in before she could make another melodramatic proclamation, "I know who you are."

"Apparently not," she muttered.

"You are cousin to Lord Winstead," he stated. "I know your name if not your face."

She gave a nod—the first gesture she'd made that even hinted of civility. Her voice, too, was slightly more tempered when she spoke again. But only slightly. "You should not have come tonight."

He paused. Then said, "I have known Charles Dunwoody for over a decade. I wished to congratulate him on his betrothal."

This did not seem to impress her. "Your presence was most distressing to my aunt and cousin."

"And for that I am sorry." He was, truly, and he was doing everything he could to set things right. But he could not share that with the Smythe-Smiths until he met with success. It would be cruel to raise the hopes of Daniel's family. And perhaps more to the point, he could not imagine they would receive him if he paid a call.

"You're sorry?" Lady Sarah said scornfully. "I find that difficult to believe."

Again, he paused. He did not like to respond to provocation with immediate outburst. He never had, which made his behavior with Daniel all the more galling. If he hadn't been drinking, he would have behaved rationally, and none of this would have happened. He certainly would not have been standing here in a darkened corner of Charles Dunwoody's parents' home, in the company of a woman who had obviously sought him out for no other reason than to hurl insults at his head.

"You may believe what you wish," he replied. He owed her no explanations.

For a moment neither spoke, then Lady Sarah said, "They left, in case you were wondering."

He tilted his head in query.

"Aunt Virginia and Honoria. They left as soon as they realized you were here."

Hugh did not know what she intended with her statement. Was he meant to feel guilty? Had they wanted to remain at the party? Or was this more of an insult? Perhaps Lady Sarah was trying to tell him that he was so repellent that her cousins could not tolerate his presence.

So he said nothing. He did not wish to make an incorrect reply. But then something niggled at his brain. A puzzle of sorts. Nothing more than an unanswered question, but it was so strange and out of place that he had to know the answer. And so he asked, "What did you mean earlier, fourteen men?"

Lady Sarah's mouth flattened into a grim line. Well, more grim, if such a thing were possible.

"When you first saw me," he reminded her, although he rather thought she knew precisely what he was talking about, "you said something about fourteen men."

"It was nothing," she said dismissively, but her

eyes shifted the tiniest bit to the right. She was lying. Or embarrassed. Probably both.

"Fourteen is not nothing." He was being pedantic, he knew, but she'd already tried his patience in every way *but* the mathematical. $14 \neq 0$, but more to the point, why did people bring things up if they didn't want to talk about them? If she hadn't intended to explain the comment, she bloody well should have kept it to herself.

She stepped rather noticeably to the side. "Please," she said, "go."

He didn't move. She'd piqued his curiosity, and there was little in this world more tenacious than Hugh Prentice with an unanswered question.

"You have just spent the last hour ordering me out of your way," she ground out.

"Five minutes," he corrected, "and while I do long for the serenity of my own home, I find myself curious about your fourteen men."

"They were not *my* fourteen men," she snapped.

"I should hope not," he murmured, then added, "not that I would judge."

Her mouth fell open.

"Tell me about the fourteen men," he prodded.

"I told you," she insisted, her cheeks flushing a satisfactory shade of pink, "it was nothing."

"But I'm curious. Fourteen men for supper? For tea? It's too many for a team of cricket, but—"

"Stop!" she burst out.

He did. Quirked a brow, even.

"If you must know," she said, her voice clipped with fury, "there were fourteen men who became engaged to be married in 1821."

There was a very long pause. Hugh was not an unintelligent man, but he had no idea what this had to do with anything. "Did all fourteen men become married?" he asked politely.

She stared at him.

"You said fourteen became engaged to be married."

"It doesn't matter."

"It does to them, I would imagine."

He'd thought they were done with histrionics, but Lady Sarah let out a cry of frustration. "You don't understand anything!"

"Oh, for the love of—"

"Do you have any idea of what you've done?" she demanded. "While you sit in your comfortable home, all cozy in London—"

"Shut up," he said, only he had no idea if he'd said it aloud. He just wanted her to stop. Stop talking, stop arguing, stop everything.

But instead she stepped forward and, with a venomous glare, demanded, "Do you know many lives you have ruined?"

He took a breath. Air, he needed air. He did not need to listen to this. Not from her. He knew precisely how many lives he'd ruined, and hers was not one of them.

But she would not let up. "Have you no conscience?" she hissed.

And finally, he snapped. Without a thought to his leg, he stepped forward until they were close enough for her to feel the heat of his breath. He backed her against the wall, trapping her with nothing but the fury of his presence. "You do not know me," he bit off. "You do not know what I think or what I feel or what measure of hell I visit each and every day of my life. And the next time you feel so wronged—you, who do not even bear the same surname as Lord Winstead—you would do well to remember that one of the lives I have ruined is my own."

And then he stepped away. "Good night," he said, as pleasantly as a summer day.

For a moment he thought they might finally be done, but then she said the one thing that could redeem her.

"They are my family."

He closed his eyes.

"They are my family," she said in a choked voice, "and you have hurt them beyond repair. For that, I can never forgive you."

"Neither," he said, his words for his ears alone, "can I."

Chapter Four

Back at Fensmore
In the drawing room with Honoria, Sarah,
Harriet, Elizabeth, Frances, and Lord Hugh
Right where we left off . . .

IT WAS A rare moment when silence fell on a gathering of Smythe-Smith cousins, but that was exactly what happened after Lord Hugh gave a polite bow and exited the drawing room.

The five of them—the four Pleinsworth sisters and Honoria—remained mute for several seconds, glancing at each other as they waited for a suitable amount of time to pass.

You could almost hear them all counting, Sarah thought, and indeed, as soon as she reached ten in her own head, Elizabeth announced, "Well *that* wasn't very subtle."

Honoria turned. "What do you mean?"

"You *are* trying to make a match of Sarah and Lord Hugh, aren't you?"

"Of course not!" Honoria exclaimed, but Sarah's negative howl was considerably louder.

"Oh, but you should!" Frances said with a delighted clap of her hands. "I like Lord Hugh very much. It's true that he can be a little eccentric, but he's terribly clever. And he's a very good shot."

All eyes swung back to Frances. "He shot Cousin Daniel in the shoulder," Sarah reminded her.

"He's a very good shot when he's sober," Frances clarified. "Daniel said so."

"I cannot begin to imagine the conversation that revealed such a fact," Honoria said, "nor do I wish to, this close to the wedding." She turned resolutely back to Sarah. "I have a favor to ask of you."

"Please say it does not involve Hugh Prentice."

"It involves Hugh Prentice," Honoria confirmed. "I need your help."

Sarah made a great show of sighing. She was going to have to do whatever Honoria asked; they both knew that. But even if Sarah had to go down without a fight, she was not going to do so without a complaint.

"I am very much afraid that he will not feel welcome at Fensmore," Honoria said.

Sarah could find nothing objectionable about that statement; if Hugh Prentice did not feel welcome, it was hardly her problem *and* nothing more than he deserved. But she could be diplomatic when the occasion warranted, so she remarked, "I think it is much more likely he will isolate himself. He's not very friendly."

"I find it more likely that he's shy," Honoria said.

Harriet, still seated at the desk, gasped with delight. "A brooding hero. The very best kind! I shall write him into my play!"

"The one with the unicorn?" Frances asked.

"No, the one I've just thought of this afternoon." Harriet pointed the feather end of her quill toward Sarah. "With the heroine who is not too pink or green."

"He shot your cousin," Sarah snapped, whipping around to face her younger sister. "Does no one *remember* that?"

"It was such a long time ago," Harriet said.

"And I think he's sorry," Frances declared.

"Frances, you are eleven," Sarah said sharply. "You are hardly able to judge a man's character."

Frances's eyes slitted. "I can judge *yours*."

Sarah looked from sister to sister, then back at Honoria. Did no one realize what an awful person Lord Hugh was? Forget for the moment (as if one could) that he had nearly destroyed their family. He was horrid. One had only to speak with him for two minutes before—

"He does often seem uncomfortable at gatherings," Honoria admitted, breaking into Sarah's inner rant, "but that is all the more reason for us to go out of our way to make him feel welcome. I—" Honoria cut herself off, looked about the room, took in Harriet, Elizabeth, and Frances, all watching her with great and unconcealed interest, and said, "Excuse me, please." She took Sarah's arm and steered her out of the drawing room, down the hall, and into another drawing room.

"Am I to be Hugh Prentice's nanny?" Sarah demanded once Honoria had closed the door.

"Of course not. But I am asking you to make sure that he feels a part of the festivities. Perhaps this evening, in the drawing room before supper," Honoria suggested.

Sarah groaned.

"He's likely to be off in a corner, standing by himself."

"Perhaps he likes it that way."

"You're so good at talking to people," Honoria said. "You always know what to say."

"Not to him."

"You don't even know him," Honoria said. "How terrible could it be?"

"Of course I've met him. I don't think there is anyone left in London I haven't met." Sarah considered this, then muttered, "Pathetic though that seems."

"I didn't say you hadn't met him, I said you do not *know* him," Honoria corrected. "There is quite a difference."

"Very well," Sarah said, somewhat grudgingly. "If you wish to split hairs."

Honoria just tilted her head, forcing Sarah to keep talking.

"I don't *know* him," Sarah said, "but what I've met of him, I don't particularly like. I *have* tried to be amiable during these last few months."

Honoria gave her a most disbelieving look.

"I have!" Sarah protested. "I wouldn't say I've tried very hard, but I must tell you, Honoria, the man is not a sparkling conversationalist."

Now Honoria looked as if she might laugh, which only fueled Sarah's irritation.

"I have tried to speak with him," Sarah ground out, "because that is what people *do* at social functions. But he never replies how he ought."

"How he ought?" Honoria echoed.

"He makes me uncomfortable," Sarah said with a sniff. "And I'm fairly certain he does not like me."

"Don't be silly," Honoria said. "Everyone likes you."

"No," Sarah said, quite frankly, "everyone likes *you*. I, on the other hand, lack your kind and pure heart."

"What are you talking about?"

"Merely that while you look for the best in everyone, I take a more cynical view of the world. And I . . ." She paused. How to say it? "There are people in this world who find me quite annoying."

"That's not true," Honoria said. But it was an automatic reply. Sarah was quite sure that given more time to consider the statement, Honoria would realize that it was quite true.

Although she would have said the same thing anyway. Honoria was marvelously loyal that way.

"It is true," Sarah said, "and it does not bother me. Well, not very much, anyway. It certainly does not bother me about Lord Hugh, given that I return the sentiment in spades."

Honoria took a moment to wade through

Sarah's words, then rolled her eyes. Not very much, but Sarah knew her too well to miss the gesture. It was the closest her kind and gentle cousin ever came to a screaming fit.

"I think you should give him a chance," Honoria said. "You've never even had a proper conversation with him."

There had been nothing proper about it, Sarah thought darkly. They had nearly come to blows. And she certainly hadn't known what to say to him. She felt ill every time she recalled their meeting at the Dunwoody engagement fête. She'd done nothing but spout clichés. She might have even stamped her foot. He probably thought her an utter imbecile, and the truth was, she rather thought she'd acted like one.

Not that she cared what he thought of her. That would ascribe far too much importance to his opinion. But in that awful moment in the Dunwoody library—and in the few brief words they'd exchanged since—Hugh Prentice had reduced her to someone she didn't much like.

And *that* was unforgivable.

"It's not up to me to say who you will or will not get on with," Honoria continued after it became clear that Sarah was not going to comment, "but I'm sure you can find the strength to endure Lord Hugh's company for one day."

"Sarcasm becomes you," Sarah said suspiciously. "When did that happen?"

Honoria smiled. "I knew I could depend upon you."

"Indeed," Sarah muttered.

"He's not so dreadful," Honoria said, patting her on the arm. "I think he's rather handsome, actually."

"It doesn't matter if he's handsome."

Honoria leapt on that. "So you think he *is* handsome."

"I *think* he's quite strange," Sarah shot back, "and if you are trying to play matchmaker . . ."

"I'm not!" Honoria held up her arms in mock surrender. "I swear it. I was merely making an observation. I think he has very nice eyes."

"I'd like him better if he had a vestigial toe," Sarah muttered. Maybe she *should* write a book.

"A vestigial—*what*?"

"Yes, his eyes are perfectly nice," Sarah said obediently. It was true, she supposed. He did have very nice eyes, green as grass, and piercingly intelligent. But nice eyes did not a future husband make. And no, she did not view every single man through the lens of eligibility—well, not very much, and certainly not *him*—but it was clear that despite her protestations, Honoria was casting her thoughts in that direction.

"I will do this for you," Sarah said, "because you know I would do anything for you. Which means I would throw myself in front of a moving carriage if it came to that." She paused, giving Honoria time to absorb *that* before continuing with a grand sweep of her arm. "And if I would throw myself in front of a moving carriage, it stands to reason that I would also consent to an activity that does not require the taking of my own life."

Honoria looked at her blankly.

"Such as sitting next to Lord Hugh Prentice at your wedding breakfast."

It took Honoria a moment to take that in. "How very . . . logical."

"And by the way, it's two days I must suffer his company, not one." She wrinkled her nose. "Just to be clear."

Honoria smiled graciously. "Then you shall entertain Lord Hugh this evening before supper?"

"Entertain," Sarah repeated sardonically. "Shall I dance? Because you know I'm not going to play the pianoforte."

Honoria laughed as she headed for the door. "Just be your usual charming self," she said, poking her face back in the room for one last second. "He will love you."

"God forbid."

"He works in strange ways . . ."

"Not that strange."

"Methinks the lady—"

"*Don't* say it," Sarah cut in.

Honoria's brows rose. "Shakespeare certainly knew what he was talking about."

Sarah threw a pillow at her.

But she missed. It was that kind of a day.

Later that day

CHATTERIS HAD ARRANGED for target shooting that afternoon, and as this was one of the few

sports in which Hugh could still participate, he
decided to head down to the south lawn at the appointed time. Or rather, thirty minutes before the
appointed time. His leg was still annoyingly stiff,
and he found that even with his cane to aid him,
he was walking more slowly than usual. There
were remedies to ease the pain, but the salve that
had been put forth by his doctor smelled like
death. As for laudanum, he could not tolerate the
dullness of mind it brought on.

All that was left was drink, and it was true that
a snifter or two of brandy seemed to loosen the
muscle and suppress the ache. But he rarely allowed himself to over-imbibe; just look what had
happened the last time he'd got drunk. He also
tried his best to avoid spirits until nightfall at the
earliest. The few times he'd given in and gulped
something down, he'd been disgusted with himself for days.

He had so few methods with which to measure his strength. It had become a point of honor
to make it through to dusk with only his wits to
battle the pain.

Stairs were always the most difficult, and he
paused at the landing to flex and straighten his
leg. Maybe he shouldn't bother. He hadn't even
made it halfway to the south lawn and already
the familiar dull throb was pulsing through his
thigh. No one would be the wiser if he just turned
around and went back to his room.

But damn it, he *wanted* to shoot. He wanted to
hold a gun in his hand and raise his arm straight

and true. He wanted to squeeze the trigger and feel the recoil as it shook through his shoulder. Most of all he wanted to hit the bloody bull's-eye.

So he was competitive. He was a man, it was to be expected.

There would be whispers and furtive looks, he was sure. It would not go unnoticed that Hugh Prentice was holding a pistol in the vicinity of Daniel Smythe-Smith. But Hugh was rather perversely looking forward to that. Daniel was, too. He had said as much when they'd talked at breakfast.

"Ten pounds if we can make someone faint," Daniel had declared, right after he'd done a rather fine falsetto imitation of one of Almack's patronesses, complete with a hand to the heart and a stellar collection of just about every expression of feminine outrage known to man.

"Ten pounds?" Hugh murmured, glancing at him over his cup of coffee. "To me or to you?"

"To both," Daniel said with a cheeky grin. "Marcus is good for it."

Marcus gave him a look and turned back to his eggs.

"He's getting very stuffy in his old age," Daniel said to Hugh.

To Marcus's credit, all he did was roll his eyes.

But Hugh had smiled. And he had realized that he was enjoying himself more than any time in recent memory. If the gentlemen were shooting, he was damn well going to join them.

It took at least five minutes to make his way down to the ground floor, however, and once there, he decided that it would be best to cut through one of Fensmore's many salons instead of taking the long way round to the south lawn.

Over the past three and a half years, Hugh had become remarkably adept at ferreting out every possible shortcut.

Third door on the right, then in, turn left, cross the room, and exit through the French doors. As an added benefit, he could take a moment to rest on one of the sofas. Most of the ladies had gone off to the village, so it was unlikely that anyone would be there. By his estimation he had a quarter of an hour before the shooting was due to start.

The drawing room wasn't terribly large, just a few seating arrangements. There was a blue chair facing him that looked comfortable enough. He couldn't see over the back of the sofa that sat opposite it, but there was probably a low table between them. He could put his leg up for a moment, and no one would be the wiser.

He made his way over, but he must not have been paying proper attention, because his cane clipped the edge of the table, which led directly to his shin clipping the edge of the table, which in turn led to a most creative string of curses clipping out of his mouth as he turned around to sit.

That was when he saw Sarah Pleinsworth, asleep on the sofa.

Oh, bloody hell.

He'd been having a better than average day, the pain in his leg notwithstanding. The last thing he needed was a private audience with the oh-so dramatic Lady Sarah. She'd probably accuse him of something nefarious, follow that with a trite declaration of hatred, then finish up with something about those fourteen men who had become engaged during the season of 1821.

He still didn't know what that was supposed to be about.

Or why he even recalled it. He'd always had a good memory, but really, couldn't his brain let go of the truly useless?

He had to get through the room without waking her up. It was not easy to tiptoe with a cane, but by God that was what he would do if that was what it took to make it through the room unnoticed.

Well, there went his hopes of resting his leg. Very carefully, he edged out from behind the low wooden table, careful not to touch anything but carpet and air. But as anyone who had ever stepped outside knew, air could move, and apparently he was breathing too hard, because before he made it past the sofa, Lady Sarah woke from her slumber with a shriek that startled him so much that he fell back against another chair, toppled over the upholstered arm, and landed awkwardly on the seat.

"What? What? What are you doing?" She blinked rapidly before spearing him with a glare. "*You.*"

It was an accusation. It absolutely was.

"Oh, you gave me a fright," she said, rubbing her eyes.

"Apparently." He swore under his breath as he tried to swing his legs over to the front of the chair. "Ow!"

"What?" she asked impatiently.

"I kicked the table."

"Why?"

He scowled. "I didn't do it on purpose."

She seemed only then to realize that she was lounging most casually along the length of the sofa and, with a flurry of movement, straightened herself to a more proper upright position. "Excuse me," she said, still flustered. Her dark hair was falling from its coiffure; he deemed it best not to point this out.

"Please accept my apology," he said stiffly. "I did not mean to startle you."

"I was reading. I must have fallen asleep. I . . . ah . . ." She blinked a few more times, then her eyes finally seemed to focus. On him. "Were you sneaking up on me?"

"*No*," he said, with perhaps more speed and fervor than was polite. He motioned to the door that led outside. "I was just cutting through. Lord Chatteris has made arrangements for target shooting."

"Oh." She looked suspicious for about one second more, then this clearly gave way to embarrassment. "Of course. There is no reason you would be sneak— That is to say—" She cleared her throat. "Well."

"Well."

She waited for a moment, then asked pointedly, "Don't you plan to continue to the lawn?"

He stared at her.

"For the shooting," she clarified.

He shrugged. "I'm early."

She did not seem to care for that answer. "It's quite pleasant outside."

He glanced out the window. "So it is." She was trying to get rid of him, and he supposed she deserved a certain measure of respect for not even trying to hide it. On the other hand, now that she was awake—and he was seated in a chair, resting his leg—there seemed no reason to hurry onward.

He could endure anything for ten minutes, even Sarah Pleinsworth.

"Do you plan to shoot?" she asked.

"I do."

"With a gun?"

"That's how one usually does it."

Her face tightened. "And you think this is prudent?"

"Do you mean because your cousin will be there? I assure you, he will have a gun as well." He felt his lips curve into an emotionless smile. "It will be almost like a duel."

"Why do you joke about such things?" she snapped.

He let his gaze land rather intently on hers. "When the alternative is despair, I generally prefer humor. Even if it is of the gallows variety."

Something flickered in her eyes. A hint of understanding, perhaps, but it was gone too quickly to be sure he'd seen it. And then she pursed her lips, an expression so prim it was clear he'd imagined that brief moment of sympathy.

"I want it known that I do not approve," she said.

"Duly noted."

"And"—she lifted her chin and turned slightly away—"I think it is a very bad idea."

"How is that different from a lack of approval?"

She just scowled.

He had a thought. "Do you find it bad enough to faint?"

She snapped back to attention. "What?"

"If you swoon on the lawn, Chatteris must give Daniel and me ten pounds each."

Her lips formed an O and then froze in that position.

He leaned back and smiled lazily. "I could be persuaded to offer you a twenty percent cut."

Her face moved, but she remained without words. Damn, but it was good fun to bait her.

"Never mind," he said. "We'd never carry it off."

Her mouth finally closed. Then opened again. Of course. He should have known her silence could be only fleeting.

"You don't like me," she said.

"Not really, no." He probably should have lied, but somehow it seemed that anything less than the truth would have been even more insulting.

"And I don't like you."

"No," he said mildly, "I didn't think you did."

"Then why are you here?"

"At the wedding?"

"In the *room*. Lud, you're obtuse." The last bit she said to herself, but his hearing had always been fairly sharp.

He rarely trotted his injury out as a trump card, but it seemed a good time. "My leg," he said with slow deliberation. "It hurts."

There was a delicious silence. Delicious for him, that was. For her, he imagined it was awful.

"I'm sorry," she mumbled, looking down before he could ascertain the extent of her flush. "That was very rude of me."

"Think nothing of it. You've done worse."

Her eyes flared.

He brought the tips of his fingers together, his hands making a hollow triangle. "I remember our previous encounter with unpleasant accuracy."

She leaned forward in fury. "You chased my cousin and aunt from a party."

"They *fled*. There is a difference. And I did not even know they were there."

"Well, you should have done."

"Clairvoyance has never been one of my talents."

He could see her straining to control her temper, and when she spoke, her jaw barely moved. "I know that you and Cousin Daniel have patched things up, but I'm sorry, I cannot forgive you for what you did."

"Even if he has?" Hugh asked softly.

She shifted uncomfortably, and her mouth pressed into several different expressions before she finally said, "He can afford to be charitable. His life and happiness have been restored."

"And yours has not." He did not phrase it as a question. It was a statement, and an unsympathetic one at that.

She clamped her mouth shut.

"Tell me," he demanded, because bloody hell, it was time they got to the bottom of this. "What, precisely, have I done to you? Not to your cousin,

not to your other cousin, but to you, Lady Sarah
Whatever your other names are Pleinsworth."

She glared at him mutinously, then got to her
feet. "I'm leaving."

"Coward," he murmured, but he stood as well.
Even she deserved the respect of a gentleman.

"Very well," she said, the color in her cheeks
rising with barely restrained anger. "I was supposed to make my debut in 1821."

"The year of the fourteen eligible gentlemen." It
was true. He forgot almost nothing.

She ignored this. "After you chased Daniel out
of the country, my family had to go into seclu-
sion."

"It was my father," Hugh said sharply.

"What?"

"My father chased Lord Winstead out of the
country. I had nothing to do with it."

"It doesn't matter."

His eyes narrowed, and with slow deliberate-
ness he said, "It does to me."

She swallowed uncomfortably, her entire bearing rigid. "Because of the duel," she said, rephras-
ing so that the blame could be put back squarely
on him, "we did not return to town for an entire
year."

Hugh choked back a laugh, finally understanding her silly little mind. She was blaming
him for the loss of her London season. "And
those fourteen eligible gentlemen are now forever lost to you."

"There is no reason to be so mocking."

"You have no way of knowing that one would

have proposed," he pointed out. He did like things to be logical, and this was . . . not.

"There is no way of knowing that one wouldn't have done," she cried. Her hand flew to her chest, and she took a jerky step back, as if surprised by her own reaction.

But Hugh felt no sympathy. And he could not stave off the unkind chuckle that burst from his throat. "You never cease to astonish me, Lady Sarah. All this time, you've been blaming *me* for your unmarried state. Did it ever occur to you to look somewhere closer to home?"

She let out an awful choke and her hand came to her mouth, not so much to cover it as to hold something in.

"Forgive me," he said, but they both knew that what he'd said was unforgivable.

"I thought I did not like you because of what you did to my family," she said, holding herself so rigid that she shook, "but that's not it at all. You are a terrible person."

He stood very still, the way he'd been taught since birth. A gentleman was always in control of his body. A gentleman didn't flail his arms or spit or fidget. He did not have much left in his life, but he had this—his pride, his bearing. "I shall endeavor not to press myself into your company," he said stiffly.

"It's too late for that," she bit off.

"I beg your pardon?"

Her eyes bored into his. "My cousin, if you recall, has requested that we sit together at the wedding breakfast."

Apparently he did forget some things. Bloody hell. He had promised Lady Honoria. There was no getting out of it. "I can be civil if you can," he said.

She shocked him then, holding out her hand to seal their agreement. He took it, and in that moment when her hand lay in his, he had the most bizarre urge to bring her fingers to his lips.

"Have we a truce, then?" she said.

He looked up.

That was a mistake.

Because Lady Sarah Pleinsworth was gazing up at him with an expression of uncommon and (he was quite sure) uncharacteristic clarity. Her eyes, which had always been hard and brittle when turned in his direction, were softer now. And her lips, he realized now that she wasn't hurling insults at him, were utter perfection, full and pink, and touched with just the right sort of curve. They seemed to tell a man that she knew things, that she knew how to laugh, and if he only laid down his soul for her, she would light up his world with a single smile.

Sarah Pleinsworth.

Good God, had he lost his mind?

Chapter Five

Later that night

WHEN SARAH CAME down for supper, she was
feeling a bit better about having to spend the
evening with Hugh Prentice. The row they'd
had that afternoon had been awful, and she
could not imagine they would ever choose to be
friends, but at least they'd got everything out in
the open. If she was to be forced to remain at his
side for the duration of the wedding, he would
not think she was doing so out of any desire for
his company.

And he would behave properly as well. They
had struck a bargain, and whatever his faults, he
did not seem the type to go back on his word. He
would be polite, and he would put on a good show
for Honoria and Marcus, and once this ridiculous

month of weddings was over, they would never need speak with each other again.

After five minutes in the drawing room, however, it became delightfully clear that Lord Hugh was not yet present. And Sarah had looked. No one was going to accuse her of shirking her duty.

Sarah had never much liked standing alone at gatherings, so she joined her mother and aunts over by the fireplace. As expected, they were nattering on about the wedding. Sarah listened with half an ear; after five days at Fensmore, she could not imagine there was any detail she had not yet heard about the upcoming ceremony.

"It is a pity the hydrangeas aren't in season," her aunt Virginia was saying. "The ones we grow at Whipple Hill are just the shade of lavender-blue we need for the chapel."

"It's blue-lavender," Aunt Maria corrected, "and you must see that hydrangeas would have been a terrible mistake."

"A mistake?"

"The colors are far too variable," Aunt Maria continued, "even on a cultivated shrub. You would never have been able to guarantee the shade ahead of time, and what if they did not match Honoria's dress perfectly?"

"Surely no one would expect perfection," Aunt Virginia replied. "Not with flowers."

Aunt Maria sniffed. "I always expect perfection."

"Especially from flowers," Sarah said with a little chuckle. Aunt Maria had named her daughters Rose, Lavender, Marigold, Iris, and Daisy. Her son, whom Sarah privately thought might be the luckiest child in England, was called John.

But Aunt Maria, though generally kindhearted, had never had much of a sense of humor. She blinked a few times in Sarah's direction before giving a little smile and saying, "Oh yes, of course."

Sarah still wasn't sure if Aunt Maria had got the joke. She decided not to press the matter. "Oh, look! There's Iris!" she said, relieved to see her cousin enter the room. Sarah had never been as close to Iris as she was to Honoria, but they were all three almost the same age, and Sarah had always enjoyed Iris's dry wit. She imagined the two of them would be spending more time together now that Honoria was getting married, especially since they shared a profound loathing for the family musicale.

"Go," her mother said, nodding in Iris's direction. "You don't want to stay here with the matrons."

She really didn't, so with a grateful smile to her mother, Sarah made her way over to Iris, who was standing near the doorway, quite obviously looking for someone.

"Have you seen Lady Edith?" Iris asked without preamble.

"Who?"

"Lady Edith Gilchrist," Iris clarified, referring to a young lady neither of them knew very well.

"Wasn't she recently engaged to the Duke of Kinross?"

Iris waved this off as if the recent loss of an

eligible duke was of no consequence. "Is Daisy down?" she asked.

Sarah blinked at the sudden change of subject. "Not that I have seen."

"Thank *God*."

Sarah's eyes widened at Iris's rather fast use of the Lord's name, but she would never criticize. Not about Daisy.

Daisy was best in very small doses. There was simply no getting around that.

"If I make it through these weddings without murdering her, it will be a small miracle," Iris said darkly. "Or a large . . . something."

"I told Aunt Virginia not to put the two of you in a bedchamber together," Sarah said.

Iris dismissed this with a flick of her head as she continued to glance about the drawing room. "There was nothing to be done about that. Sisters will be put together. They need to conserve rooms. I'm used to it."

"Then what is wrong?"

Iris swung around to face her, her pale eyes large and furious in her similarly pale face. Sarah had once heard a gentleman call Iris colorless— she had light blue eyes, pale strawberry blond hair, and skin that was practically translucent. Her brows were pale, her lashes were pale, everything about her was pale—until one got to know her.

Iris was as fierce as they came. "She wants to *play*," she seethed.

For a moment Sarah did not comprehend. And then—terrifyingly—she did. "No!" she gasped.

"She brought her violin up from London," Iris confirmed.

"But—"

"And Honoria has already moved *her* violin to Fensmore. And of course every great house has a pianoforte." Iris clenched her jaw; she was quite obviously repeating Daisy's words.

"But your cello!" Sarah protested.

"You'd think, wouldn't you?" Iris fumed. "But no, she's thought of everything. Lady Edith Gilchrist is here, and she brought *her* cello. Daisy wants me to borrow it."

Instinctively, Sarah whipped her head around, looking for Lady Edith.

"She's not here yet," Iris said, all business, "but I need to find her the moment she gets in."

"Why would Lady Edith bring a cello?"

"Well, she plays," Iris said, as if Sarah had not considered that.

Sarah resisted the urge to roll her eyes. Well, almost. "But why would she bring it *here*?"

"Apparently, she's quite good."

"What has that got to do with anything?"

Iris shrugged. "I expect she likes to practice every day. Many great musicians do."

"I wouldn't know," Sarah said.

Iris gave her a commiserating look, then said, "I need to find her before Daisy does. Under no circumstances may she permit Daisy to borrow her cello on my behalf."

"If she's that good, she probably wouldn't want to lend it out. At least not to one of us." Sarah grimaced. Lady Edith was relatively new to London, but surely she knew of the Smythe-Smith musicale.

"I'm apologizing in advance for abandoning you," Iris said, keeping her eyes on the open doorway. "I shall probably bolt midsentence the moment I see her."

"I may have to bolt first," Sarah told her. "I have been assigned duties of my own for the evening."

Her tone must have belied her distaste, because Iris turned to her with renewed interest.

"I'm to be nanny to Hugh Prentice," Sarah said, sounding rather burdened as the words clipped out of her mouth. But it was a good kind of burdened. If she was going to have a dreadful evening, at least she could boast about it in advance.

"Nanny to— Oh, my."

"Don't laugh," Sarah warned.

"I wasn't going to," Iris clearly lied.

"Honoria insisted. She thinks he won't feel welcome if one of us doesn't see to his happiness and inclusion."

"And she asked you to nanny him?" Iris gave her a dubious stare, always an unsettling expression. There was something about Iris's eyes, that watery pale blue and the lashes so fine they were almost invisible. She could be rather unnerving.

"Well, no," Sarah admitted, "not in so many words." Not in any words, to be truthful, and in fact, Honoria had specifically *denied* those words, but it did make for a better story to call herself a nanny.

At functions such as these, one had to have something good about which to complain. It was rather like those boys at Cambridge she'd met last spring. They only seemed happy when they'd been able to moan about how much work they had to do.

"What does she want you to do?" Iris asked.

"Oh, this and that. I'm to sit with him tomorrow at the wedding breakfast. Rupert's taken ill," she added as an aside.

"Well, that's good, at least," Iris murmured.

Sarah acknowledged this with a brief nod as she continued. "And she specifically asked me to entertain Lord Hugh before supper."

Iris glanced over her shoulder. "Is he here yet?"

"No," Sarah said with a happy sigh.

"Don't get too complacent," Iris warned. "He'll be down. If Honoria asked you to watch out for him, she will have asked him—quite specifically—to come to supper."

Sarah stared at Iris in horror. Honoria had *said* she wasn't trying to make a match of the two of them . . . "Surely you don't think—"

"No, no," Iris said with a snort, "she wouldn't dare try to play matchmaker. Not with you."

Sarah's lips came together to ask her what she meant by *that*, but before she could make a sound, Iris added, "You know Honoria. She likes everything to be neat and tidy. If she wants you to look after Lord Hugh, she'll make sure he's here to need looking after."

Sarah considered this for a moment, then gave a nod of concurrence. Honoria *was* like that. "Well," she declared, because she always did like a declarative *well*. "It's going to make for a miserable two days, but I promised Honoria, and I always keep my obligations."

If Iris had been sipping a drink, she would have sprayed it across the room. *"You?"*

"What do you mean, *me*?" Sarah demanded. Iris looked as if she was about to chortle with amusement.

"Oh, please," Iris said, in that scornful way one could adopt only with family and still hope to be on speaking terms the next day, "you are the last person who can claim to keep all of her obligations."

Sarah drew back, deeply affronted. "I beg your pardon."

But if Iris saw Sarah's distress, she did not notice. Or did not care. "Does your memory not stretch back to last April?" Iris prompted. "April the fourteenth, to be precise?"

The musicale. Sarah had backed out the afternoon of the performance. "I was ill," she protested. "There was no way I could have played."

Iris did not say a word. She didn't have to. Sarah was lying, and they both knew it.

"Very well, I wasn't ill," Sarah admitted. "At least not very ill."

"It's nice of you to finally admit it," Iris said in an annoyingly superior voice.

Sarah shifted her weight uncomfortably. It had been the two of them that spring, plus Honoria and Daisy. Honoria had been happy to play as long as she was with family, and Daisy was convinced that she was well on her way to becoming a virtuoso. Iris and Sarah, on the other hand, had held many conversations debating the various methods of death by musical instrument. Gallows humor. It had been the only way they'd been able to get through the dread.

"I did it for you," she finally said to Iris.

"Oh, really."

"I thought the entire performance would be canceled."

Iris was clearly unconvinced.

"I did!" Sarah insisted. "Who would have ever thought Mama would drag poor Miss Wynter into the performance? Although it did turn out well for her, didn't it?"

Miss Wynter—Miss Anne Wynter, who was going to marry Cousin Daniel in two weeks and become the Countess of Winstead—had made the mistake of once telling Sarah's mother that she could play the pianoforte. Lady Pleinsworth, apparently, had not forgotten this.

"Daniel would have fallen in love with Miss Wynter regardless," Iris retorted, "so don't try to soothe your conscience with that."

"I wasn't. I was merely pointing out that I never could have foreseen—" She let out an impatient breath. None of this sounded the way it did in her head. "Iris, you must know that I was trying to save you."

"You were trying to save yourself."

"I was trying to save both of us. It just— It did not work the way I planned."

Iris regarded her coolly. Sarah waited for her to respond, but she didn't. She just stood there, drawing out the moment like soft treacle candy, stretched into a ropy swing. Finally, Sarah could take it no more, and she gave in with, "Just say it."

Iris raised a brow.

"Whatever it is you're so keen to tell me. Obviously there is something."

Iris's lips parted, then closed, as if she were taking time to choose the correct words. Finally, she said, "You know that I love you."

It was not what Sarah had expected. Unfortunately, neither was what came next.

"I will always love you," Iris continued. "In fact, I will probably even always like you, and you know I cannot say that about most of our family. But you can be terribly selfish. And the worst part of it is, you don't even see it."

It was the strangest thing, Sarah thought. She wanted to say something. She *needed* to say something, because that's what she did when faced with something she didn't like. Iris couldn't call her selfish and expect Sarah to just stand there and listen.

And yet that was what she seemed to be doing.

She swallowed, and she felt her tongue dart out to moisten her lips, but she could not form words. All she could do was think *No.* It wasn't true. She loved her family. She would do anything for them. That Iris could stand there and call her selfish . . .

It cut deep.

Sarah stared at her cousin's face, sensing the precise moment when Iris moved on, when the fact that she'd just called Sarah selfish was no longer the most consequential thing in the world.

As if anything could be more consequential.

"There she is," Iris said briskly. "Lady Edith. I need to get to her before Daisy does." She took a step, then turned and said, "We can talk about this later. If you want."

"I'd rather not, thank you," Sarah replied tightly, finally hauling her personality out of whatever hole it had just jumped into. But Iris didn't hear her. She'd already turned her back and was making her way toward Lady Edith. Sarah was left alone in the corner, as awkward as a jilted bride.

And that—of course—was when Hugh Prentice arrived.

Chapter Six

THE STRANGE THING was, Sarah thought she was angry.

She thought she was furious with Iris, who ought to have been more sensitive to the feelings of others. If Iris had felt the need to call her selfish, at the very least she could have done so in a more private setting.

And then to abandon her! Sarah did understand the need to intercept Lady Edith before Daisy descended upon her, but still, Iris should have said she was sorry.

But then, as Sarah stood in her corner, wondering how long she could pretend that she had not noticed Lord Hugh's arrival, she took an unexpected breath.

And choked back a sob.

Apparently she was something other than

angry, and she was in grave danger of crying, right here in the crowded Fensmore drawing room.

She turned swiftly, determined to examine the large, gloomy portrait that had been keeping her company. The subject appeared to be an unpleasant gentleman from Flanders, seventeenth century, if Sarah's eye for fashion was correct. How he managed to look so proud in that ridiculous pleated collar she would never know, but he was staring down his beaky nose in a manner that told her clearly that none of *his* cousins would dare to call him selfish to his face, and if they did, he would not cry about it.

Sarah curled her lip and glared at him. It was probably a testament to the skill of the artist that he seemed to glare right back at her.

"Has the gentleman done something to offend?"

It was Hugh Prentice. Sarah knew his voice well enough by now. Honoria must have sent him over. She could not imagine why he might seek out her company otherwise.

They had promised to be civil, not eager.

She turned. He was standing about two feet from her, impeccably dressed for supper. Except for his cane. It was scuffed and scratched, the wood grain dull from overuse. Sarah wasn't sure why she found this so interesting. Surely Lord Hugh traveled with a valet. His boots had been buffed to a high shine, and his cravat was expertly tied. Why would his cane be denied the same careful treatment?

"Lord Hugh," she said, relieved that her voice sounded almost normal as she offered a small curtsy.

He didn't say anything right away. He turned back to the portrait, his chin tilted up as his eyes swept over it. Sarah was glad he was not looking at her with such examination; she was not sure she could manage another dissection of her faults so soon after the first.

"That collar looks most uncomfortable," Lord Hugh said.

"That was my first thought as well," Sarah replied, before she remembered that she did not like him, and more to the point, he was her burden for the evening.

"I expect we should be glad that we live in modern times."

She did not respond; it was not the sort of statement that required it. Lord Hugh continued to scrutinize the painting, at one point leaning in, presumably to examine the brushwork. Sarah did not know if he'd realized she needed time to compose herself. She could not imagine that he had; he didn't seem the type of man to notice such things. Either way, she was grateful. By the time he turned to face her, the choking feeling in her chest had eased, and she was no longer in danger of embarrassing herself in front of several dozen of her cousin's most important wedding guests.

"The wine is very good tonight, I'm told," she said. It was an abrupt start to conversation, but it was polite and innocuous, and most importantly, it was the first thing that had popped into her head.

"You're told?" Lord Hugh echoed.

"I haven't had any myself," Sarah explained. An awkward pause, and then: "Actually, no one told me. But Lord Chatteris is renowned for his cellars. I cannot imagine the wine would be anything but good."

Good heavens, this was a stilted conversation. But no matter; Sarah would soldier on. She would not shirk her duties tonight. If Honoria looked her way; if *Iris* looked her way—

No one would be able to say that she had not kept her promises.

"I try not to drink in the company of the Smythe-Smiths," Lord Hugh said, almost off-handedly. "It rarely ends well for me."

Sarah gasped.

"I jest," he said.

"Of course," she replied quickly, mortified to have been revealed as so unsophisticated. She should have got the joke. She would have done, if she weren't still so upset about Iris.

Dear Lord, she said to herself (and Anyone Else who might be listening), *please bring this evening to an end with uncanny speed*.

"Isn't it interesting," Lord Hugh asked slowly, "all that is wrought by societal convention?"

Sarah turned to him, even though she knew she'd never be able to discern his meaning from his expression. He tilted his head to the side, the movement rearranging the shadows on his impassive face.

He was handsome, Sarah realized in a strange burst of awareness. It wasn't just the color of his eyes. It was the way he looked at a person, unwavering and sometimes unnerving. It lent him an air of intensity that was difficult to ignore. And his mouth—he rarely smiled, or at least he rarely smiled at *her*, but there was something rather wry about it. She supposed some people might not find that attractive, but she . . .

Did.

Dear Lord, she tried again, *forget uncanny. Nothing less than the supernatural would be speedy enough.*

"Here we are," he continued, motioning elegantly with his hand to the rest of the guests, "trapped in a room with, oh, how many others would you say?"

She had no idea where he was going with this, but she hazarded a guess. "Forty?"

"Indeed," he replied, although she could tell by the quick sweep of his eyes across the room that he disagreed with her estimation. "And their collective presence means that you"—he leaned in, just an inch—"whom we have already established finds me loathsome, are being quite polite."

"I'm not being polite because there are forty other people in the room," she said, her brows arching. "I'm being polite because my cousin requested it of me."

The corner of his mouth moved. It might have been amusement. "Did she realize what a challenge this might pose?"

"She did not," Sarah said tightly. Honoria knew that Sarah did not care for Lord Hugh's company, but she did not seem to comprehend the extent of her distaste.

"I must commend you, then," he said with a wry nod, "for keeping your protestations to yourself."

Something lovely and familiar clicked back into place, and Sarah finally began to feel more like herself. Her chin rose a very proud half of an inch. "I did not."

To her great surprise, Lord Hugh made a noise that might have been a smothered laugh. "And she saddled you with me, anyway."

"She worries that you might not feel welcome here at Fensmore," Sarah said, in just the sort of tone that said this was not a shared concern.

His brows rose, and again he almost smiled. "And she thinks *you* are the person to welcome me?"

"I never told her of our previous meeting," Sarah admitted.

"Ah." He gave a condescending nod. "It all begins to make sense."

Sarah clenched her teeth in a largely unsuccessful attempt to keep from snorting. How she *hated* that tone of voice. That *oh-I-see-how-your-pretty-little-female-mind-works* tone of voice. Hugh Prentice was hardly the only man in England to employ it, but he seemed to have honed the skill to a razor-fine edge. Sarah could not imagine how anyone tolerated his company for more than a few minutes. Yes, he was rather nice to look at, and yes, he was (she was told) exceptionally intelligent, but by God, the man was like fingernails on slate.

She leaned forward. "It is a testament to my

love for my cousin that I have not found some way to poison your tooth powder."

He leaned forward. "The wine might have been an effective substitute," he said, "were I drinking. That was why you suggested it, was it not?"

She refused to give ground. "You are mad."

He gave a one-shouldered shrug and backed away as if the charged moment between them had never occurred. "I'm not the one who brought up poison."

Her mouth fell open. His tone was precisely the one she might use while discussing the weather.

"Angry?" he murmured politely.

Not so much angry as baffled. "You make it very difficult to be nice to you," she told him.

He blinked. "Was I meant to offer you my tooth powder?"

Good heavens, he was frustrating. And the worst part was, she wasn't even sure if he was joking now. Nevertheless, she cleared her throat and said, "You were *meant* to have a normal conversation."

"I'm not sure the two of us have normal conversations."

"I can assure you, *I* do."

"Not with me." This time he did smile. She was sure of it.

Sarah straightened her shoulders. Surely the butler must be calling them in to supper soon. Perhaps she ought to start offering her prayers to *him*, since the other Him didn't seem to be listening.

"Oh, come now, Lady Sarah," Lord Hugh said.

"You must admit that our first meeting was anything but normal."

She pressed her lips together. She hated to acknowledge his point—any of his points, really—but he did have one.

"And since then," he added, "we have met but a handful of times, and always in a most superficial manner."

"I had not noticed," she said tightly.

"That it was superficial?"

"That we had met," she lied.

"Regardless," he continued, "this is only the second time we have exchanged more than two sentences with each other. The first I believe you instructed me to remove the world of my presence."

Sarah winced. That had not been her finest moment.

"And then tonight . . ." His lips moved into a seductive smile. "Well, you did mention poison."

She leveled a flat stare in his direction. "You should mind your tooth powder."

He chuckled at that, and a little electric thrill jolted through her veins. She might not have got the best of him, but she had definitely scored an acknowledged point. Truth be told, she was starting to enjoy herself. She still disliked him, only partly on principle, but she had to admit that she was having, perhaps, just the tiniest amount of fun.

He was a worthy adversary.

She hadn't even realized she *wanted* a worthy adversary.

Which did not mean—good God, if she was blushing at her own thoughts she was going to hurl herself out the window—that she wanted *him*. Any worthy adversary would do.

Even one without such nice eyes.

"Is something wrong, Lady Sarah?" Lord Hugh inquired.

"No," she replied. Too quickly.

"You look agitated."

"I'm not."

"Of course," he murmured.

"I'm—" She cut herself off, then said disgruntledly, "Well, now I am."

"And here I hadn't even been trying," he said.

Sarah had all sorts of retorts to that, but none which would leave him without an obvious parry of his own. Maybe what she *really* wanted was an only slightly less worthy adversary. Just enough brains to keep it interesting, but not so much that she would not always win.

Hugh Prentice would never be *that* man.

Thank God.

"Well, this looks like an awkward conversation!" came a new voice.

Sarah turned her head, not that she needed to see the speaker to recognize her identity. It was the Countess of Danbury, the most terrifying old dragon of the ton. She had once managed to destroy a violin with nothing but a cane (and, Sarah was convinced, sleight of hand). But her true weapon, as everyone knew, was her devastating wit.

"Awkward, yes," Lord Hugh said with a respectful bow. "But growing less so with each passing second now that you are here."

"Pity," the elderly lady replied, adjusting her grip on her cane. "I find awkward conversations to be very diverting."

"Lady Danbury," Sarah said, dipping into a curtsy, "what a lovely surprise to see you this evening."

"What are you talking about?" Lady Danbury demanded. "This should be no surprise at all. Chatteris is my great-grandnephew. Where else would I be?"

"Ehrm," was all Sarah got out before the countess demanded, "Do you know why I made my way across the entire room, specifically to join the two of you?"

"I cannot imagine," Lord Hugh said.

Lady Danbury shot a sideways glance at Sarah, who quickly put in, "Nor I."

"I have found that happy people are dull. You two, on the other hand, looked ready to spit nails. Naturally I came right over." She looked from Hugh to Sarah and then said plainly, "Entertain me."

This was met with dumbfounded silence. Sarah stole a look at Lord Hugh and was relieved to see that his usual bored expression had been cracked with surprise.

Lady Danbury leaned forward and said in a loud whisper, "I have decided to like you, Lady Sarah."

Sarah was not at all certain this was a good thing. "You have?"

"Indeed. And so I will give you some advice." She nodded toward Sarah as if granting an audience to a serf. "You may feel free to share it at will."

Sarah's eyes darted to Lord Hugh's, although why she thought he might come to her aid she could not say.

"Our current conversation notwithstanding," Lady Danbury continued imperiously, "I have observed you to be a young lady of reasonable wit."

Reasonable? Sarah felt her nose wrinkling as she tried to figure *that* out. "Thank you?"

"It was a compliment," Lady Danbury confirmed.

"Even the reasonable part?"

Lady Danbury snorted. "I don't know you *that* well."

"Well, then, thank you," Sarah said, deciding this was an excellent time to be gracious, or at the very least, obtuse. She glanced over at Lord Hugh, who looked mildly amused, and then back at Lady Danbury, who was eyeing her as if she expected her to say something more.

Sarah cleared her throat. "Ehrm, was there any reason you wished me to know of your regard?"

"What? Oh, yes." Lady Danbury thumped her cane on the ground. "Despite my advancing age, I forget nothing." She paused. "Except occasionally what I've just said."

Sarah kept her face fixed with a blank smile and tried to tamp down a gnawing sense of dread.

Lady Danbury let out a dramatic sigh. "I suppose one can't reach the age of seventy without making a few concessions to it."

Sarah suspected that seventy missed the mark by at least a decade, but there was no way she was going to make this opinion public.

"What I was *going* to say," Lady Danbury continued, her voice dripping with the long-suffering tones of the endlessly interrupted (despite the fact that she was the only one who had been talking), "is that when you expressed surprise at my presence, which we both know was nothing more than a feeble attempt to make conversation, and *I* said, 'Where else would I be?' *you* should have said, 'Apparently you don't find polite conversation very diverting.'"

Sarah's lips parted and hung there in an astonished oval for a full two seconds before she said, "I am afraid I can't follow you."

Lady Danbury fixed her with a vaguely aggravated stare before saying, "I had told you that I found awkward conversations to be very diverting, and *you* said that nonsense about being surprised to see me, then *I* quite rightly called you foolish."

"I don't believe you called her foolish," Lord Hugh murmured.

"Didn't I? Well, I thought it." Lady Danbury thumped her cane on the carpet and turned back to Sarah. "At any rate, I was only trying to be helpful. There's never any point spouting useless platitudes. Makes you seem a bit like a wooden post, and you don't want that, do you?"

"It really depends on the location of the wooden post," Sarah replied, wondering how many wooden posts one might find in, say, Bombay.

"Well done, Lady Sarah," Lady Danbury applauded. "Keep sharpening that tongue. I expect you'll wish to keep your wits about you this evening."

"I generally wish to keep my wits about myself every evening."

Lady Danbury gave an approving nod. "And you—" She turned to Lord Hugh, much to Sarah's delight. "Don't think I've forgotten you."

"I believe you said you forget nothing," he said.

"So I did," Lady Danbury replied. "Rather like your father in that regard, I expect."

Sarah gasped. Even for Lady Danbury, this was audacious.

But Lord Hugh proved to be more than her match. His expression did not change in the least as he said, "Ah, but that is not the case at all. My father's memory is relentlessly selective."

"But tenacious."

"Also relentlessly."

"Well," Lady Danbury declared, thumping her cane on the carpet. "I expect it's time to call him off."

"I have very little control over my father, Lady Danbury."

"No man is without all resources."

He tipped his head in a tiny salute. "I did not say that I was."

Sarah's eyes flicked back and forth so fast she was getting dizzy.

"This nonsense has gone on long enough," Lady Danbury announced.

"On that point, we are in agreement," Lord

Hugh replied, but to Sarah's ears, they were still sparring.

"It is good to see you at this wedding," the elderly countess said. "I hope it portends peaceful times to come."

"As Lord Chatteris is not my great-grandnephew, I can only assume that I was invited out of friendship."

"Or to keep an eye on you."

"Ah," Lord Hugh said, one corner of his mouth sliding into a wry curve, "but that would be counterproductive. One would assume that the only dastardly deed for which I might need monitoring would involve Lord Winstead, who, as we both know, is here at the wedding."

His face resumed its normal inscrutable mask, and he regarded Lady Danbury unblinkingly until she said, "I believe that is quite the longest sentence I have ever heard you utter."

"Have you heard him utter many sentences?" Sarah inquired.

Lady Danbury turned to her with a hawkish expression. "I'd quite forgotten you were there."

"I have been uncharacteristically quiet."

"Which brings me to my original point," Lady Danbury declared.

"That we are awkward?" Lord Hugh murmured.

"Yes!"

This, predictably, was met with an awkward pause.

"You, Lord Hugh," Lady Danbury declared, "have been abnormally taciturn since the day you were born."

"You were there?" he queried.

Lady Danbury's face screwed up, but it was obvious she appreciated an excellent riposte, even when directed at her. "How do you put up with him?" she asked Sarah.

"I rarely have to," Sarah replied with a shrug.

"Hmmph."

"She has been assigned to me," Lord Hugh explained.

Lady Danbury's eyes narrowed. "For someone so uncommunicative, you're quite pithy this evening."

"It must be the company."

"I do tend to bring out the best in people." Lady Danbury smiled slyly and swung around to face Sarah. "What do you think?"

"Without a doubt you bring out the best in me," Sarah proclaimed. She'd always known when to say what someone else wanted to hear.

"I must say," Lord Hugh said in a dry tone, "I find *this* conversation diverting."

"Well, you would, wouldn't you?" Lady Danbury retorted. "It's not as if you've had to tax your brain to keep up with me."

Sarah felt her lips part again as she tried to sort that one out. Had Lady Danbury just called him clever? Or was she insulting him by saying that he hadn't added anything of interest to the conversation?

And what did it mean that *Sarah* had to tax her brain to keep up with her?

"You look perplexed, Lady Sarah," Lady Danbury said.

"I find myself fervently hoping that we will soon be called in to supper," Sarah admitted.

Lady Danbury snorted with amusement.

Emboldened, Sarah said to Lord Hugh, "I believe I have begun to pray to the butler."

"If there are to be replies, you'll certainly hear his before anyone else's," he said.

"Now *this* is more like it," Lady Danbury announced. "Look at the two of you. You're positively bantering."

"Bantering," Lord Hugh repeated, as if he could not quite grasp the word.

"It's not as entertaining for *me* as an awkward conversation, but I imagine you prefer it." Lady Danbury pressed her lips together and glanced about the room. "I suppose I shall have to find someone else to entertain me now. It's quite a delicate balance, you know, finding awkwardness without stupidity." She thumped her cane on the carpet, hmmphed, and departed.

Sarah turned to Lord Hugh. "She's mad."

"I might point out that you recently said the same thing to me."

Sarah was sure there were a thousand different responses to that, but she managed to think of precisely none of them before Iris suddenly appeared. Sarah clenched her teeth. She was still very annoyed with her.

"I found her," Iris announced, her face still grim with latent determination. "We are saved."

Sarah could not find enough charity within herself to say something bright and congratulatory. She did, however, nod.

Iris gave her a queer look, punctuated with a tiny shrug.

"Lord Hugh," Sarah said, with perhaps a bit more emphasis than was strictly necessary, "may I present my cousin, Miss Smythe-Smith? Formerly Miss Iris Smythe-Smith," she added, for no reason other than her own sense of annoyance. "Her elder sister was recently wed."

Iris started, clearly only just realizing that he'd been standing next to her cousin. This did not surprise Sarah; when Iris had her mind set on something she rarely noticed anything she deemed irrelevant.

"Lord Hugh," Iris said, recovering quickly.

"I am most relieved to hear that you are saved," Lord Hugh said.

Sarah took some satisfaction in the fact that Iris did not appear to know how to respond.

"From plague?" Lord Hugh inquired. "Pestilence?"

Sarah could only stare.

"Oh, I know," he said in quite the jolliest tone she'd ever heard from him. "Locusts. There's nothing like a good infestation of locusts."

Iris blinked several times, then lifted a finger as if she'd just thought of something. "I'll leave you, then."

"Of course you will," Sarah muttered.

Iris gave her an almost imperceptible smirk, then made her departure, snaking fluidly through the crowd.

"I must confess to curiosity," Lord Hugh said once Iris had disappeared from view.

Sarah just stared ahead. He wasn't the sort to let her silence stop him, so there didn't seem much need to reply.

"From what dreadful fate did your cousin save you?"

"Not you, apparently," Sarah muttered before she could control her tongue.

He chuckled at that, and Sarah decided there was no reason not to tell him the truth. "My cousin Daisy—that's Iris's younger sister—was trying to organize a special performance of the Smythe-Smith Quartet."

"Why should that be a problem?"

Sarah took a moment to phrase her query. "You have not attended one of our musicales, then?"

"I have not had the pleasure."

"Pleasure," Sarah repeated, tucking her chin back toward her neck as she tried to choke down her disbelief.

"Is something wrong?" Lord Hugh asked.

She opened her mouth to explain, but just then the butler came in and called them in for supper.

"Your prayers are answered," Lord Hugh said wryly.

"Not all of them," she muttered.

He offered her his arm. "Yes, you're still stuck with me, aren't you?"

Indeed.

Chapter Seven

The following afternoon

AND SO THE Earl of Chatteris and Lady Honoria Smythe-Smith were joined in holy matrimony. The sun was shining, the wine was flowing, and judging by the laughter and smiles at the wedding breakfast (which had long since metamorphosed into a wedding luncheon), a good time was being had by all.

Even Lady Sarah Pleinsworth.

From where Hugh was sitting at the head table (rather by himself; everyone else had got up to dance), she was the very embodiment of carefree English womanhood. She spoke easily to the other guests, she laughed often (but never too loudly), and when she danced, she looked so bloody happy it nearly lit the room on fire.

Hugh had once liked to dance.

He'd been good at it, too. Music was not so very different from mathematics. It was all just patterns and sequences. The only difference was that they hung in the air instead of on a piece of paper.

Dancing was a grand equation. One side was sound, the other movement. The dancer's job was to make them equal.

Hugh might not have *felt* music, the way the choral master at Eton had insisted he must, but he certainly understood it.

"Hullo, Lord Hugh. Would you like some cake?"

Hugh looked up and smiled. It was little Lady Frances Pleinsworth, holding two plates. One had a gigantic slice of cake, the other a merely enormous one. Both had been liberally frosted with lavender-hued icing and tiny candy violets. Hugh had seen the cake in all its glory before it had been cut; he had immediately begun to wonder how many eggs such a gateau might have required. When that had proved an impossible calculation, he'd started thinking about how long it would have taken to make the confection. Then he'd moved on to—

"Lord Hugh?" Lady Frances said, cutting into his thoughts. She lifted one of the plates a few inches higher in the air, reminding him of why she'd come over.

"I do like cake," he said.

She sat down next to him, setting the plates on the table. "You looked lonely."

Hugh smiled again. It was the sort of thing an adult would never have said aloud. And precisely the reason he'd rather have been chatting with her than anyone else in the room. "I was alone, not lonely."

Frances frowned, considering that. Hugh was just about to explain the difference when she cocked her head and asked, "Are you sure?"

"Alone is a state of being," he explained, "whereas lonely is—"

"I know that," she cut in.

He regarded her. "Then I'm afraid I do not understand your question."

She cocked her head to the side. "I was just wondering if a person always knows when he is lonely."

Budding little philosopher, she was. "How old are you?" he asked, deciding that he would not be surprised if she opened her mouth and said she was actually forty-two.

"Eleven." She jabbed a fork into her cake, expertly picking the icing from between the layers. "But I'm very precocious."

"Clearly."

She didn't say anything, but he saw her smiling around her fork as she took a bite.

"Do you like cake?" she asked, delicately dabbing the corner of her mouth with a napkin.

"Doesn't everyone?" he murmured, not pointing out that he'd already said he did.

She glanced down at his untouched plate. "Then why haven't you eaten any?"

"I'm thinking," he said, his eyes sweeping across the room and settling on the laughing form of her eldest sister.

"You can't eat and think at the same time?" Frances asked.

It was a dare if ever he'd heard one, so he hauled his attention back to the slab of cake in front of him, took a huge bite, chewed, swallowed, and said, "541 times 87 is 47,067."

"You're making that up," Frances said instantly.

He shrugged. "Feel free to check the answer yourself."

"I can't very well do so *here*."

"Then you'll have to take my word for it, won't you?"

"As long as you realize that I *could* check your answer if I had the proper supplies," Frances said pertly. Then she frowned. "Did you truly figure that out in your head?"

"I did," he confirmed. He took another bite of cake. It really was quite tasty. The icing seemed to have been flavored with actual lavender. Marcus had always liked sweets, he recalled.

"That's *brilliant*. I wish I could do that."

"It occasionally comes in handy." He ate more cake. "And sometimes does not."

"I'm very good at maths," Frances said in a matter-of-fact voice, "but I can't do it in my head. I need to write everything down."

"There's nothing wrong with that."

"No, of course not. I'm much better than Elizabeth." Frances gave a lofty smile. "She hates that I am, but she knows it's true."

"Which one is Elizabeth?" Hugh probably should have remembered which sister was which, but the memory that captured every word on a page was not always so dependable with names and faces.

"My next oldest sister. She is occasionally unpleasant, but for the most part we get on well."

"Everyone is occasionally unpleasant," he told her.

That stopped her short. "Even you?"

"Oh, especially me."

She blinked a few times, then must have decided she preferred the earlier strain of conversation, because when she opened her mouth again it was to ask, "Do you have any brothers or sisters?"

"I have one brother."

"What is his name?"

"Frederick. I call him Freddie."

"Do you like him?"

Hugh smiled. "Very much so. But I don't get to see him very often."

"Why not?"

Hugh didn't want to think about all the reasons why not, so he settled on the only one that was suitable for her ears. "He doesn't live in London. And I do."

"That's too bad." Frances poked her fork in her cake, idly smearing the icing. "Perhaps you can see him at Christmas."

"Perhaps," Hugh lied.

"Oh, I forgot to ask," she said. "Are you better at arithmetic than he is?"

"I am," Hugh confirmed. "But he doesn't mind."

"Neither does Harriet. She's five years older than I am, and I'm still better than she is."

Hugh gave a nod, having no other reply.

"She likes to write plays," Frances continued. "She doesn't care about numbers."

"She should," Hugh said, glancing back out at the wedding celebration. Lady Sarah was now dancing with one of the Bridgerton brothers. The angle was such that Hugh could not be sure which one. He recalled that three of the brothers were married, but one was not.

"She's very good at it," Frances said.

She is, Hugh thought, still watching Sarah. She danced beautifully. One could almost forget her waspish mouth when she danced like that.

"She's even putting a unicorn in the next one."

A uni— "What?" Hugh turned back to Frances, blinking.

"A unicorn." She gave him a frighteningly steady look. "You *are* familiar with them?"

Good Lord, was she poking fun at him? He'd have been impressed if it wasn't so patently ridiculous. "Of course."

"I'm mad for unicorns," Frances said with a blissful sigh. "I think they're brilliant."

"Nonexistently brilliant."

"So we *think,*" she replied with suitable drama.

"Lady Frances," Hugh said in his most didactic voice, "you must be aware that unicorns are creatures of myth."

"The myths had to come from somewhere."

"They *came* from the imaginations of bards."

She shrugged and ate cake.

Hugh was dumbfounded. Was he really debating the existence of unicorns with an eleven-year-old girl?

He tried to drop the matter. And found he could not. Apparently he *was* debating the existence of unicorns with an eleven-year-old girl.

"There has never been a recorded sighting of a unicorn," he said, and to his great irritation, he realized that he sounded as prim and stiff as Sarah Pleinsworth had when she'd been all snippy about his plans to shoot targets with her cousin.

Frances lifted her chin. "I have never seen a lion, but that doesn't mean they don't exist."

"You may have never seen a lion, but hundreds of other people have done."

"You can't prove that something *doesn't* exist," she countered.

Hugh paused. She had him there.

"Indeed," she said smugly, recognizing the exact moment he'd been forced to capitulate.

"Very well," he said, giving her an approving nod. "I cannot prove that unicorns don't exist, but *you* cannot prove they do."

"True," she said graciously. Her mouth pursed and then did an unnerving little twist. "I like you, Lord Hugh."

For a second she sounded exactly like Lady Danbury. Hugh wondered if he ought to be afraid.

"You don't speak to me as if I were a child," she said.

"You *are* a child," he pointed out. She'd used the subjunctive form of "to be," which would imply that she *wasn't* actually a child.

"Well, yes, but you don't speak to me as if I were an idiot."

"You're not an idiot," he said. And she'd used

the subjunctive correctly that time. But he didn't make mention of that.

"I *know*." She was starting to sound somewhat exasperated.

He stared at her for a moment. "Then what is your point?"

"Just that— Oh, hullo, Sarah." Frances smiled over Hugh's shoulder, presumably at the current bane of his existence.

"Frances," came the now familiar voice of Lady Sarah Pleinsworth. "Lord Hugh."

He stood, even though it was awkward, with his leg.

"Oh, you don't need to—" Sarah began.

"I do," Hugh cut in sharply. The day he could no longer rise to his feet in the presence of a lady was— Well, quite honestly he did not want to ponder it.

She gave a tight—and possibly embarrassed—smile, then walked around him to sit in the chair on the other side of Frances. "What were the two of you talking about?"

"Unicorns," Frances answered promptly.

Sarah's lips came together in what appeared to be an attempt to maintain a straight face. "Really?"

"Really," Hugh said.

She cleared her throat. "Did you reach any conclusions?"

"Just that we must agree to disagree," he said. He added a placid smile. "As so often occurs in life."

Sarah's eyes narrowed.

"Sarah doesn't believe in unicorns, either,"

Frances said. "None of my sisters do." She gave a sad little sigh. "I am quite alone in my hopes and dreams."

Hugh watched Sarah roll her eyes, then said, "I have a feeling, Lady Frances, that the only thing you are alone in is being showered with the love and devotion of your family."

"Oh, I'm not alone in that," Frances said brightly, "although as the youngest, I do enjoy certain benefits."

Sarah made a snorting sound.

"It's true, then?" Hugh murmured, looking her way.

"She would be quite dreadful if she weren't so innately marvelous," Sarah said, smiling at her sister with obvious affection. "My father spoils her abominably."

"He does," Frances said happily.

"Is your father here?" Hugh asked curiously. He did not think he'd ever met Lord Pleinsworth.

"No," Sarah replied. "He deemed it too far a journey from Devon. He rarely leaves home."

"He doesn't like to travel," Frances put in.

Sarah nodded. "He'll be at Daniel's wedding, though."

"Is he bringing the dogs?" Frances asked.

"I don't know," Sarah replied.

"Mama will—"

"—kill him, I know, but—"

"Dogs?" Hugh cut in. Because really, it had to be asked.

The two Pleinsworth sisters looked at him as if they'd quite forgotten he was there.

"Dogs?" he repeated.

"My father," Sarah said, delicately picking her way across her words, "is rather fond of his hounds."

Hugh glanced over at Frances, who nodded.

"How many dogs?" Hugh asked. It seemed a logical question.

Lady Sarah appeared reluctant to admit to a number, but her younger sister had no such compunctions. "Fifty-three at last count," Frances said. "But it's probably more by now. They're always having puppies."

Hugh failed to locate an appropriate response.

"Of course he can't fit them all in one carriage," Frances added.

"No," Hugh managed to reply. "I don't imagine he could."

"He has often said that he finds animals to be better company than humans," Sarah said.

"I cannot say that I disagree," Hugh said. He saw Frances open her mouth to speak and quickly silenced her with a pointed finger. "Unicorns do *not* count."

"I was *going* to say," she said with feigned affront, "that I wish he *would* bring the dogs."

"Are you mad?" Sarah demanded, right as Hugh murmured, "All fifty-three of them?"

"He probably wouldn't bring them all," Frances told Hugh before turning to Sarah. "And no, I'm not mad. If he brought the dogs, I'd have someone to play with. There are no other children here."

"You have me," Hugh found himself saying.

The two Pleinsworth sisters fell utterly silent.

Hugh had a feeling that this was not a common occurrence.

"I suspect you'd have a difficult task recruiting me for a game of Oranges and Lemons," he said with a shrug, "but I'm happy to do something that does not require much use of my leg."

"Oh," Frances said. She blinked a few times. "Thank you."

"This has been the most entertaining conversation I've had at Fensmore," he told her.

"Really?" Frances asked. "But hasn't Sarah been assigned to keep you company?"

There was a very awkward silence.

Hugh cleared his throat, but Sarah spoke first. "Thank you, Frances," she said with great dignity. "I appreciate your taking my place at the head table while I danced."

"He looked lonely," Frances said.

Hugh coughed. Not because he was embarrassed, but because he was . . . Bloody hell, he didn't know what he was feeling just then. It was damned disconcerting.

"Not that he *was* lonely," Frances said quickly, shooting him a conspiratorial glance. "But he did look so." She glanced back and forth between her sister and Hugh, apparently only just realizing she might be caught in the middle of an uncomfortable moment. "And he needed cake."

"Well, we all need cake," Hugh put in. He could not have cared less if Lady Sarah was put out, but there was no need for Lady Frances to feel ill at ease.

"I need cake," Sarah announced.

It was just the thing to move the conversation forward. "You haven't had any?" Frances asked in amazement. "Oh, but you must. It's absolutely brilliant. The footman gave me a piece with extra flowers."

Hugh smiled to himself. Extra flowers, indeed. The decorations had turned Lady Frances's tongue purple.

"I was dancing," Sarah reminded her.

"Oh, yes, of course." Frances pulled a face and turned to Hugh. "It is another great sorrow of being the only child at a wedding. No one dances with me."

"I assure you I would," he said in all seriousness. "But alas . . ." He motioned to his cane.

Frances gave a sympathetic nod. "Well, then, I'm very glad I was able to sit with you. It's no fun sitting alone while everyone else is dancing." She stood and turned to her sister. "Shall I get you some cake?"

"Oh, that won't be necessary."

"But you just said you wanted some."

"She said she *needed* some," Hugh said.

Sarah looked at him as if he'd sprouted tentacles.

"I remember things," he said simply.

"I'll get you cake," Frances decided, and walked off.

Hugh entertained himself by counting to see how long it would take for Lady Sarah to cut through the silence and speak to him after her sister departed. When he reached forty-three seconds (give or take a few; he didn't have a timepiece for a truly accurate measure) he realized that he was going to have to be the adult of the duo, and he said, "You like to dance."

She started, and when she turned to him, he realized instantly from her expression that while he had been measuring an awkward pause in the conversation, she had merely been sitting in companionable silence.

He found this strange. And perhaps even unsettling.

"I do," she said abruptly, still blinking with surprise. "The music is delightful. It really does make one stand up and— I beg your pardon." She flushed, the way everyone did when they said something that might possibly refer to his injured leg.

"I used to like to dance," he said, mostly to be contrary.

"I— ah—" She cleared her throat. "Ehrm."

"It's difficult now, of course."

Her eyes took on a vague expression of alarm, so he smiled placidly and took a sip of his wine.

"I thought you did not drink in the presence of the Smythe-Smiths," she said.

He took another sip—the wine *was* quite good, just as she'd promised the night before—and turned to her with every intention of responding with a dry jest, but when he saw her sitting there, her skin still pink and dewy from her recent exertions, something turned within him, and the little knot of anger he worked so hard to keep buried burst forth and began to bleed.

He was never going to dance again.

He was never going to ride a horse or climb a tree or stride purposefully across a room and sweep a lady off her feet. There were a thousand things he'd never do, and you'd think it would have been a man who'd reminded him of this—an able-bodied man who could hunt and box and do all those bloody things a man was meant to do, but no, it was *her*, Lady Sarah Pleinsworth, with her fine eyes and nimble feet, and every bloody smile she'd bestowed upon her dance partners that morning.

He didn't like her. He really didn't, but by God, he'd have sold a piece of his soul right then to dance with her.

"Lord Hugh?" Her voice was quiet, but it held a tiny trace of impatience, just enough to alert him that he'd been silent for too long.

He took another sip of his wine—more of a swig this time, really—and said, "My leg hurts." It didn't. Not much, anyway, but it might as well have done. His leg seemed to be the reason for everything in his life; surely a glass of wine was no exception.

"Oh." She shifted in her seat. "I'm sorry."

"Don't be," he said, perhaps more brusquely than he'd intended. "It isn't your fault."

"I know *that*. But I can still be sorry that it pains you."

He must have given her a dubious look, because she drew back defensively and said, "I'm not inhuman."

He looked at her closely, and somehow his eyes dipped down the line of her neck to the delicate planes of her collarbone. He could see every breath, every tiny motion along her skin. He cleared his throat. She was most definitely human.

"Forgive me," he said stiffly. "I was of the opinion that you thought my suffering was no more than I deserve."

Her lips parted, and he could practically see his statement running through her mind. Her discomfort was palpable, until finally she said, "I may have felt that way, and I cannot imagine I will ever bring myself to think charitably of you, but I am trying to be a less . . ." She stopped, and her head moved awkwardly as she sought words. "I am trying to be a better person," she finally said. "I do not wish you pain."

His brows rose. This was not the Sarah Pleinsworth with whom he was familiar.

"But I don't like you," she suddenly blurted.

Ah. There she was. Hugh actually took some comfort in her rudeness. He was feeling unaccountably weary, and he did not have the energy to figure out this deeper, more nuanced Sarah Pleinsworth.

He might not like the overly dramatic young miss who made grand and loud pronouncements, but right then . . . he preferred her.

Chapter Eight

SHE REALLY COULD see over the entire room from up here at the head table, Sarah thought. It gave one the opportunity to stare quite shamelessly (as one did at events such as these) at the bride. The happy bride, dressed in pale lavender silk and a radiant smile. One could, perhaps, shoot dagger eyes at that happy bride (with no intention, of course, that the happy bride actually see those dagger eyes). But it was, after all, Honoria's fault that Sarah was stuck up here, sitting next to Lord Hugh Prentice, who, after apparently having a lovely conversation with her younger sister, had turned unpleasant and surly.

"I do bring out the best in you, don't I?" Sarah muttered without looking at him.

"Did you say something?" he asked. He didn't look at her, either.

"No," she lied.

He shifted in his seat, and Sarah glanced down long enough to realize that he was adjusting the position of his leg. He seemed to be most comfortable with it stretched out before him; she'd noticed that the previous night at supper. But whereas that table had been laden with guests, this one was quite empty save for the two of them, and there was plenty of room to—

"It doesn't hurt," he said, not turning even an inch in her direction.

"I beg your pardon?" she said, since she had *not* been looking at his leg. In fact, after she had noticed that he was holding it quite straight, she had been quite purposefully looking at at least six other things.

"The leg," Hugh said. "It doesn't hurt right now."

"Oh." It was on the tip of her tongue to retort that she had not inquired about his leg, but even she knew when good manners called for restraint. "The wine, I imagine," she finally said. He hadn't had much, but if he said that it helped with the pain, who was she to doubt him?

"It is difficult to bend," he said. And then he did look at her, full straight and green. "In case you were wondering."

"Of course not," she said quickly.

"Liar," he said softly.

Sarah gasped. Of course she had been lying, but it had been a *polite* lie. Whereas his calling her out on it had been most assuredly not polite.

"If you want to know about it," Hugh said, cutting off a small bite of cake with the side of his fork, "just ask."

"Very well," Sarah said sharply, "are you missing any great big chunks of flesh?"

He choked on his cake. This gave her great satisfaction.

"Yes," he said.

"Of what size?"

He looked like he might smile again, which had not been her intention. He glanced down at his leg. "I'd say about two cubic inches."

She gritted her teeth. What sort of person answered in cubic inches?

"About the size of a very small orange," he added. Condescendingly. "Or a somewhat massive strawberry."

"I know what a cubic inch is."

"Of course you do."

And the bizarre thing was, he didn't sound the least bit condescending when he said *that*.

"Did you injure your knee?" she asked, because drat it all, now she was curious. "Is that why you cannot bend it?"

"I can bend it," he replied, "just not very well. And no, there was no injury to the knee."

Sarah waited several seconds, then said, primarily between her teeth, "Why, then, can't you bend it?"

"The muscle," he said, letting one of his shoulders rise and fall in a shrug. "I suspect it doesn't stretch the way it ought, given that it's missing two cubic inches of, what did you call it?" His voice grew unpleasantly droll. "Ah yes, a chunk of flesh."

"You told me to ask," she ground out.

"So I did."

Sarah felt her mouth tighten. Was he *trying* to make her feel like a heel? If there were any official society rules for how a gentlewoman was meant to behave with a partially crippled man, they had not been taught to her. She was fairly certain, however, that she was supposed to pretend that she did not notice his infirmity.

Unless he required assistance. In which case she *was* supposed to notice his limp, because it would be unforgivably insensitive to stand aside and watch him flounder. But either way, she probably wasn't supposed to ask questions.

Such as why he couldn't bend his leg.

But *still*. Wasn't it his duty as a gentleman not to make her feel awful about it when she flubbed?

Honoria owed her one for this. Honoria probably owed her three.

Three of what, she wasn't sure, but something large. Something very large.

They sat there for another minute or so, then Hugh said, "I don't think your sister is coming back with cake." He motioned very slightly with his head. Frances was waltzing with Daniel. The expression on her face was one of utter delight.

"He has always been her favorite cousin," Sarah remarked. She still wasn't really looking at Hugh, but she sort of *felt* him nod in agreement.

"He has an easy way with people," Hugh said.

"It is a talent."

"Indeed." He took a sip of his wine. "One that you possess as well, I understand."

"Not with everyone."

He smiled mockingly. "You refer to me, I presume."

It was on the tip of her tongue to say, *Of course not*, but he was too intelligent for that. Instead she sat in stony silence, feeling very much like a fool. A rude fool.

He chuckled. "You should not chastise yourself for your failure. I am a challenge for even the most affable of people."

She turned, staring at his face with utter confusion. And disbelief. What sort of man said such a thing? "You seem to get on well with Daniel," she finally replied.

One of his brows rose, almost like a dare. "And yet," he said, leaning slightly toward her, "I shot him."

"To be fair, you were dueling."

He almost smiled. "Are you defending me?"

"No." Was she? No, she was simply making conversation. Which, according to him, she was supposed to be good at. "Tell me," she said, "did you mean to hit him?"

He froze, and for a moment Sarah thought she'd gone too far. When he spoke, it was with quiet amazement. "You are the first person ever to ask me that."

"That can't be possible." Because really, didn't everything hinge on that one detail?

"I don't believe I realized it until this moment, but no, no one has ever thought to ask if I meant to shoot him."

Sarah held her tongue for a few seconds. But only just. "Well, did you?"

"Mean to shoot him? No. Of course not."

"You should tell him that."

"He knows."

"But—"

"I said that no one had asked me," he cut in. "I did not say that I had never offered the information myself."

"I expect his shot was accidental as well."

"We were neither of us in our right minds that morning," he said, his tone utterly devoid of inflection.

She nodded. She didn't know why; she wasn't really agreeing to anything. But it felt as if she should respond. It felt as if he deserved a response.

"Nevertheless," Lord Hugh said, staring straight ahead, "I was the one to call for the duel, and I was the one who shot first."

She looked down at the table. She did not know what to say.

He spoke again, quietly, but with unmistakable conviction. "I have never blamed your cousin for my injury."

And then, before she could even think about how to respond, Lord Hugh stood so abruptly that his injured leg bumped into the table, splashing a bit of wine out of someone's forgotten glass. When Sarah looked up, she saw him wince.

"Are you all right?" she asked carefully.

"I'm fine," he said in a curt voice.

"Of course you are," she muttered. Men were always "fine."

"What is that supposed to mean?" he snapped.

"Nothing," she lied, coming to her feet. "Do you need assistance?"

His eyes blazed with fury that she'd even asked, but just as he started to say, "No," his cane clattered to the floor.

"I'll get that for you," Sarah said quickly.

"I can—"

"I've already *got* it," she ground out. Good Lord, the man was making it difficult for her to be a considerate human being.

He let out a breath, and then, even though he was clearly loath to do so, he said, "Thank you."

She handed him the cane, and then, very carefully, asked, "May I accompany you to the door?"

"It's not necessary," he said brusquely.

"For you, perhaps," she shot back.

That seemed to pique his curiosity. One of his brows rose in question, and Sarah said, "I believe you are aware that I have been tasked with your welfare."

"You should really stop flattering me, Lady Sarah. It will go to my head."

"I will not shirk my duty."

He looked at her for a long moment, then sent a pointed glance toward the twenty or so wedding guests who were currently dancing.

Sarah took a steadying breath, trying not to rise to his bait. She probably shouldn't have abandoned him at the table, but she had been feeling merry, and she liked to dance. Surely Honoria hadn't meant that she must remain at his side for every moment of the wedding. Besides, there had been several other people left at the table when she'd got up. And she'd come back when she'd realized he'd been all alone with only Frances for company.

Although truth be told, he did seem to prefer Frances.

"It is strange," he murmured, "being a young woman's duty. I can't say I have ever before had the pleasure."

"I made a promise to my cousin," Sarah said in a tight voice. To say nothing of Iris and her judgmental ways. "As a gentleman, you should allow me to at least attempt to fulfill that promise."

"Very well," he said, and his voice was not angry. Nor was it resigned, or amused, or anything she could discern. He held out his arm, as any gentleman would, but she hesitated. Was she supposed to take it? Would it set him off balance?

"You won't knock me over," he said.

She took his arm.

He tilted his head toward hers. "Unless, of course, you push."

She felt herself flush.

"Oh, come now, Lady Sarah," he said, looking down at her with a condescending expression. "Surely you can take a joke. Especially when it's at my expense."

Sarah forced her lips into a tight smile.

Lord Hugh chuckled, and they headed for the door, making faster progress than she would have expected. His limp was pronounced, but he had clearly figured out how best to compensate for it. He must have had to relearn how to walk, she realized with amazement. It would have taken months, maybe years.

And it would have been painful.

Something akin to admiration began to flutter within her. He was still rude and annoying, and she certainly did not enjoy his company, but for the first time since that fateful duel three and a half years earlier, Sarah found that she admired him. He was strong. No, not in that *watch-how-effortlessly-I-can-toss-a-young-lady-onto-a-horse* way, although for all she knew he was that, too. She did have her hand on his arm, and there was nothing soft about him.

Hugh Prentice was strong on the inside, where it truly counted. He'd have to be, to come back from such an injury.

She swallowed, her eyes finding focus somewhere across the room even as she continued in step next to him. She felt unsettled, as if the floor had suddenly dropped an inch to the right, or the air had gone thin. She had spent the last few years detesting this man, and while this anger had not consumed her, it had, in some small way, defined her.

Lord Hugh Prentice had been her excuse. He had been her constant. When the world tipped and changed around her, he had remained her steady object of disgust. He was cold, he was heartless, he was without conscience. He had ruined her cousin's life and never apologized for it. He was horrible in a way that meant nothing else in life could ever be *that* bad.

And now she had found something within him

to admire? *That* was unlike her. Honoria was the one who found the good in people; Sarah held the grudge.

And she did not change her mind.

Except, apparently, when she did.

"Will you dance to your heart's content once I've left?" Lord Hugh suddenly asked.

Sarah started, so lost in the tumult of her thoughts that his voice hit too loudly at her ears. "I hadn't thought about it, honestly," she said.

"You should," he said quietly. "You're a lovely dancer."

Her lips parted in surprise.

"Yes, Lady Sarah," he said, "that was a compliment."

"I hardly know what to do with it."

"I'd recommend accepting it gracefully."

"And do you base this upon personal experience?"

"Certainly not. I almost never accept compliments with grace."

She looked up at him, expecting to see a sly look, maybe even a mischievous one, but his face remained as impassive as ever. He wasn't even looking at her.

"You're a very odd man, Lord Hugh Prentice," she said quietly.

"I know," he said, and they steered around Sarah's enormous great-uncle (and his remarkably tall wife) to reach the ballroom door. Before they could make their escape, however, they were intercepted by Honoria, who was still radiating such happiness that Sarah thought her cheeks must ache from smiling. Frances was standing at her side, holding her hand and basking in the bridal glow.

"You're not leaving so soon!" Honoria exclaimed.

And then, just to prove that it was impossible to make an unnoticed exit in a room full of Smythe-Smiths, Iris suddenly materialized on Honoria's other side, flushed and out of breath from the Scottish reel that had just ended.

"Sarah," Iris said with a tipsy giggle. "And Lord Hugh. Together. Again."

"Still," Hugh corrected, much to Sarah's mortification. He gave Iris a polite bow, then turned to Honoria and said, "It has been a delightful wedding, Lady Chatteris, but I must go to my room for a rest."

"And I must accompany him," Sarah announced.

Iris snorted a laugh.

"Not to his room," she said quickly. Good Lord. "Just to the stairs. Or maybe—" Did he need help on the stairs? Was she supposed to offer it? "Er, up the stairs if you—"

"As far as you wish to take me," he said, his benevolent statement clearly meant to tease.

Sarah tightened her fingers on his arm, hopefully to the point of pain.

"But I don't wish for you to leave yet," Honoria exclaimed.

"They do make a lovely pair," Iris said with a smile.

"You are too kind, Iris," Sarah ground out.

"It was lovely seeing you, Lord Hugh," Iris said, with a slightly too-fast curtsy. "I'm afraid you will have to excuse me. I promised Honoria I would find Cousin Rupert and dance with him. Must keep my commitments, you know!" She gave a jaunty wave and scooted away.

"Thank heavens for Iris," Honoria said. "I don't know what Rupert has been eating this morning, but no one wants to stand near him. It is so comforting to know that I can count upon my cousins."

And the dagger that Iris had just thrust into Sarah's heart got a neat little twist. If Sarah had thought she might divest herself of Lord Hugh anytime soon, she was clearly mistaken.

"You should thank her later," Honoria continued, directing her words toward Sarah. "I know how much you and Cousin Rupert don't . . . ah . . ." Her voice trailed away as she remembered that Lord Hugh was standing across from her. It was never polite to air family differences in public, even if she had made him aware of the rift just the day before. "Well," she declared, after clearing her throat. "Now you don't have to dance with him."

"Because Iris is," Frances put in helpfully, as if Sarah had not quite grasped that.

"We really must be going," Sarah said.

"No, no, you can't," Honoria said. She took Sarah's hands in her own. "I want you to be here. You are my dearest cousin."

"But only because I'm too young," Frances sotto-voiced to Hugh.

"Please," Honoria said, then turned her face

toward Hugh. "And you, too, Lord Hugh. It would mean so much to me."

Sarah gritted her teeth. If this were anyone else, she would have thrown up her arms and stalked off. But Honoria wasn't trying to play the matchmaker. She wasn't that sly, and even if she were, she would never be that obvious. Rather, the bride's bliss was such that she wanted everyone to be just as happy as she was, and she could not imagine that anyone could be happier than they were right here in this very room.

"I am sorry, Lady Chatteris," Lord Hugh murmured, "but I fear I must rest my leg."

"Oh, but then you must make your way to the drawing room," Honoria replied instantly. "We are serving cake there for guests who do not wish to dance."

"Sarah hasn't had cake!" Frances exclaimed. "I was supposed to get some for her."

"It's all right, Frances," Sarah assured her, "I—"

"Oh, you must have cake," Honoria said. "Mrs. Wetherby worked with the cook for weeks to get the recipe just right."

Sarah did not doubt it. Honoria was mad for sweets; she always had been.

"I'll come with you," Frances said.

"That would be lovely, but—"

"And Lord Hugh can come, too!"

At that, Sarah turned to Frances with suspicion. Honoria might simply be trying to make the entire world as ecstatic as she was, but Frances's motives were rarely so pure.

"Very well," Sarah acquiesced before she realized it was really Lord Hugh's place to do so.

"Marcus and I will be going to the drawing room soon to greet people there," Honoria said.

"As you wish, my lady," Hugh said with a little bow. Nothing in his voice betrayed irritation or impatience, but Sarah was not fooled. Strange that she'd got to know him well enough in the last day to realize that he was absolutely furious. Or at the very least, mildly annoyed.

And yet his face was as stony as ever.

"Shall we?" he murmured. Sarah nodded, and they continued toward the door. Once in the hall, however, he paused and said, "You need not accompany me to the drawing room."

"Oh, I do," she muttered, thinking of Iris, who was rubbing it in, and Honoria, who was not, and even Frances, who fully expected her to be there when she arrived with cake. "But if you wish to leave, I shall make your excuses."

"I promised the bride."

"So did I."

He looked at her for a moment longer than was comfortable, then said, "I don't suppose you're the sort to break your promises?"

He was lucky she'd released his arm. She'd probably have snapped his bone in two. "No."

Again, he stared at her. Or maybe it wasn't a stare, but it was very strange the way he so frequently let his eyes linger on her face before he spoke. He did this with other people, too; she'd noticed it the night before.

"Very well, then," he said. "I believe we are expected in the drawing room."

She glanced at him, then returned to face forward. "I do like cake."

"Were you planning to deny yourself merely to avoid me?" he asked as they continued down the hall.

"Not exactly."

He gave her a sideways look. "Not exactly?"

"I was going to return to the ballroom once you left," she admitted. "Or have some sent to my room." A moment later she added, "And I wasn't trying to avoid you."

"Weren't you?"

"No, I—" She smiled to herself. "Not exactly."

"Not exactly?" he echoed. Again.

She didn't clarify. She couldn't, because she wasn't even sure what she'd meant. Just that, maybe, she didn't completely detest him any longer. Or at least not enough to deny herself cake.

"I have a question," she said.

He cocked his head, indicating that she should proceed.

"Yesterday, when we were in the drawing room, when you, erh . . ."

"Woke you up?" he supplied.

"Yes," she said, wondering why it had felt embarrassing to say it. "Well, after, I mean. You said something about ten pounds."

He chuckled, a low, rich sound that was born deep in his throat.

"You wanted me to pretend to swoon," she reminded him.

"Could you have done?" he asked.

"Faked a swoon? I should hope so. It's a talent every lady should possess." She shot him a cheeky grin, then asked, "Did Marcus really offer you ten pounds if I fainted on the lawn?"

"No," Lord Hugh admitted. "Your cousin Daniel felt that the sight of us both armed with pistols might be enough to make a lady swoon."

"Not just me," she felt compelled to clarify.

"Not just you. And then Daniel announced that Lord Chatteris would pay us each ten pounds if we managed it."

"Marcus agreed to this?" Sarah could not think of anything less like him, except possibly jumping onto a stage and dancing a jig.

"Of course not. Can you imagine such a thing?" Lord Hugh smiled then, a real, true one that curved more than just the corners of his mouth. It reached his eyes, sparkling in those green depths, and for the most staggering, *horrifying* moment, he turned almost handsome. No, not that. He'd always been handsome. When he smiled, he turned . . .

Lovable.

"Oh, dear God," she choked out, jumping back. She'd never kissed a man, never even *wanted* to, and she was starting with Hugh Prentice?

"Is something wrong?"

"Ehrm, no. I mean, yes. I mean, there was a spider!"

He looked down at the floor. "A spider?"

"It went that way," she said quickly, pointing to the left. And sort of to the right as well.

Lord Hugh frowned, leaning on his cane as his body swayed to one side to better glance down the hall.

"I'm terrified of them," Sarah said. It wasn't quite true, but almost so. She certainly did not like them.

"Well, I don't see it now."

"Should I go find someone?" she blurted, thinking that a trip across the house, perhaps all the way to the servants quarters, might not be such a bad idea. If she could not see Hugh Prentice, this madness would have to end, wouldn't it? "You know," she went on, making it all up as she went along, "to search it out. And kill it. Good heavens, there could be a nest."

"I am sure the maids of Fensmore would never allow such a thing to come to pass."

"Nevertheless," she squeaked. And then she winced, because the squeak had been awful.

"Perhaps it would be easier to ring for a footman?" He motioned to the drawing room, which was just a few feet away.

She nodded, because of course he was correct, and already she felt herself returning to normal. Her heartbeat was slowing, and as long as she did not look at his mouth, the urge to kiss him was gone. Mostly.

She straightened her shoulders. She could do this. "Thank you for your kind escort," she said, and stepped into the drawing room.

It was empty.

"Well, this is very strange," she said.

Hugh's lips pressed together. "Indeed."

"I'm not sure . . . ," Sarah began, but she didn't have to figure out what to say next, because Lord Hugh had turned to her with slightly narrowed eyes. "Your cousin," he began. "She wouldn't—"

"No!" Sarah exclaimed. "I mean, no," she said in a much more appropriate voice. "Iris maybe, but not Hon—" She cut herself off. The last thing she wanted was for him to think any of the Smythe-Smiths were trying to throw them together.

"Look!" she said, her voice coming out over-bright and loud. She flittered her hand toward a table to the left. "Empty plates. There were people here. They're just gone now."

He didn't say anything.

"Should we sit down?" she asked awkwardly.

He still didn't say anything. He did turn his head, though, to more directly face her.

"And wait?" she offered. "Since we said we would?" She felt ridiculous. And uncommonly fidgety. But now she felt as if she had to prove something to herself, that she could be in the same room as him and feel perfectly normal.

"Frances will be expecting us to be here," she added, since Lord Hugh had seemingly gone mute. She supposed he was just thinking, but really, couldn't he think and make idle conversation at the same time? She did it all the time.

"After you, Lady Sarah," he said. Finally.

She made her way over to a blue and gold sofa, the same one, she realized, she'd been sleeping on the day before when he'd woken her up. She was tempted to glance behind her as she walked to make sure that he did not need her assistance.

Which was ridiculous, because she knew he didn't need her assistance, at least not in such a simple endeavor as this.

But she wanted to, and when she finally reached the sofa and sat down, she was unaccountably relieved to be able to look up at him. He was only a few steps behind, and a moment later he was seated in the blue chair he had occupied the day before.

Déjà vu, she thought, except everything was different now. Everything except where they were sitting. It had taken only a day, and her world had been turned upside down.

Chapter Nine

"Déjà vu," Lady Sarah quipped, and Hugh was thinking that very thing, except it wasn't quite the same. The table was not where it had been the day before. He'd thought it had looked off when he sat down.

"Is something the matter?" she asked.

He had a feeling he was frowning. "No, just . . ." He shifted in his seat. How difficult would it be to move the table? It was still covered with half-empty plates that the servants must not have realized were ready to be removed. But surely he could shove those aside. . . .

"Oh!" Lady Sarah said suddenly. "You need to stretch out your leg. Of course."

"I think the table is not quite where it was yesterday," he said.

She looked down at the table and then back at him.

"I had room to extend my leg," he clarified.

"So you did," she said briskly. She stood, and he almost groaned. He placed his hands on the arms of the chair, getting ready to push himself up, but Lady Sarah placed one hand lightly over his and said, "No, please do not feel you must rise."

He looked down at her hand, but just as quickly as it had appeared, it was gone, and she started to move the dishes to a different table.

"Don't," he said, finding no joy in watching her perform menial tasks on his behalf.

She ignored him. "There," she said, placing her hands on her hips as she surveyed the partially cleared table. She looked up. "Would it be more comfortable to have your foot on the floor or on the table?"

Good God. He couldn't believe she was even asking. "I'm not going to put my foot on the table."

"Would you do so at your home?"

"Of course, but—"

"Then you have answered my question," she said pertly, turning back to the dirty dishes.

"Lady Sarah, stop."

She kept clearing and did not bother to look at him. "No."

"I insist." It was too strange. Lady Sarah Pleinsworth was clearing away dirty dishes and preparing to move furniture. Even more astonishing was that she was doing it in order to help *him*.

"Be quiet and allow me to help you," she said. Rather sternly, too.

His lips parted with surprise, and she must have taken a bit of pleasure in his astonishment, because her lips formed a smile, and then that smile turned smug.

"I'm not helpless," he muttered.

"I didn't think you were." Her dark eyes sparkled, and as she turned back to the task of clearing the dishes, realization thundered through him like a hot desert wind.

I want her.

His breath caught.

"Is something wrong?" she called out.

"No," he croaked. But he still wanted her.

She looked up. "You sounded funny. As if . . . well, I don't know what." She resumed clearing the dishes, speaking as she worked. "Maybe as if you were in pain."

Hugh held silent, trying not to stare at her as she moved through the drawing room. Dear God, *what* had happened to him? Yes, she was very attractive, and yes, the velvet bodice of her dress was fitted in such a way that a man could not help but be aware of the exact—exactly perfect—shape of her breasts.

But this was Sarah Pleinsworth. He had hated her less than twenty-four hours ago. He might *still* hate her a little bit.

And he bloody well didn't know what a hot desert wind felt like. Where the *hell* had that come from?

Sarah set the final dish down and turned to look at him. "I think what we need to do is get your foot on the table, and then pull the whole thing toward you so it will support the rest of your leg."

He didn't move for a moment. He couldn't. He was still trying to figure out what the hell was going on.

"Lord Hugh," she said expectantly. "Your leg?"

There was no stopping her, he realized, so he imparted a silent apology to his hosts and set his booted foot on the table.

It did feel good to stretch out the leg.

"Hold on," Sarah said, coming back around to his side of the table. "It's not supporting your knee." She moved next to him and pulled the table closer, but it set the whole thing at a diagonal. "Oh, sorry," she said, scooting around the back of his chair. "Just a moment."

She stepped sideways through the space between the sofa and his chair, squeezing herself into a spot right next to him. They were not touching, but he could feel her warmth, pulsing off her skin.

"If you'll just excuse me," she said under her breath.

He turned his head.

He really shouldn't have done so.

Lady Sarah had bent over to get a bit of leverage, and that dress . . . the dip of the neckline . . . so close to him . . .

He shifted in his seat again, and this time it had nothing to do with his injury.

"Can you lift it a bit?" Sarah asked.

"What?"

"Your leg." She wasn't looking at him, thank God, because he could not stop looking at her. The shadow between her breasts was so close, and the scent of her was swirling around him—lemons and honeysuckle and something far more earthy and sensual.

She had been dancing all morning. Out of breath and dizzy with exertion. Just the thought of it made him so desperate for her that he thought he might stop breathing.

"Do you need help?" she asked.

Dear God, yes. He hadn't been with a woman since his injury, and the truth was, he hadn't really wanted to. He had the same needs as any man, but it was so bloody hard to imagine anyone desiring him with his ruined leg that he'd not allowed himself to feel it for anyone else.

Until now, when it had hit him like—

Oh, bloody hell, not a hot desert wind. Anything but a hot desert wind.

"Lord Hugh," Sarah said impatiently, "did you hear me? If you lift your leg, it will be easier for me to pull the table in."

"Sorry," he muttered, and he lifted his leg an inch.

She pulled at the table, but it rubbed against the upper of his boot and caught a little, forcing her to take a step to maintain her balance.

She was so close now he could reach out and touch her. His fingers clamped down on the arms of his chair lest they give in to desire.

He wanted to touch her hand, to feel her fingers curl around his, and then he wanted to bring it to his lips. He would kiss the inside of her wrist, feel her pulse thrumming beneath her pale skin.

And then—oh, dear God, this was not the time

for an erotic daydream, but he could not seem to help himself—then he would lift her arms above her head, the motion arching her back, so that when he pressed her body against his, he would feel all of her, every dip and curve. And then he would reach beneath her skirt and slide his hand up her leg to the sensitive crook of her hip.

He wanted to know the exact temperature of her, and then he wanted to know it again, when she was hot and flushed with desire.

"There we are," she said, straightening back up. It was nearly impossible to think that she was oblivious to his distress, that she could not know that he was within inches of losing control.

She smiled, having got the table into the position she wanted. "Is that better?"

He nodded, not trusting himself to speak.

"Are you all right? You look a bit flushed."

Oh, dear God.

"Can I get you anything?"

You.

"No!" he blurted, rather too loudly. How the bloody hell had this happened? He was staring at Sarah Pleinsworth like a randy schoolboy, and all he could think about was the shape of her lips, the color.

He wanted to know the texture.

She placed a hand on his forehead. "May I?" she asked, but she was already touching him before she finished her query.

He nodded. What else could he have done?

"You really don't look well," she murmured. "Perhaps when Frances arrives with the cake, we can ask her to fetch you some lemonade. You might find it refreshing."

He nodded again, forcing his mind to focus on Frances. Who was eleven. And liked unicorns.

And should not, under any circumstances, enter the room while he was in such a state.

Sarah removed her hand from his forehead and frowned. "You're a little warm," she said, "but not overmuch."

He could not imagine how that was possible. Just moments ago, he'd thought he might go up in flames.

"I'm fine," he said, almost cutting her off. "I just need more cake. Or lemonade."

She looked at him as if he'd sprouted an extra ear. Or turned a different color.

"Is something wrong?" he asked.

"No," she said, although she didn't sound as if she entirely meant it. "You just don't sound like yourself."

He tried to keep his tone light as he said, "I wasn't aware we knew each other well enough to make that determination."

"It is strange," she agreed, sitting back. "I think it's just that— Never mind."

"No, tell me," he urged. Conversation was a very good idea. It kept his mind off other things, and more importantly, it ensured that she was sitting on her sofa and not bending over him in his chair.

"You often pause before you speak," she said.

"Is that a problem?"

"No, of course not. It's just . . . different."

"Perhaps I like to consider my words before I use them."

"No," she murmured. "That's not it."

A small laugh escaped his lips. "Are you saying I don't consider my words before I use them?"

"No," she said, laughing in turn. "I'm sure you do. You're very clever, as I'm sure you know that I know."

This made him smile.

"I can't really explain it," she continued. "But when you look at a person— No, let's not be unnecessarily vague— When you look at *me* before you speak, there is frequently a moment of silence, and I don't think it's because you are picking and choosing your words."

He watched her intently. Now *she* had fallen silent, and *she* was the one who was trying to decide what she thought. "It's something in your face," she finally said. "It just doesn't look like you are trying to decide what to say." She looked up quite suddenly, and the contemplative expression left her face. "I'm sorry, that was quite personal."

"No apology is needed," he said quietly. "Our world is filled with meaningless conversations. It is an honor to participate in one that is not."

Her cheeks took on a faint blush of pride, and she looked away almost shyly. He realized in that moment that he, too, knew her well enough to know that this was not a frequent expression on her face.

"Well," she said, folding her hands in her lap. She cleared her throat, then cleared it again. "Perhaps we should— Frances!"

The last of this was said with great fervor and, he thought he detected, some relief.

"I'm sorry that took so long," Frances said as she came into the room. "Honoria tossed her bouquet, and I didn't want to miss it."

Sarah straightened like a shot. "Honoria tossed the bouquet when I wasn't there?"

Frances blinked a few times. "I suppose she did. But I shouldn't worry about it. You'd never have outrun Iris."

"Iris ran?" Sarah's mouth fell open, and Hugh could only describe the expression on her face as a mix of horror and glee.

"She leapt," Frances confirmed. "Harriet was knocked to the floor."

Hugh covered his mouth.

"Do not stifle your laughter on my account," Sarah said.

"I didn't realize Iris had set her cap for someone," Frances said, looking down at the cake. "May I have a bite of yours, Sarah?"

Sarah motioned with her hand to go ahead and answered, "I don't think she has."

Frances licked a bit of icing off the end of her fork. "Perhaps she thinks the bridal bouquet will hasten her discovery of her true love."

"If that were the case," Sarah said wryly, "I might have leapt in front of Iris."

"Do you know how the tradition of the bridal bouquet toss was formed?" Hugh asked.

Sarah shook her head. "Are you asking me because you know, or are you asking me because you want to know?"

He ignored her slight sarcasm and said, "Brides are considered to be good luck, and many centuries ago young women who wanted a piece of that luck tried quite literally to get a piece of it by tearing off bits of her gown."

"That's barbaric!" Frances exclaimed.

He smiled at her outburst. "I can only deduce that some clever soul realized that if the bride could offer a different token of her romantic success, it might prove beneficial to her health and well-being."

"I should say so," Frances said. "Think of all the brides who must have been *trampled*."

Sarah chuckled and reached out to take what was left of her cake. Frances had made significant progress on the icing. Hugh started to tell her to take his; he'd already had a piece back when he'd been watching her dance. But with his leg on the table, he couldn't bend forward enough to slide his plate in front of hers.

So he just watched as she took a bite and listened while Frances chattered on about nothing in particular. He felt remarkably content, and he might have even closed his eyes briefly, until he heard Frances say:

"You've got a bit of icing."

He opened his eyes.

"Right here," Frances was saying to Sarah, motioning to her own mouth.

There were no napkins; Frances hadn't thought to bring them. Sarah's tongue darted out of her mouth and licked the corner of her lips.

Her tongue. Her lips.

His downfall.

Hugh yanked his foot off the table and came awkwardly to his feet.

"Is something wrong?" Sarah asked.

"Please give my apologies to Lady Chatteris," he said stiffly. "I know she wanted me to wait for her, but I really do need to rest my leg."

Sarah blinked with confusion. "Weren't you just—"

"It's different," he interrupted, even thought it wasn't, really.

"Oh," she said, and it was a very ambiguous *oh*. She could have been surprised or delighted or even disappointed. He couldn't hear the difference. And the truth was, he shouldn't want to be able to hear it, because he had no business lusting for a woman like Lady Sarah Pleinsworth.

No business at all.

Chapter Ten

The next morning

THE FENSMORE DRIVE was one long line of carriages as wedding guests prepared to depart Cambridgeshire and travel southwest to Berkshire, more specifically to Whipple Hill, the country home of the Earls of Winstead. It would be, as Sarah had once put it, the Great and Terrible Caravan of British Aristocracy. (Harriet had, quill in hand, insisted that such a term required capitalization.)

As London was only a bit out of the way, some of the guests who had been relegated to the nearby inns chose to return to town. But most had elected to turn the dual celebration into a three-week-long traveling house party.

"Good gracious," Lady Danbury had declared

upon receiving her invitations to both weddings, "do they really think I'm going to reopen my town house for ten days between weddings?"

No one had dared to point out that Lady Danbury's country estate was located in Surrey, which was even more directly between Fensmore and Whipple Hill than London.

But Lady Danbury's point was a valid one. The ton was a far-flung society this time of year, with most people in the north or the west, or more pertinently, somewhere other than Cambridgeshire and Berkshire and points between. Hardly anyone saw reason in opening their London houses for less than two weeks when they could enjoy the hospitality of someone else.

Although it must be said, that opinion was not shared by everyone.

"Remind me," Hugh said to Daniel Smythe-Smith as they walked through Fensmore's entrance hall, "why am I not going home?"

It was a three-day journey from Fensmore to Whipple Hill, two if one wanted to push it, which no one did. Hugh supposed it meant less overall time in a carriage than returning to London and then heading out to Berkshire a week later, but still, it was going to be a mad journey. Someone (Hugh was not sure who—it certainly wasn't Daniel; he'd never had a head for such things) had plotted the route, marked all the inns (along with how many rooms each held) and figured out where everyone must sleep.

Hugh hoped no one not planning to attend the Chatteris-Smythe-Smith-Wynter weddings was out on the roads this week because there would not be a room to be had.

"You're not going home because your home is dull," Daniel told him with a slap to his back. "And you don't own a carriage, so if you were to return to London, you'd have to find a seat with one of my mother's friends."

Hugh opened his mouth to speak, but Daniel wasn't done yet. "And that's to say nothing of getting to Whipple Hill *from* London. There might be room with my mother's former nanny, but if not, you could try booking a seat on the mail coach."

"Are you done?" Hugh asked.

Daniel held up a finger as if he had one last thing to say, then brought it back down. "Yes," he said.

"You are a cruel man."

"I speak the truth," Daniel replied. "Besides, why wouldn't you want to come to Whipple Hill?"

Hugh could think of one reason.

"The festivities begin as soon as we arrive," Daniel continued. "It shall be continuous and magnificent frivolity until the wedding."

It was difficult to imagine a man with a soul lighter and more filled with joy than Daniel Smythe-Smith's. Hugh knew that part of this was due to Daniel's upcoming nuptials with the beautiful Miss Wynter, but truthfully, Daniel had always been a man who made friends easily and laughed often.

Knowing that he had destroyed the life of such a man, Hugh had found it that much more difficult when Daniel had been exiled to Europe.

Hugh was still amazed that Daniel had returned to his position in England with grace and good humor. Most men would have burned for revenge.

But Daniel had thanked him. He had thanked him for finding him in Italy, and then he had thanked him for calling off his father's witch hunt, and then finally, he had thanked him for his friendship.

There was nothing, Hugh thought, that he would not do for this man.

"What would you do in London, anyway?" Daniel asked, motioning for Hugh to follow him down the drive. "Sit about and do sums in your head?"

Hugh gave him a look.

"I tease because I admire."

"Really."

"It's a brilliant skill," Daniel insisted.

"Even if it did get you shot and run out of the country?" Hugh asked. It was true what he'd said to Lady Sarah—sometimes gallows humor was the only choice.

Daniel stopped in his tracks, and his expression turned somber.

"You do realize," Hugh said, "that my aptitude with numbers is precisely the reason I have always excelled at cards."

Daniel's eyes seemed to darken, and when he blinked, his face took on an air of quiet resignation. "It's done, Prentice," he said. "It's over, and our lives are restored."

Yours is, Hugh thought, then loathed himself for thinking it.

"We were both idiots," Daniel said quietly.

"We may have both been idiots," Hugh replied, "but only one of us called for the duel."

"I did not have to accept."

"Of course you did. You wouldn't have been able to show your face if you had not." It was a stupid code of honor among the young gentlemen of London, but it was sacrosanct. If a man was accused of cheating at cards, he had to defend himself.

Daniel placed his hand on Hugh's shoulder. "I have forgiven you, and you, I think, have forgiven me."

Hugh had not, in fact, but that was only because there was nothing to forgive.

"What I wonder," Daniel continued softly, "is if you have forgiven yourself."

Hugh did not reply, and Daniel did not press him to. Instead, his voice returned to its previous jovial tones, and he declared, "Let us go to Whipple Hill. We shall eat, some of us shall drink, and we shall all be merry."

Hugh gave a brief nod. Daniel no longer drank spirits. He said he had not touched them since that fateful night. Hugh sometimes thought he should follow his example, but there were evenings when he needed something to take the teeth out of the pain.

"Besides," Daniel said, "you have to be there early, anyway. I've decided you must join the wedding party."

That stopped Hugh cold. "I beg your pardon?"

"Marcus shall be my best man, of course, but I

think I need a few more gentlemen to stand up for me. Anne has a veritable flotilla of ladies."

Hugh swallowed, wishing he weren't so damned uncomfortable accepting such an honor. Because it *was* an honor, and he wanted to say that he was grateful, and it meant so much to him, and he'd forgotten just how steadying it felt to have a true friend.

But all he could manage was a jerky nod. He hadn't been lying to Sarah the day before. He didn't know how to accept compliments graciously. He supposed one had to think one deserved them.

"It's settled then," Daniel said. "Oh, and by the by, I've found you a spot in my favorite carriage."

"What does that mean?" Hugh asked suspiciously. They'd exited the house and were nearly down the steps to the drive.

"Let's see," Daniel said, ignoring his query. "Right . . . there." He motioned with a flick of his hand to a relatively small black carriage fifth in line down the drive. There was no crest, but it was clearly well made and cared for. Probably the secondary coach of one of the noble families.

"Whose carriage is that?" Hugh demanded. "Tell me you did not put me with Lady Danbury."

"I did not put you with Lady Danbury," Daniel replied, "although truth be told, she would probably be an excellent traveling companion."

"Who, then?"

"Climb up and see."

Hugh had spent an entire afternoon and most of a night convincing himself that his crazed lust for Sarah Pleinsworth had been brought on by momentary madness which had been brought on by . . . something. Maybe more momentary madness. However it had happened, a full day at close quarters with her could not be a good idea.

"Winstead," he said in a warning voice. "Not your cousin. I'm telling you, I've already—"

"Do you know how many cousins I have? Do you really think you could avoid all of them?"

"*Winstead.*"

"Don't worry, I've put you with the best of the lot, I promise."

"Why do I feel as if I'm being led to slaughter?"

"Well," Daniel admitted, "you will be outnumbered."

Hugh swung around. "What?"

"Here we are!"

Hugh looked up just as Daniel wrenched open the door.

"Ladies," Daniel said grandly.

Out popped a head. "Lord Hugh!"

It was Lady Frances.

"Lord Hugh."

"Lord Hugh."

And her sisters, apparently. Although not, as far as Hugh could tell, Lady Sarah.

Hugh finally exhaled.

"Some of my finest hours have been spent with these three ladies," Daniel said.

"I believe today's journey is to be nine hours," Hugh said dryly.

"It will be nine very fine hours." Daniel leaned closer. "But if I might offer some advice," he whispered, "don't try to follow everything they say. You'll get vertigo."

Hugh paused on the step up. "What?"

"In you go!" Daniel gave him a push. "We shall see you when we stop for our luncheon."

Hugh opened his mouth to protest, but Daniel had already slammed the door shut.

Hugh glanced about the interior of the coach. Harriet and Elizabeth sat facing forward, a large pile of books and papers on the seat between them. Harriet was trying to balance a lap desk on her knees and had a quill tucked behind her ear.

"Wasn't that nice of Daniel to put you in the coach with us?" Frances said, as soon as Hugh had settled into his seat next to her. Or rather, it was a bit before he was settled; he was coming to realize that she was not a particularly patient child.

"Indeed," Hugh murmured. He supposed he was thankful, actually. Better Lady Frances than some stuffy old lady or a gentleman with a cheroot. And surely her sisters would be tolerable.

"I asked him specially," Frances continued. "I had such a nice time at the wedding yesterday." She turned to her sisters. "We ate cake together."

"I saw," Elizabeth said.

"Do you mind riding backwards?" Frances asked. "Harriet and Elizabeth both get sick if they do."

"Frances!" Elizabeth protested.

"It's true. What would be more embarrassing, my telling Lord Hugh that you get sick from riding backwards, or actually getting sick from riding backwards?"

"I would prefer the former myself," Hugh said.

"Are you going to chatter the whole way?" Harriet asked. Of the three, she looked the most like Sarah. Her hair was a few shades lighter, but the shape of her face was the same, and so was her smile. She looked at Hugh with a hint of embarrassment. "I beg your pardon. I was addressing my sisters, of course. Not you."

"Think nothing of it," he said with a light smile. "But as it happens, I don't intend to chatter the whole way."

"I was planning to write," Harriet continued, moving a small sheaf of papers onto her lap desk.

"You can't do that," Elizabeth said. "You'll get ink everywhere."

"No, I won't. I'm developing a new technique."

"For writing in the carriage?"

"It involves less ink. I promise. And did anyone remember to pack biscuits? I always get hungry before we stop for lunch."

"Frances brought some. And you know Mother will have a fit if you get ink on—"

"Watch your elbows, Frances."

"So sorry, Lord Hugh. I hope that didn't hurt. And I didn't bring any biscuits. I thought Elizabeth was going to do so."

"Did you sit on my doll?"

"Oh, bother. I knew I should have eaten a bigger breakfast. Stop looking at me like that. I'm not going to get ink on the cush—"

"Your doll is right here. How does one use less ink?"

Hugh could only stare. There appeared to be

sixteen different conversations going on at once. With only three participants.

"Well, I just jot down the main ideas—"

"Do the main ideas have unicorns?"

Hugh had been completely unable to track who was saying what until *that*.

"Not the unicorns again," Elizabeth groaned. She looked over at Hugh and said, "Please forgive my sister. She is obsessed with unicorns."

Hugh glanced down at Frances. She'd gone rigid with anger and was glaring at her sister. He didn't really blame her; Elizabeth's tone had been as older-sibling as it got, two parts condescension and one part derision. And while he didn't really hold that against her—he would have been the same at her age, he was sure—he was seized by a sudden urge to be a little girl's hero.

He couldn't remember the last time he'd been anyone's hero.

"I rather like unicorns," he said.

Elizabeth looked stunned. "You do?"

He shrugged. "Doesn't everyone?"

"Yes, but you don't *believe* in them," Elizabeth said. "Frances thinks they are real."

Out of the corner of his eye he saw Frances eyeing him nervously.

"I certainly cannot prove that they *don't* exist," he said.

Frances let out a squeak.

Elizabeth looked as if she'd been staring into the sun too long.

"Lord Hugh," Frances said, "I—"

"*Mama!*"

Frances stopped midsentence and they all looked toward the carriage door. It was Sarah's voice, just outside the carriage, and she did not sound happy.

"Do you think she's going to ride with us?" Elizabeth whispered.

"Well, she did on the way here," Harriet replied.

Lady Sarah. In the carriage. Hugh was not sure he could imagine a more diabolical torture.

"It's here with your sisters or with Arthur and Rupert," came the voice of Lady Pleinsworth. "I'm sorry, but we just don't have room in . . ."

"I won't get to sit with you," Frances told Hugh apologetically. "They won't all three fit on the other side."

Lady Sarah would be sitting next to him. Apparently there *was* a more diabolical torture.

"Don't worry," Harriet assured him, "Sarah doesn't get sick riding backwards."

"No, it's fine," they all heard Sarah say, "I don't mind riding with them, but I was hoping—"

The door was wrenched open. Sarah was already halfway up the step, her back to the carriage as she continued to speak with her mother. "It's just that I'm tired, and—"

"It's time to depart," Lady Pleinsworth cut in firmly. She gave her daughter a little shove. "I won't be the one to hold everyone up."

Sarah let out an impatient exhale as she backed into the carriage and turned around and—

Saw him.

"Good morning," Hugh said.

Her mouth hung open in surprise.

"I'll move over," Frances grumbled. She got up and moved across the carriage, trying to take the window seat from Elizabeth before ending up, arms crossed, in the center.

"Lord Hugh," Sarah said, clearly at a loss. "I, ehrm . . . What are you doing here?"

"Don't be rude," Frances scolded.

"I'm not being rude. I'm just surprised." She sat down in the spot Frances had vacated. "And curious."

Hugh reminded himself that she had no idea what had happened the day before. Because *nothing* had happened. It had all been in his head. And perhaps a few other parts of his body. But the important thing was, she didn't know, and she would never know, because it was going to go away.

Momentary madness, by definition, was momentary.

All the same, it took some effort not to notice that her hip was only a few inches from his.

"To what do we owe the pleasure of your company, Lord Hugh?" Sarah asked as she untied her bonnet.

She definitely had no idea. There was no way she'd have used the word *pleasure*, otherwise.

"Your cousin informed me that he had saved me a spot in the best carriage of the trip," he said.

"The caravan," Frances corrected.

He pulled his eyes off Sarah to look at her youngest sister. "I beg your pardon?"

"The Great and Terrible Caravan of British Aristocracy," Frances said pertly. "It's what we call it."

He felt himself grin, and when he next breathed, it sounded like a laugh. "That's . . . excellent," he said, finally settling on a word.

"Sarah thought of it," Frances said with a shrug. "She's very clever, you know."

"Frances," Sarah warned.

"She is," Frances said in the worst imitation of a whisper Hugh had ever heard.

Sarah's eyes flitted this way and that, the way they did when she was uncomfortable, and then finally she leaned forward to glance out the window. "Aren't we meant to be leaving soon?"

"The Great and Terrible Caravan," he murmured.

She turned to him with suspicion in her eyes.

"I like it," he said simply.

Her lips parted, and she had that look about her, as if she was planning a long sentence, but instead she said, "Thank you."

"Oh, here we go!" Frances said happily.

The wheels of the carriage began to turn beneath them. Hugh sat back and allowed the motion to lull him into quietude. He'd never minded coach travel before his injury. It had always put him to sleep. It still did; the only problem was that there was rarely enough room to extend his leg, and it hurt like the devil the following day.

"Will you be all right?" Lady Sarah asked quietly.

He tilted his head toward her and murmured, "All right?"

Her eyes went fleetingly to his leg.

"I'll be fine."

"Won't you need to stretch it?"

"We'll be stopping for lunch."

"But—"

"I will be fine, Lady Sarah," he cut in, but to his own surprise, his words held no bite of defensiveness. He cleared his throat. "Thank you for your concern."

Her eyes narrowed, and he could tell that she was trying to decide if she believed him. He didn't want to give her any cause to think him anything but perfectly comfortable, so he glanced idly over at the three youngest Pleinsworth sisters, squeezed in a row. Harriet was tapping the feathered end of a quill against her forehead, and Elizabeth had pulled out a small book. Frances was leaning past her, trying to see out the window.

"We haven't even left the drive," Elizabeth said, not taking her eyes from her book.

"I just want to *see*."

"There is nothing *to* see."

"There will be."

Elizabeth flipped a page with crisp precision. "You're not going to be like this the whole— Ow!"

"It was an accident," Frances insisted.

"She kicked me," Harriet said, to no one in particular.

Hugh watched the exchange with some humor, well aware that what was amusing now would be agonizing if it went on for the next hour.

"Why don't you try to see out Harriet's window?" Elizabeth said.

Frances sighed but did as her sister had suggested. A moment later, however, they heard the sound of paper crumpling.

"Frances!" Harriet cried.

"I'm *sorry*. I just want to look out the window."

Harriet looked over at Sarah pleadingly.

"I can't," Sarah said. "If you think you're uncomfortable now, just think how tight it would be with me there instead of Frances."

"Frances, sit still," Harriet said sharply, and she turned back to the papers on her lap desk.

Hugh felt Sarah nudge him lightly with her elbow, and when he turned, she motioned with her eyes toward her hand.

One . . . two . . . three . . .

She was discreetly counting the seconds, each finger stretching out in time.

Four . . . five . . .

"Frances!"

"Sorry!"

Hugh peeked over at Sarah, whose faint smile was decidedly smug.

"Frances, you cannot keep leaning over me like that," Elizabeth snapped.

"Then let me sit at the window!"

All eyes turned to Elizabeth, who finally let out a hugely irritated huff as she crouched in the middle of the carriage to allow Frances to slide over to the window. Hugh watched with interest as Elizabeth wiggled about far more than was necessary to find a comfortable position, reopened her book, and glared at the words.

He looked at Sarah. She looked back with an expression that said, *Just you wait*.

Frances did not disappoint.

"I'm bored."

Chapter Eleven

SARAH SIGHED, TORN between amusement and embarrassment that Lord Hugh was about to witness a classic Pleinsworth spat.

"For the love of— Frances!" Elizabeth glared at her younger sister as if she might take her head off. "It hasn't been more than five minutes since we switched places!"

Frances gave a helpless shrug. "But I'm bored."

Sarah stole a glace at Hugh. He seemed to be trying not to laugh. Which she supposed was the best she could hope for.

"Can't we *do* something?" Frances pleaded.

"I am," Elizabeth ground out, holding up her book.

"You *know* that's not what I meant."

"Oh, no!" Harriet cried out.

"I knew you were going to spill the ink!" Elizabeth yelled. Then she let out a shriek, "Don't get it on me!"

"Stop moving so much!"

"I can help!" Frances said excitedly, leaping into the fray.

Sarah was just about to intervene when Lord Hugh reached forward, grabbed Frances by the collar, and hauled her across the carriage, where he deposited her unceremoniously onto Sarah's lap.

It was rather magnificent, really.

Frances gaped.

"You should stay out of it," he advised.

Sarah, meanwhile, was dealing with an elbow to her lungs. "I can't breathe," she gasped.

Frances adjusted her position. "Better?" she asked brightly.

Sarah's reply was a huge gulp of air. Somehow she managed to twist her head to the side so that she was facing Lord Hugh. "I would compliment you on a superior extrication except that I seem to have lost all feeling in my legs."

"Well, at least you're breathing now," he said.

And then—heaven help her—she started to laugh. There was something so ludicrous about being complimented for breathing. Or maybe it was just that one *had* to laugh when the best thing about one's situation was that one was still breathing.

And so she did. She laughed. She laughed so hard and so long that Frances slid right off her lap to the floor. And then she kept on laughing until the tears were running down her face, and Elizabeth and Harriet stopped their bickering and stared, astounded.

"What's wrong with Sarah?" Elizabeth asked.

"It was something about having trouble breathing," Frances said from the floor.

Sarah let out a little shriek of laughter at that, then clutched her chest, gasping, "Can't breathe. Laughing too hard."

Like all good laughter, it was contagious, and before long the whole carriage was giggling, even Lord Hugh, whom Sarah could never have imagined laughing like that. Oh, he smirked, and occasionally he chuckled, but right then, as the Pleinsworth carriage rolled south toward Thrapstone, he was as undone as the rest of them.

It was a glorious moment.

"Oh my," Sarah finally managed to say.

"I don't even know what we're laughing about," Elizabeth said, still grinning from ear to ear.

Sarah finished wiping the tears from her eyes and tried to explain. "It was— He said— oh, never mind, it would never be as funny in the retelling."

"I've got the ink cleaned up, at least," Harriet said. She pulled a sheepish face. "Well, except for my hands."

Sarah looked over and winced. Only one of Harriet's fingers seemed to have been spared.

"You look as if you've got the plague," Elizabeth said.

"No, I think that's on your neck," Harriet replied, taking no offense whatsoever. "Frances, you should get off the floor."

Frances looked up at Elizabeth, who had slid back into the seat by the window. Elizabeth sighed and moved to the center.

"I'm just going to get bored again," Frances said as soon as she was settled.

"No, you're not," Hugh said firmly.

Sarah turned to look at him, amused and impressed. It took a brave man to take on the Pleinsworth girls.

"We shall find something to do," he announced.

She waited for him to realize that could never be enough of an answer. Apparently her sisters were doing the same, for at least ten seconds passed before Elizabeth asked him, "Have you any suggestions?"

"He's brilliant with numbers," Frances said. "He can multiply monstrously huge sums in his head. I've seen him do it."

"I can't imagine you will find it entertaining to quiz me at maths for nine hours," he said.

"No, but it might be entertaining for the next ten minutes," Sarah said, and she meant every word. How was it possible that she did not know this about him? She knew that he was very clever; Daniel and Marcus had both said so. She also knew that he had been considered unbeatable at cards. After all that had happened, there was no way she could not know *that*.

"How monstrously huge?" she asked, because truly, she wanted to know.

"At least four digits," Frances said. "That's what he did at the wedding breakfast. It was brilliant."

Sarah peered over at Hugh. He seemed to be blushing. Well, maybe just a little bit. Or maybe not. Maybe she just wanted him to be blushing. There was something quite appealing about the notion.

But then she caught something else in his expression. She didn't know how to describe it, except that she suddenly knew . . .

"You can do more than four digits," she said with wonder.

"It is a talent," he said, "that has brought me as much trouble as it has benefit."

"May I quiz you?" Sarah asked, trying to keep some of the eagerness out of her voice.

He leaned toward her with a bit of smirk. "Only if I can quiz *you*."

"Spoilsport."

"I might call you the same."

"Later," she said firmly. "You are going to show me later." She was *fascinated* by this newly revealed talent of Lord Hugh's. Surely he wouldn't mind one little equation. He'd done it for Frances.

"We can read one of my plays," Harriet suggested. She started rifling through the stack of papers on her lap. "I have the one I started just last night. You know, the one with the heroine who is not too pink—"

"And not too green!" Frances and Elizabeth finished excitedly.

"Oh," Sarah said with great dismay. "Oh oh oh oh. *No*."

Lord Hugh turned to her with some amusement. "Not too pink or green?" he murmured.

"It is a description of me, I'm afraid."

"I . . . see."

She gave him a look. "Laugh. You know you want to."

"She is also not too fat or thin," Frances said helpfully.

"It's not *actually* Sarah," Harriet explained. "Just a character I've modeled upon her."

"Quite closely," Elizabeth added. With a grin.

"Here you are," Harriet said, holding a small stack of papers across the carriage. "I have only one copy, so you'll have to share."

"Does this masterpiece have a name?" Hugh inquired.

"Not yet," Harriet replied. "I've found that I often must complete a play before I know what to call it. But it will be something terribly romantic. It's a love story." She paused, her mouth twisting in thought. "Although I'm not sure it will have a happy ending."

"This is a romance?" Lord Hugh said with a dubious quirk of his brow. "And I'm meant to be the hero?"

"We can't really use Frances," Harriet said with no sarcasm whatsoever. "And I've only got the one copy, so if Sarah is the heroine you've got to be the hero, since you're sitting next to her."

He looked down. "My name is Rudolfo?"

Sarah nearly spit out a laugh.

"You're Spanish," Harriet said. "But your mother was English, so you speak it perfectly."

"Do I have an accent?"

"Of course."

"Can't imagine why I asked," he murmured. And then, to Sarah: "Oh, look. Your name is Woman."

"Typecast again," Sarah quipped.

"I hadn't thought of a proper name yet," Harriet explained, "but I didn't want to hold up the entire manuscript. It could take me weeks to think of the right name. And by then I might have forgotten all of my ideas."

"The creative process is a peculiar thing, indeed," Lord Hugh murmured.

Sarah had been reading ahead while Harriet was speaking, and she was developing serious misgivings. "I'm not certain this is a good idea," she said, tugging the second page out of the pile so she could read further.

No, it definitely wasn't a good idea.

"Reading in a moving carriage is always a risk," Sarah said quickly. "Especially riding backwards."

"You never get sick," Elizabeth reminded her.

Sarah looked ahead to page three. "I might."

"You don't have to actually *do* the things in the play," Harriet said. "This isn't a true performance. It's just a reading."

"Should I be reading ahead?" Lord Hugh asked Sarah.

Wordlessly, she handed him page two.

"Oh."

And page three.

"*Oh.*"

"Harriet, we cannot do this," Sarah said firmly.

"Oh, *please*," Harriet pleaded. "It would be so helpful. That's the problem with writing plays. One needs to hear the words said aloud."

"You know that I have never been good at acting out your plays," Sarah said.

Lord Hugh looked at her quizzically. "Really?"

Something about his expression did not sit well with her. "What does that mean?"

He gave a little shrug. "Just that you're very dramatic."

"Dramatic?" She did not like the way that sounded.

"Oh, come now," he said, with far more condescension than was healthy in a closed carriage, "surely you don't see yourself as quiet and meek."

"No, but I don't know that I'd go so far as *dramatic.*"

He looked at her for a moment, then said, "You do enjoy making pronouncements."

"It's true, Sarah," Harriet put in. "You do."

Sarah whipped her head around and fixed such a look onto her sister's face that it was a wonder she didn't wither on the spot.

"I'm not reading this," she said, clamping her mouth shut.

"It's just a kiss," Harriet exclaimed.

Just a kiss?

Frances's eyes opened nearly as wide as her mouth. "You want Sarah to kiss Lord Hugh?"

Just a kiss. It could never be just a kiss. Not with him.

"They wouldn't actually *do* the kiss," Harriet said.

"Does one *do* a kiss?" Elizabeth asked.

"No," Sarah bit off. "One does not."

"We wouldn't tell anyone," Harriet tried.

"This is highly inappropriate," Sarah said in a

tight voice. She turned to Lord Hugh, who had not uttered a word for some time. "Surely you agree with me."

"I surely do," he said, his words strangely clipped.

"There. You see, we are not reading this." Sarah thrust the pages back at Harriet, who retrieved them with great reluctance.

"Would you do it if Frances read the part of Rudolfo?" Harriet asked in a small voice.

"You just said—"

"I know, but I really want to hear it aloud."

Sarah crossed her arms. "We are not reading the play, and that is final."

"But—"

"I said *no*," Sarah exploded, feeling the last remnants of her control snapping in two. "I am not kissing Lord Hugh. Not here. Not now. Not ever!"

An appalled silence fell across the carriage.

"I beg your pardon," Sarah muttered. She could feel a flush rising from the throat to the tip of her head. She waited for Lord Hugh to say something horribly clever and cutting, but he did not utter a word. Neither did Harriet. Or Elizabeth or Frances.

Finally Elizabeth made an awkward noise with her throat and said, "I'll just read my book, then."

Harriet reshuffled her papers.

Even Frances turned to the window and looked out without a word about boredom.

Of Lord Hugh, Sarah did not know. She could not bring herself to look at him. Her outburst had been ugly, the insult unforgivable. *Of course* they weren't going to kiss in the carriage. They wouldn't have kissed even if they'd been performing the play in a drawing room. Like Harriet had said, there would have been some sort of narration, or perhaps they would have leaned in (but kept a respectable six inches apart) and kissed air.

But she was already so aware of him, in ways that confused as much as they infuriated. Just reading ahead that their characters would kiss . . .

It had been too much.

The journey continued in silence. Frances eventually fell asleep. Harriet stared into space. Elizabeth kept reading, although every now and then she'd look up, her eyes flicking from Sarah to Hugh and back again. After an hour, Sarah thought that Lord Hugh might have fallen asleep, too; he had not moved even once since they'd gone silent, and she could not imagine it was comfortable for his leg to remain in the same position for so long.

But when she chanced a peek, he was awake. The only sign that he saw her looking at him was a tiny change in his eyes.

He did not say anything.

Nor did she.

Finally she felt the wheels of the carriage slowing, and when she peered out the window she saw that they were approaching an inn with a cheery little sign that said, *The Rose and Crown, est. 1612.*

"Frances," she said, glad to have a logical reason to speak. "Frances, it's time to wake up. We're here."

Frances blinked groggily and leaned on Elizabeth, who did not utter a complaint.

"Frances, are you hungry?" Sarah persisted. She leaned forward and jostled her knee. The carriage had come to a complete stop, and all Sarah could think about was escape. She had been trying so hard to keep still, to keep quiet. It felt as if she hadn't drawn a breath in hours.

"Oh," Frances finally said with a yawn. "Did I fall asleep?"

Sarah nodded.

"I'm hungry," Frances said.

"You should have remembered the biscuits," Harriet said.

Sarah would have scolded her for such a petty comment except that it was a relief to hear something so perfectly normal.

"I didn't know I was supposed to bring the biscuits," Frances whined, coming to her feet. She was small for her age and could stand in the carriage without crouching.

The door to the carriage swung open, and Lord Hugh took his cane and stepped out without a word.

"You did know," Elizabeth said. "I told you."

Sarah moved toward the door.

"You're stepping on my cloak!" Frances howled.

Sarah looked out. Lord Hugh was holding up his hand to help her down.

"I'm not stepping on anything."

Sarah took his hand. She didn't know what else she could possibly do.

"Get off my— Oh!"

There was a shriek, and then someone stumbled hard into Sarah. She lurched forward, her free hand swinging wildly for balance, but to no avail. She fell, first onto the step, and then onto the hard ground, taking Lord Hugh down with her.

She let out a cry as a splinter of pain shot through her ankle. *Calm down*, she told herself, *it's just the surprise*. It was like stubbing one's toe. It hurt like the dickens for one second, and then you realized it was the surprise more than anything.

So she held her breath and waited for the pain to subside.

It didn't.

Chapter Twelve

FOR A MOMENT, Hugh had thought himself whole again.

He was not entirely sure what had happened inside the carriage, but moments after Sarah placed her warm hand in his, she let out a cry and came toppling toward him.

He held out his arms to catch her. It was the most natural thing in the world, except that he was a man with a ruined leg, and men with ruined legs should never forget what they are.

He caught her, or at least he thought he did, but his leg could not support their combined weight, not when amplified by the force of her fall. He did not have time to feel pain; his muscle simply crumpled, and his leg buckled beneath him.

So it didn't really matter if he caught her or not. They both crashed to the ground, and for a moment Hugh could do nothing but gasp. The impact had sucked the very breath from his body, and his leg . . .

He bit down on the inside of his cheek. Hard. Strange how one pain could lessen the intensity of another. Or at least it usually did. This time it did nothing. He tasted blood and still his leg felt shot through with needles.

Cursing under his breath, he forced himself to his hands and knees so that he could get to Sarah, who was sprawled on the ground next to him.

"Are you all right?" he asked urgently.

She nodded, but it was that jerky, unfocused type of nod that said that no, she was not all right.

"Is it your leg?"

"My ankle," she whimpered.

Hugh knelt beside her, his leg screaming in agony at being overbent. He would need to get Sarah into the Rose and Crown, but first he should check to see if she had broken the bone. "May I?" he said, his hands hovering near her foot.

She nodded, but before he could even touch her, they were surrounded. Harriet had jumped down from the carriage, and then Lady Pleinsworth had run out from the inn, and God knows who else was pressing in, and pushing him out. Finally Hugh just hauled himself to his feet and backed up, leaning heavily on his cane.

The muscle in his thigh felt as if someone had impaled him with a burning knife, but even so, it was a familiar sort of pain. He hadn't done anything new to his leg, it seemed to tell him; he'd just pushed it to the limit.

Two gentlemen arrived on the scene—Sarah's cousins, he thought—and then Daniel was there, pushing them away.

Taking charge.

Hugh watched as he checked her ankle, then he watched as Sarah put her arms around his neck.

And still he watched as Daniel swept through the crowd and carried her into the inn.

Hugh would never be able to do that. Forget riding, forget dancing, and hunting, and all those things he mourned since a bullet had mangled his thigh. None of those seemed to matter anymore.

He would never gather a woman in his arms and carry her away.

He had never felt like less of a man.

The Rose and Crown Inn
An hour later

"How many?"

Hugh looked up just as Daniel slid onto the stool next to him in the barroom at the inn.

"How many drinks?" Daniel clarified.

Hugh took a gulp of his ale, and then another, because that was what it took to finish the mug. "Not enough."

"Are you drunk?"

"Sadly, no." Hugh signaled to the innkeeper for another.

The innkeeper looked over. "One for you, too, m'lord?"

Daniel shook his head. "Tea, if you will. It's early yet."

Hugh smirked.

"Everyone is in the dining room," Daniel told him.

All two hundred of us, Hugh almost said, but then he remembered that they were splitting up between inns for lunch. He supposed he should be thankful for small favors. Only one-fifth of the traveling party would have seen his humiliation.

"Do you want to join us?" Daniel asked.

Hugh looked over at him.

"I didn't think so."

The innkeeper set another mug of ale in front of Hugh. "The tea'll be ready soon, m'lord."

Hugh lifted the mug to his lips and downed about a third of it in one gulp. There wasn't nearly enough alcohol in the stuff. It was taking him far too long to squash his brain into nothingness.

"Did she break it?" he asked. He had not intended to ask questions, but this he had to know.

"No," Daniel said, "but it's a nasty sprain. It's swollen, and she's in quite a lot of pain."

Hugh nodded. He knew all about that. "Can she travel?"

"I think so. We'll have to put her in a different carriage. She'll need to elevate the leg."

Hugh took another long drink.

"I didn't see what happened," Daniel said.

Hugh went still. Slowly, he turned to his friend. "What are you asking me?"

"Just what happened," Daniel said, his mouth twisting with disbelief at Hugh's overreaction.

"She fell out of the carriage. I failed to catch her."

Daniel stared at him for several seconds, then said, "Oh, for God's sake, you're not blaming yourself, are you?"

Hugh did not reply.

One of Daniel's hands waved forth in question. "How could you have caught her?"

Hugh gripped the edge of the bar.

"Bloody hell," Daniel muttered. "It's not always about your leg. I probably would have missed, too."

"No," Hugh spat. "You would not have missed."

Daniel was quiet for a moment, then said, "Her sisters were squabbling. Apparently one of them knocked into her inside the carriage. That was why she fell."

It didn't really matter why she fell, Hugh thought, and he took another drink.

"So it was really more like she was thrown."

Hugh hauled his attention off his drink for long enough to snarl, "Do you have a point?"

"She must have come from the carriage with considerable force," Daniel said, and Hugh supposed he was speaking in a patient voice. But Hugh wasn't in the mood to give points for patience. He was in the mood to drink, and to feel sorry for himself, and snap the head off whoever was stupid enough to approach. He finished his ale, slammed the mug down, and signaled for another. The innkeeper was quick to comply.

"Are you sure you want to drink that?" Daniel asked.

"Quite."

"I seem to recall," Daniel said in an excruciatingly quiet voice, "you once telling me you did not drink until nightfall."

Did Daniel think Hugh had forgotten? Did he think Hugh would have sat here and downed pint after pint of bad ale if there were any other way to kill the pain? It wasn't just his leg this time. Bloody hell, how was he supposed to be a man when his goddamned leg couldn't hold him up?

Hugh felt his heart quicken with fury, and he heard his breath turn to short, angry puffs. There were a hundred different things he could have said to Daniel in that moment, but only one truly expressed what he felt.

"Piss off."

There was a very long silence, then Daniel stepped down from the stool. "You are in no state to ride the rest of the day in a carriage with my young cousins."

Hugh curled his lip. "Why the hell do you think I'm drinking?"

"I am going to pretend you did not say that," Daniel said quietly, "and I suggest that when you're sober you do the same." He walked to the door. "We leave in one hour. I will have someone inform you which carriage you may ride in."

"Just leave me," Hugh said. Why not? He didn't need to be at Whipple Hill right away. He could bloody well marinate at the Rose and Crown for the week.

Daniel smiled humorlessly. "You'd like that, wouldn't you?"

Hugh shrugged, trying to be insolent. But all it did was set him off-balance, and he nearly slid off his stool.

"One hour," Daniel said, and he walked away.

Hugh slumped over his drink, but he knew that in one hour, he would be standing in front of the Rose and Crown, preparing for the next leg of the journey. If anyone else—anyone at all—had stood before him and ordered him to be ready in an hour, he would have marched out of the inn and never turned back.

But not Daniel Smythe-Smith. And he suspected Daniel knew that.

Whipple Hill
nr. Thatcham
Berkshire
Six days later

THE RIDE TO Whipple Hill had been nothing short of miserable, but now that she was here, it occurred to Sarah that perhaps she had been lucky to have spent her first three days with a swollen ankle trapped in the Pleinsworth coach. The ride might have bumped and jostled, but at least she'd had a logical reason to remain off her feet. More to the point, everyone else was stuck in one place on their bottoms, as well.

No longer.

Daniel was determined that the week leading up to his wedding should be the stuff of legend, and he had planned every imaginable diversion and entertainment. There would be outings and charades and dancing and a hunt and at least twelve other wondrous pastimes that would be revealed as necessary. Sarah would not have put it past him to offer juggling lessons on the lawn. Which, by the by, she knew he could do. He'd taught himself when he was twelve and a traveling fair had passed through town.

Sarah spent her first full day in residence trapped in the room she was sharing with Harriet with her foot propped up on pillows. Her other sisters had come to visit, as had Iris and Daisy, but Honoria was still at Fensmore, enjoying a few days of privacy with her new husband before traveling down. And while Sarah appreciated her relatives stopping by to entertain her, she was less enthralled by their breathless accounts of all the amazingly fabulous events taking place outside her bedroom door.

Her second day at Whipple Hill passed in much the same manner, except that Harriet took pity on her and promised to read her all five acts of *Henry VIII and the Unicorn of Doom*, which had been recently renamed *The Shepherdess, the Unicorn, and Henry VIII*. Sarah could not understand why; there was no mention of a shepherdess anywhere. She had nodded off for only a few minutes. Surely she could not have missed a character pivotal enough to merit a mention in the title of the play.

The third day was the worst. Daisy brought her violin.

And Daisy knew no short pieces.

So when Sarah awoke on her fourth day at Whipple Hill, she swore to herself that she would descend the grand staircase and join the rest of humanity or die trying.

She did, actually, swear this. And she must have done so with great conviction, because the housemaid paled and crossed herself.

But make it down she did, only to find that half the ladies had departed for the village. And the other half were about to.

The men planned to hunt.

It had been rather mortifying to arrive at breakfast in the arms of a footman (she had not specified how she would descend the grand staircase), so as soon as all of the other guests had departed, she rose to her feet and took a gingerly step. She could put a little weight on the ankle as long as she was careful.

And leaned against a wall.

Maybe she'd go to the library. She could find a book, sit down, read. No need to use her feet at all. The library wasn't so far.

She took another step.

It wasn't *completely* across the house.

She groaned. Who was she trying to fool? At this rate it was going to take her half the day to make it to the library.

What she needed was a cane.

She stopped. This made her think of Lord Hugh. She had not seen him in nearly a week. She supposed she shouldn't have found this odd; they were only two of over a hundred people who'd made the journey from Fensmore to Whipple

Hill. And it went without saying that he would not come to visit her while she convalesced in her bedroom.

Still, she'd been thinking of him. When she was lying in bed with her foot on the pillows, she wondered how long he'd had to do the same. When she'd got up in the middle of the night and crawled to the chamber pot, she'd started to wonder . . . and then she'd cursed the biological unfairness of it all. A man wouldn't have needed to crawl to the chamber pot, now, would he? He could probably use the blasted thing in bed.

Not that she was imagining Lord Hugh in bed.

Or using a chamber pot, for that matter.

But still, how had he done it? How did he still do it? How did he manage the everyday tasks of life without wanting to tear his hair out and scream to the heavens? Sarah hated being so dependent on everyone else. Just this morning she'd had to ask a maid to find her mother, who'd then decided that a footman was the correct person to carry her down to breakfast.

All she wanted was to go somewhere on her own two feet. Without informing anyone of her plans. And if she had to suffer through shooting pain every time she put weight on her foot, then so be it. It was worth it just to get out of her room.

But back to Lord Hugh. She knew that his leg bothered him after too much use, but did he feel pain every time he took a step? How was it possible she had not asked him this? They had walked together, certainly no long distances, but still, she should have known if he was in pain. She should have *asked*.

She hobbled a bit farther down the hall, then finally gave up and sat down in a chair. Someone would be along eventually. A maid . . . a footman . . . It was a busy house.

She sat, tapping a tune on her leg with her hands. Her mother would have a fit if she saw her like this. A lady was meant to sit still. A lady should speak softly and laugh musically and do all sorts of things that had never come naturally to Sarah. It was remarkable, really, that she loved her mother so well. By all rights, they should have wanted to kill each other.

After a few minutes Sarah heard someone moving around the corner. Should she call out? She did need help, but—

"Lady Sarah?"

It was him. She didn't know why she was so surprised. Or pleased. But she was. Their last conversation had been awful, but when she saw Lord Hugh Prentice coming toward her down the hall, she was so happy to see him that it was astonishing.

He reached her side, then looked up and down the hall. "What are you doing here?"

"Resting, I'm afraid." She kicked her foot out an inch or so. "My ambitions outstripped my abilities."

"You shouldn't be up and about."

"I just spent three days practically tied to my bed."

Was it her imagination, or did he suddenly look somewhat uncomfortable?

She kept talking. "And three more before that trapped in a coach—"

"As did we all."

She pressed her lips together peevishly. "Yes, but the rest of you were able to get out and walk around."

"Or limp," he said dryly.

Her eyes flew to his face, but whatever emotions he hid behind his eyes, she could not interpret them.

"I owe you an apology," he said stiffly.

She blinked. "For what?"

"I let you fall."

She looked at him for a moment, utterly stunned that he might blame himself for what was so obviously an accident.

"Don't be ridiculous," she assured him. "I would have fallen no matter what. Elizabeth was stepping on Frances's hem, and Frances was tugging, and then Elizabeth moved her foot, and—" She waved her hand. "Well. Never you mind. Somehow Harriet was the one who came tumbling into me. If it had been only Frances, I daresay I might have been able to catch my balance."

He did not say anything, and still she found herself unable to interpret his expression.

"It was on the step, you know," she heard herself say. "That was when I injured my ankle. Not when I landed." She had no idea why this might make a difference, but she'd never been talented at censoring her words when she was nervous.

"I owe you an apology as well," she added haltingly.

He looked at her in question.

She swallowed. "I was very unkind to you in the carriage."

He started to say something, probably, "Don't be silly," but she cut him off.

"I overreacted. It was very . . . embarrassing, Harriet's play. And I just want you to know that I'm sure I would have acted the same way with anyone. So really, you shouldn't feel insulted. At least, not personally."

Good God, she was babbling. She'd never been good at apologies. Most of the time she simply refused to give them.

"Are you joining the gentlemen for the hunt?" she blurted out.

The corner of his mouth tightened and his brows rose into a wry expression as he said, "I cannot."

"Oh. *Oh*." Stupid fool, what had she been thinking? "I'm so sorry," she said. "That was terribly insensitive of me."

"You don't need to dance around it, Lady Sarah. I am lame. It is a fact. And it is certainly not your fault."

She nodded. "Still, I'm sorry."

For the barest second he looked unsure of what to do, then, in a quiet voice, he said, "Apology accepted."

"I don't like that word, though," she said.

His brows rose.

"Lame." She scrunched her nose. "It makes you sound like a horse."

"Have you an alternative?"

"No. But it's not my job to solve the world's problems, merely to state them."

He stared at her.

"*I jest.*"

And then, finally, he smiled.

"Well," she said, "I suppose I only jest a little. I don't have a better word for it, and I probably cannot solve the world's problems, although to be fair, no one has given me the opportunity to do so." She looked up with slyly narrowed eyes, almost daring him to comment.

To her great surprise, he only laughed. "Tell me, Lady Sarah, what do you plan to do with yourself this morning? Somehow I doubt your intention is to sit in the hall all day."

"I thought I might read in the library," she admitted. "It's silly, I know, since that's what I've been doing in my room these past few days, but I'm desperate to be anywhere but that bedchamber. I think I would go read in a wardrobe just for the change of scenery."

"It would be an interesting change of scenery," he said.

"Dark," she agreed.

"Woolly."

She pressed her lips together in what turned out to be a failed attempt to hold back laughter. "Woolly?" she echoed.

"That's what you'd find in my wardrobe."

"I find myself alarmed by a vision of sheep." She paused, then winced. "And of what Harriet might do with such a scene in one of her plays."

He held up a hand. "Let us change the subject."

She cocked her head to the side, then realized she was smiling flirtatiously. So she stopped smiling. But she still felt unaccountably flirtatious.

So she smiled again, because she liked smiling, and she liked feeling flirtatious, and most of all because she knew he would know that she wasn't *actually* flirting with him. Because she wasn't. She was just feeling flirtatious. It was a result of having been cooped up in that room for so long with no one but sisters and cousins.

"You were on your way to the library," he said.

"I was."

"And you started out at . . ."

"The breakfast room."

"You did not make it very far."

"No," she admitted, "I didn't."

"Did it perhaps occur to you," he asked in careful tones, "that you should not be walking on that foot?"

"It did, as a matter of fact."

He quirked a brow. "Pride?"

She gave him a glum nod of confirmation. "Far too much of it."

"What shall we do now?"

She looked down at her traitorous ankle. "I suppose I need to find someone to carry me there."

There was a long pause, long enough for her to look up. But he had turned away, so all she saw was his profile. Finally, he cleared his throat and asked, "Would you like to borrow my cane?"

Her lips parted in surprise. "But don't you need it?"

"Not for shorter distances. It helps," he said, before she could point out that she'd never seen him without it, "but it is not strictly necessary."

She was about to agree to his suggestion; she even reached for the cane, but then she stopped, because he was just the sort of man to do something stupid in the name of chivalry. "You can walk without the cane," she said, looking directly into his eyes, "but does it mean that your leg will give you more pain later?"

He went quite still, and then he said, "Probably."

"Thank you for not lying to me."

"I almost did," he admitted.

She allowed herself a tiny smile. "I know."

"You have to take it now, you know." He grasped the center of the cane and held it out so the handle was within reach. "My honesty should not go unrewarded."

Sarah knew she should not allow him to do this. He might want to help her now, but later that day, his leg would hurt. Needlessly.

But somehow she knew that to refuse would cause him far more pain than anything his leg could give him later that day. He needed to help her, she realized.

He needed to help her far more than she needed help.

For a moment she could hardly speak.

"Lady Sarah?"

She looked up. He was watching her with a curious expression, and his eyes . . . How was it possible his eyes grew more beautiful each time she saw him? He wasn't smiling; the truth was, he didn't smile that often. But she saw it in his eyes. A glint of warmth, of happiness.

It hadn't been there that first day at Fensmore.

And it stunned her to her very toes how much she never wanted it to go away.

"Thank you," she said decisively, but instead of the cane, she reached toward his hand. "Help me up?"

Neither was wearing gloves, and the sudden burst of warmth on her skin made her tremble. His hand wrapped firmly around hers, and with a little tug, she found herself on her feet. Or foot, really. She was balancing on the good one.

"Thank you," she said again, somewhat alarmed at how breathless she sounded.

Wordlessly, he held out the cane, and she took it, curling her fingers around the smooth handle. It felt almost intimate, holding this object that had practically become an extension of his body.

"It's a bit tall for you," he said.

"I can make do." She tested out a step.

"No, no," he said, "you need to lean into it a bit more. Like this." He stepped behind her and placed his hand over hers on the handle of the cane.

Sarah stopped breathing. He was so close that she could feel his breath, warm and ticklish on the tip of her ear.

"Sarah?" he murmured.

She nodded, needing a moment to find her voice again. "I-I think I have it now."

He stepped away, and for a moment all she

could feel was the loss of his presence. It was startling, and disconcerting, and . . .

And it was cold.

"Sarah?"

She shook herself out of her odd reverie. "Sorry," she mumbled. "Woolgathering."

He grinned. Or maybe it was a smirk. A friendly one, but still smirkish.

"What is it?" She'd never seen him smile like that.

"Just wondering where the wardrobe was."

It took her a moment—she was sure she would have got it instantly if she'd not been so befuddled—and then she grinned right back. And then: "You called me Sarah."

He paused. "So I did. I apologize. It was unconsciously done."

"No," she said quickly, jumping atop his final words. "It's fine. I like it, I think."

"You think?"

"I do," she said firmly. "We are friends now, I think."

"You think." This time he was definitely smirking.

She tossed him a sarcastic glance. "You could not resist, could you?"

"No," he murmured, "I think not."

"That was so dreadful it was almost good," she told him.

"And that was such an insult I almost feel complimented."

She felt her lips tighten at the corners. She was trying not to smile; it was a battle of the wits, and somehow she knew that if she laughed, she lost. But at the same time, losing wasn't such a terrible prospect. Not in this.

"Come along," he said with mock severity. "Let's see you walk to the library."

And she did. It wasn't easy, and it wasn't painless—truthfully, she shouldn't have been up and about yet—but she did it.

"You're doing very well," he said as they neared their destination.

"Thank you," she said, ridiculously pleased by his praise. "It's marvelous. Such independence. It was just awful having to rely on someone to carry me about." She looked over her shoulder at him. "Is that how you feel?"

His lips curved in a wry expression. "Not exactly."

"Really? Because—" Her throat nearly closed. "Never mind." What an *idiot* she was. Of course it hadn't felt the same for him. She was using the cane to get her through the *day*. He would never be without it.

From that moment forward she no longer wondered why he did not smile very often. Instead, she marveled that he ever did.

Chapter Thirteen

The blue drawing room
Whipple Hill
Eight o'clock in the evening

WHEN IT CAME to social engagements, Hugh never knew which was worse: to be early and exhaust himself having to rise every time a lady appeared, or to arrive late, only to be the center of attention while he limped into the room. This evening, however, his injury had made the decision for him.

He had not been lying when he told Sarah that his leg would most likely pain him that night. But he was glad she had taken the cane. It was, he thought with a surprising lack of bitterness, the closest he would ever come to sweeping her into his arms and carrying her to safety.

Pathetic, but a man had to take his triumphs where he could.

By the time he entered the large drawing room at Whipple Hill, most of the other guests were already present. About seventy people, if he judged the crowd correctly. More than half of the so-called caravan were being lodged in nearby inns; they frolicked at the house during the day but were gone in the evening.

He did not bother to pretend that he was looking for anyone but Sarah the moment he limped through the door. They had spent much of the day in quiet companionship in the library, occasionally chatting but most often just reading. She had demanded that he demonstrate his mathematical brilliance (her words, not his), and he had complied. He'd always hated "performing" on demand, but Sarah had watched and listened with such obvious delight and amazement that he hadn't been able to bring himself to feel his usual discomfort.

He had misjudged her, he realized. Yes, she was overly dramatic and given to grand pronouncements, but she was not the shallow debutante he had once thought her. He was also coming to realize that her earlier antipathy toward him had not been entirely without merit. He had wronged her—inadvertently, but still. It was a fact that she would have had that first season in London if not for his duel with Daniel.

Hugh would not go so far as to agree that he had ruined her life, but now that he knew her better, it did not seem unlikely that Lady Sarah

Pleinsworth might have nabbed one of those now legendary fourteen gentlemen.

He could not, however, bring himself to regret this.

When he found her—it was her laughter, actually, that drew him to her—she was sitting on a chair in the middle of the room with her foot propped up on a small ottoman. One of her cousins was with her, the pale one. Iris, her name was. She and Sarah seemed to have an odd, somewhat competitive, relationship. Hugh would never be so bold as to think he understood more than three things about women (and probably not even that many), but it was clear to him that those two carried on complete conversations with nothing but narrowed eyes and tilts of the head.

But for now they seemed to be having a jolly time, so he made his way over and gave a polite bow.

"Lady Sarah," he said. "Miss Smythe-Smith."

Both ladies smiled and greeted him in return.

"Won't you join us?" Sarah said.

He sat in the chair to Sarah's left, taking the opportunity to extend his leg in front of him. He generally tried not to draw notice to himself by doing this in public, but she knew that he would be more comfortable this way, and more to the point, he knew that she would not be shy about telling him how he ought to sit.

"How is your ankle feeling this evening?" he asked her.

"Very well," she answered, then wrinkled her nose. "No, that's a lie. It's fairly dreadful."

Iris chuckled.

"Well, it is," Sarah said with a sigh. "I reckon I overexerted myself this morning."

"I thought you spent the morning in the library," Iris said.

"I did," Sarah told her. "But Lord Hugh very kindly lent me his cane. I walked all the way across the house on my own." She frowned at her foot. "Although after that I did absolutely nothing with it. I'm not sure why it's being so wretched."

"This sort of injury takes time to heal," Hugh said. "It may have been more than a simple sprain."

She grimaced. "It did make an awful sound when I twisted it on the step. Rather like something tearing."

"Oh, that's dreadful," Iris said with a shudder. "Why didn't you say anything?"

Sarah just shrugged, and Hugh said, "That's not a good sign, I'm afraid. It's certainly nothing permanent, but it does indicate that the injury may be deeper than originally thought."

Sarah let out a dramatic sigh. "I suppose I shall have to learn to grant audiences in my boudoir like a French queen."

Iris looked at Hugh. "I warn you, she's serious."

He did not doubt it.

"Or," Sarah continued, her eyes taking on a dangerous sparkle, "I could have someone arrange a litter to carry me about."

Hugh chuckled at her flamboyance. It was just the sort of thing that a mere week ago would have set his teeth on edge. But now that he knew her better, he could not help but be amused. She had a rather unique way of setting people at ease. He had meant it when he had said it before: it was a talent.

"Shall we feed you grapes from a golden chalice?" Iris teased.

"But of course," Sarah replied, holding her haughty expression for about two seconds before she broke into a grin.

They all laughed then, which was probably why none of them noticed Daisy Smythe-Smith until she was practically upon them.

"Sarah," she said rather officiously, "might I have a word?"

Hugh rose to his feet. He hadn't had a chance to talk with this particular Smythe-Smith yet. She looked young, still in the schoolroom but old enough to come down to supper at a family event.

"Daisy," Sarah said in greeting. "Good evening. Have you been introduced to Lord Hugh Prentice? Lord Hugh, this is Miss Daisy Smythe-Smith. She is Iris's sister."

Of course. He'd heard of this family. The Smythe-Smith Bouquet, someone had once called them. He could not remember all of their names. Daisy, Iris, probably a Rosehip and Marigold. He dearly hoped none were named Crocus.

Daisy bobbed a quick curtsy, but she clearly had no interest in him, for she immediately turned her curly blond head back to Sarah. "Since you cannot dance tonight," she said bluntly, "my mother has decided that we shall play."

Sarah blanched, and Hugh suddenly recalled that first night at Fensmore, when she had started to tell him something about her family's musicales. She had been cut off before she could finish. He never did learn what she was going to say.

"Iris won't be able to join us," Daisy continued, oblivious to Sarah's reaction. "We have no cello, and Lady Edith wasn't invited to *this* wedding, not that that would have done us any good," she said with an affronted sniff. "It was very unkind of her not to let us borrow her cello at Fensmore."

Hugh watched as Sarah threw a desperate glance at Iris. Iris, he noted, responded with nothing but sympathy. And horror.

"But the pianoforte is perfectly tuned," Daisy said, "and of course I brought my violin, so we shall make a duet of it."

Iris returned Sarah's expression with one of her own. They were having another one of those silent conversations, Hugh thought, untranslatable by anyone of the male sex.

Daisy soldiered on. "The only question is what to play. I propose Mozart's Quartet no. 1, since we do not have time to practice." She turned to Hugh. "We performed that earlier this year."

Sarah made a choking sound. "But—"

But Daisy was brooking no interruptions. "I assume you remember your part?"

"No! I don't. Daisy, I—"

"I do realize," Daisy continued, "that there are only two of us, but I don't think that will make a difference."

"You don't?" Iris asked, looking vaguely ill.

Daisy spared her sister a fleeting glance. A fleeting glance, Hugh noted, that still managed to

imbue itself with an astonishing degree of condescension and annoyance.

"We shall simply go forward without the cello
or second violin," she announced.

"*You* play the second violin," Sarah said.

"Not when there is only one violinist," Daisy
replied.

"That makes absolutely no sense," Iris put in.

Daisy let out a highly aggravated puff of air.
"Even if I play the second part, as I did last spring,
I will still be the only violinist." She waited for
affirmation, then plowed on anyway. "Which
therefore will make me the first violin."

Even Hugh knew it did not work that way.

"You cannot have a second violin without a
first," Daisy said impatiently. "It is numerically
impossible."

Oh no, Hugh thought, *she is not going to bring
numbers into this*.

"I can't play tonight, Daisy," Sarah said, with a
slow, horrified shake of her head.

Daisy's lips pinched. "Your mother said you
would."

"My mother—"

"What Lady Sarah means to say," Hugh cut in
smoothly, "is that she has already promised her
evening to me."

It seemed he was developing a taste for playing
the hero. Even to ladies who were not eleven years
old and infatuated with unicorns.

Daisy looked at him as if he were speaking another language. "I don't understand."

From the expression on Sarah's face, she didn't

either. Hugh offered his blandest smile and said, "I, too, cannot dance. Lady Sarah has offered to sit with me throughout the evening."

"But—"

"I am sure that Lord Winstead has made arrangements for tonight's music," Hugh continued.

"But—"

"And I so rarely have someone to keep me company on nights such as these."

"But—"

Good *God* the girl was persistent. "I am afraid I simply cannot allow her to break her promise to me," Hugh said.

"Oh, I could never do that," Sarah said, finally playing her role. She gave Daisy a helpless shrug. "It's a promise."

Daisy positively rooted herself to the floor, her face twitching as it began to sink in that she had been thoroughly thwarted. "Iris . . . ," she began.

"I will not play the pianoforte," Iris practically cried.

"How did you know what I was going to ask you?" Daisy asked with a petulant frown.

"You have been my sister since you were born," Iris replied testily. "Of course I knew what you were going to ask me."

"We all had to learn how to play," Daisy whined.

"And then we all stopped taking lessons when we took up strings."

"What Iris is trying to say," Sarah said, with a little glance toward Hugh before turning firmly to Daisy, "is that her skills on the pianoforte could never match yours on the violin."

Iris let out a noise that sounded suspiciously like a choke, but by the time Hugh looked at her, she was saying, "It's true, Daisy. You know it's true. I would only embarrass myself."

"Very well." Daisy finally capitulated. "I suppose I could just perform something by myself."

"No!" both Sarah and Iris shouted at once.

And it really was a shout. Enough people turned in their direction that Sarah was forced to plaster her face with an embarrassed smile and say, "So sorry."

"Whyever not?" Daisy asked. "I'm happy to do so, and there is no shortage of violin solos from which to choose."

"It is very difficult to dance to the music of a single violin," Iris quickly said.

Hugh had no idea if this was true, but he certainly wasn't going to question it.

"I suppose you're right," Daisy said. "It is really too bad. This is a family wedding, after all, and it would be so much more special to have family playing the music."

It wasn't just that it was the only unselfish thing she had said; it was that it was *completely* unselfish, and when Hugh chanced a glance at Sarah and Iris, they both wore somewhat abashed expressions on their faces.

"There will be other opportunities," Sarah said, although she did not go so far as to offer any specifics.

"Perhaps tomorrow," Daisy said with a little sigh.

Neither Sarah nor Iris said a word. Hugh wasn't even sure they breathed.

The bell sounded for dinner, and Daisy departed. As Hugh rose to his feet, Sarah said, "You should walk in with Iris. Daniel said he would carry me. I must say I'm grateful." Her nose wrinkled. "It's very strange having the footman do it."

Hugh started to say that they would wait until Daniel arrived, but the man of the hour had his usual impeccable timing, and Hugh had barely offered Iris his arm before Daniel was pulling Sarah into his and carrying her off to the dining room.

"If they weren't cousins," Iris said in that dry tone Hugh was coming to realize was uniquely hers, "that would have been very romantic."

Hugh looked at her.

"I said if they weren't cousins," she protested. "Anyway, he's so desperately in love with Miss Wynter he would not notice if an entire naked harem fell from the ceiling."

"Oh, he'd notice," Hugh said, since he was quite sure that Iris was trying to be provoking. "He just wouldn't do anything about it."

As Hugh walked into the dining room with the wrong woman on his arm, it occurred to him that he, too, wouldn't do anything about it.

If a naked harem fell from the ceiling.

Later that night
After supper

"You realize," Sarah said to Hugh, "that you're stuck with me now for the duration of the evening."

They were sitting on the lawn, under torches that somehow managed to make the air warm enough to remain outside as long as one had a coat. And a blanket.

They weren't the only ones who had taken advantage of the fine evening. A dozen chairs and lounges had been set up on the grass outside the ballroom, and at any given time about half of them were filled. Sarah and Hugh were the only people who had taken up permanent residence, though.

"If you so much as leave my side," Sarah continued, "Daisy will find me and drag me to the pianoforte."

"And would that be so very dreadful?" he asked.

She gave him a steady look, then said, "I shall make certain you are sent an invitation to our next musicale."

"I look forward to it."

"No," she said, "you don't."

"This all feels very mysterious," he said, leaning back comfortably in his chair. "It has been my experience that most young ladies are eager to demonstrate their skill at the pianoforte."

"We," she said, pausing to give the pronoun just the right amount of emphasis, "are uncommonly dreadful."

"You can't be that bad," he insisted. "If you were, you wouldn't be staging annual musicales."

"That presupposes logic." She grimaced. "And taste." There seemed no reason not to offer the unvarnished truth. He'd learn soon enough, if he ever found himself in London at the wrong time of year.

Hugh chuckled, and Sarah tipped her head toward the sky, not wishing to waste another thought on her family's infamous musicales. The night was far too lovely for that. "So many stars," she murmured.

"Do you enjoy astronomy?"

"Not really," she admitted, "but I do like looking at the stars on a clear night."

"That's Andromeda right there," he said, pointing toward a collection of stars that Sarah privately thought resembled a tipsy pitchfork more than anything else.

"What about that one?" she asked, gesturing toward a squiggle that looked like the letter W.

"Cassiopeia."

She moved her finger a bit to the left. "And that one?"

"Nothing that I'm aware of," he admitted.

"Have you ever counted them all?" she asked.

"The stars?"

"You count everything else," she teased.

"The stars are infinite. Even I can't count that high."

"Of course you can," she said, feeling lovely and mischievous, all rolled together. "It couldn't be simpler. Infinity minus one, infinity, infinity plus one."

He looked over at her with an expression that told her he knew that she knew she was being ridiculous. But still he said, "It doesn't work that way."

"It should."

"But it doesn't. Infinity plus one is still infinity."

"Well, that makes *no* sense." She sighed happily, pulling her blanket more tightly around her. She loved to dance, but truly, she could not imagine why anyone would choose to remain in the ballroom when they could be out on the lawn, celebrating the heavens.

"Sarah! And Hugh! What a delightful surprise!"

Sarah and Hugh exchanged a glance as Daniel made his way over to them, his fiancée laughingly trailing behind. Sarah still had not quite adapted to Miss Wynter's impending change of position—from her sisters' governess to Countess of Winstead and their soon-to-be cousin. It wasn't that Sarah was being a snob about it, or at least she didn't think she was. She hoped she wasn't. She liked Anne. And she liked how happy Daniel was when he was with her.

It was just all very strange.

"Where is Lady Danbury when we need her?" Hugh said.

Sarah turned to him with a curious smile. "Lady Danbury?"

"Surely we are meant to say something about this not being a surprise at all."

"Oh, I don't know," Sarah said with an arch smile. "As far as I know, no one here is my great-grandnephew."

"Have you been out here all evening?" Daniel asked once he and Anne were near.

"Indeed we have," Hugh confirmed.

"You're not too cold?" Anne inquired.

"We are well blanketed," Sarah said. "And truly, if I cannot dance, I'm delighted to be out here in the fresh air."

"You two make quite a pair this evening," Daniel said.

"I believe this is the cripples' corner," Hugh put in dryly.

"Stop saying that," Sarah scolded.

"Oh, sorry." Hugh looked over at Daniel and Anne. "She will heal, of course, so she cannot be allowed in our ranks."

Sarah sat forward. "That's not what I meant. Well, it is, but not entirely." Then, because Daniel and Anne were regarding them with confusion, she explained, "This is the third—no, the fourth time he has said that."

"Cripples' corner?" Hugh repeated, and even in the torchlight she could see that he was amused.

"If you do not stop saying that, I swear I'm leaving."

Hugh quirked a brow. "Didn't you just say that I'm stuck with you for the rest of the evening?"

"You shouldn't call yourself a cripple," Sarah returned. Her voice was growing too passionate, but she was completely unable to temper it. "It's a terrible word."

Hugh, predictably, was matter-of-fact. "It applies."

"No. It does not."

He chuckled. "Are you going to compare me to a horse again?"

"This is far more interesting than anything going on inside," Daniel said to Anne.

"No," she said firmly, "it's not. And it's certainly not any of our business." She tugged on his arm, but he was gazing longingly at Sarah and Hugh.

"It could be our business," he said.

Anne sighed and rolled her eyes. "You are such a gossip." Then she said something to him Sarah could not hear, and Daniel reluctantly allowed her to drag him away.

Sarah watched them go, somewhat confused by Anne's obvious desire to leave—did she think they needed privacy? How odd. Still, she was not done with this conversation, so she turned back to Hugh and said, "If you must, you may call yourself lame," she said, "but I forbid you to call yourself a cripple."

He drew back in surprise. And, perhaps, amusement. "You forbid me?"

"Yes. I do." She swallowed, uncomfortable by the rush of emotion within her. For the first time that evening, they were completely alone on the lawn, and she knew that if she allowed her voice to drop to its quietest register, he would still hear her. "I still don't like *lame*, but at least it's an adjective. If you call yourself a cripple, it's as if that's all you are."

He looked at her for a long moment before rising to his feet and crossing the very short distance to her chair. He leaned down, and then, so softly that she was not certain she'd heard him, he said, "Lady Sarah Pleinsworth, may I have this dance?"

* * *

HUGH WAS NOT prepared for the look in her eyes. Her face tipped up toward his, and her lips parted with a breath, and in that moment he would have sworn that the sun rose and set on her smile.

He leaned in, almost close enough for a whisper. "If I am not, as you say, a cripple, then I must be able to dance."

"Are you sure?" she whispered.

"I shall never know unless I try."

"I won't be very graceful," she said ruefully.

"That's why you are the perfect partner."

She reached out and placed her hand in his. "Lord Hugh Prentice, I would be honored to dance with you."

Carefully, she moved to the edge of her chair, then allowed him to tug her to her feet. Or rather, to her foot. It was almost comical; he was leaning on the chair, and she was leaning on him, and neither could stop their grins from extending into giggles.

When they were both upright and reasonably well balanced, Hugh listened for the strains of music wafting out along the night breeze. He heard a quadrille.

"I believe I hear a waltz," he said.

She looked up at him, clearly about to issue a correction. He placed a finger on her lips. "It must be a waltz," he told her, and he saw the instant she understood. They would never dance a reel, or a minuet, or quadrille. Even a waltz would require considerable innovation.

He reached over and plucked his cane from where it was resting against the side of his chair.

"If I put my hand here," he said, resting it on the handle, "and you put yours on mine . . ."

She followed his lead, and he placed his other hand at the small of her back. Without ever taking her eyes from his, she moved her hand to his shoulder. "Like this?" she whispered.

He nodded. "Like this."

It was the strangest, most awkward waltz imaginable. Instead of a clasped pair of hands, elegantly arched before them, they both put their weight on the cane. Not too heavily; they didn't need that much support, not while they had each other. He hummed in three-quarter time, and he led with light pressure on her back, moving the cane whenever it was time to turn.

He had not danced in nearly four years. He had not felt music flow through his body, nor savored the warmth of a woman's hand in his. But tonight . . . It was magical, almost spiritual, and he knew that there was no way he could ever thank her for this moment, for restoring a piece of his soul.

"You're very graceful," she said, gazing up at him with an enigmatic smile. This was the smile she used in London, he was certain of it. When she danced at a ball, when she looked up at her suitor and paid him a compliment, this was how she smiled. It made him feel positively normal.

He never thought he'd be so grateful for a smile.

He dipped his head toward hers and pretended to be imparting a secret. "I've been practicing for years."

"Have you now?"

"Oh, indeed. Shall we attempt a turn?"

"Oh yes, let's."

Together they lifted the cane, swung it gently to the right, then pressed the tip back down on the grass.

He leaned in. "I've been waiting for the proper moment to unleash my talent upon the world."

Her brows rose. "The proper moment?"

"The proper partner," he corrected.

"I knew there was a reason I fell out of that carriage." She laughed and looked up with a mischievous glint in her eyes. "Aren't you going to say that you knew there was a reason you didn't catch me?"

About this, however, he could not be glib. "No," he said with quiet force. "Never."

She was looking down, but he could see by the curve of her cheeks that she was pleased. After a few moments, she said, "You did break my fall."

"It appears I am good for something," he replied, happy to be back to their teasing banter. It was a safer place to be.

"Oh, I don't know about that, my lord. I suspect you're good for many things."

"Did you just 'my lord' me?"

This time, when she smiled, he heard it in her breath, right before she said, "It seems that I did."

"I cannot imagine what I have done to earn such an honor."

"Oh, it is not a question of what you have done to earn it," she said, "but what I *think* you have done to earn it."

For a moment he stopped dancing. "This may explain why I don't understand women."

At that she laughed. "It is but one of many reasons, I'm sure."

"You wound me."

"On the contrary. I know of no man who truly wishes to understand women. What would you have to complain about if you did?"

"Napoleon?"

"He's dead."

"The weather?"

"You already have that, not that you could possibly find any complaint tonight."

"No," he agreed, peering up at the stars. "It is an uncommonly fine evening."

"Yes," she said softly. "Yes, it is."

He should have been satisfied with that, but he was feeling greedy, and he did not want the dance to end, so he allowed his hand to settle more heavily on her back and said, "You did not tell me what you think I have done to earn the honor of your calling me 'your lord.'"

She glanced up at him with impudent eyes. "Well, if I were completely honest, I might admit that it just popped out of my mouth. It does lend a flirtatious air to a statement."

"You crush me."

"Ah, but I'm not going to be completely honest. Instead, I'm going to recommend that you wonder why I was feeling flirtatious."

"I shall take that recommendation."

She hummed quietly as they turned.

"You're going to make me ask, aren't you?"

"Only if you want to."

He caught her gaze and held it. "I do want."

"Very well, I was feeling flirtatious because—"

"Hold on one moment," he interrupted, because she deserved it, after making him ask. "It's time for another spin."

They executed this one perfectly, which was to say, they didn't fall down.

"You were saying," he prompted.

She looked up at him with faux severity. "I *should* claim to have forgotten my train of thought."

"But you won't."

She made a sorry little face. "Oh, but I think I have forgotten."

"*Sarah.*"

"How do you make my name sound like such a threat?"

"It doesn't really matter if it sounds like a threat," he said. "It only matters if you *think* it sounds like a threat."

Her eyes grew wide, and she burst into laughter. "You win," she said, and he was quite sure she would have thrown up her hands in defeat if they had not still been depending upon one another to stay upright.

"I think I do," he murmured.

It was the strangest, most awkward waltz imaginable, and it was the most perfect moment of his life.

Chapter Fourteen

*Several nights later, well after dark
in the guest bedchamber shared by
the Ladies Sarah and Harriet Pleinsworth*

"Are you going to read all night?"

Sarah's eyes, which had been speeding along
the pages of her novel with a most pleasurable
abandon, froze in place upon the word *forsythia*.
"Why," she said aloud (and with considerable ag-
gravation), "does that question even exist in the
realm of human activity? Of course I'm not going
to read all night. Has there ever even existed a
human being who has read all night?"

This was a question she regretted immediately,
because this was Harriet lying in bed next to her,
and if there was anyone in the world who would

respond by saying, "There probably has been," it was Harriet.

And she did.

"Well, I'm not going to," Sarah muttered, even though she'd already said as much. It was important to get the last word in a sisterly argument, even if it did mean repeating oneself.

Harriet turned onto her side, scrunching her pillow under her head. "What are you reading?"

Sarah pushed back a sigh and let her book fall closed around her index finger. This was not an unfamiliar sequence of events. When Sarah could not sleep, she read novels. When Harriet could not sleep, she pestered Sarah.

"Miss Butterworth and the Mad Baron."

"Haven't you read that before?"

"Yes, but I enjoy rereading it. It's silly, but I like it." She reopened the book, planted her eyes back on *forsythia,* and prepared to move forward.

"Did you see Lord Hugh tonight at supper?"

Sarah stuck her index finger back into the book. "Yes, of course I did. Why?"

"No reason in particular. I thought he looked very handsome." Harriet had dined with the adults that evening, much to Elizabeth's and Frances's chagrin.

The wedding was now but three days away, and Whipple Hill was a flurry of activity. Marcus and Honoria (Lord and Lady Chatteris, Sarah reminded herself) had arrived from Fensmore looking flushed and giggly and deliriously happy. It would have been enough to make Sarah want to gag, except that she had been having a rather fine time herself, laughing and bantering with Lord Hugh.

It was the oddest thing, but his was the first face she thought of when she woke in the morning. She looked for him at breakfast, and she always seemed to find him there, his plate so nearly full as to indicate that he'd arrived mere moments before she had.

Every morning, they lingered. They told themselves it was because they could not partake in the many activities that had been planned for the day (although in truth Sarah's ankle was much improved, and even if a walk to the village was still out of the question, there was no reason she could not manage bowls on the lawn).

They lingered, and she would pretend to sip at her tea, because if she actually drank as much as one normally might over the hours she sat at the table, she'd be forced to cut the conversation short.

She did not reflect upon the fact that a conversation truncated at the hour mark could not possibly be construed as short.

They lingered, and most people didn't seem to notice. The other guests came and went, taking their food from the sideboard, drinking their coffee and tea, and leaving. Sometimes Sarah and Hugh were joined in conversation, sometimes not.

And then finally, when it became past obvious that it was time for the servants to clean the breakfast room, Sarah would rise and casually mention where she thought she might take her book for the afternoon.

He would never say that he planned to join her, but he always did.

They had become friends, and if occasionally she caught herself staring at his mouth, thinking that everyone had to have a first kiss, and wouldn't it be lovely if hers was with him . . . Well, she kept such things to herself.

She was running out of novels, though. The Whipple Hill library was extensive, but it was sadly lacking in books of the kind Sarah liked to read. *Miss Butterworth* had been haphazardly shelved between *The Divine Comedy* and *The Taming of the Shrew.*

She looked back down. Miss Butterworth had not yet met her baron, and Sarah was eager for the plot to get moving.

Forsythia . . . forsythia . . .

"Did you think he looked handsome?"

Sarah let out an annoyed groan.

"Did you think Lord Hugh looked handsome?" Harriet prodded.

"I don't know, he looked like himself." The first part was a lie; Sarah did know, and she had found him heartbreakingly handsome. The second part was the truth, and was probably the reason she thought him so handsome to begin with.

"I think Frances has fallen in love with him," Harriet said.

"Probably," Sarah agreed.

"He's very kind to her."

"Yes, he is."

"He taught her to play piquet this afternoon."

It must have been while she was helping Anne

at her final dress fitting, Sarah thought. She could not imagine when else he would have had the time.

"He didn't let her win. I think she thought he would, but I think she likes that he didn't."

Sarah let out a loud, long-suffering sigh. "Harriet, what is this about?"

Harriet tucked her chin back in surprise. "I don't know. I was just making conversation."

"At"—Sarah looked vainly for a clock—"whatever time it is?"

Harriet was quiet for a full minute. Sarah managed to get from *forsythia* to *pigeon* before her sister spoke again.

"I think he likes you."

"What are you talking about?"

"Lord Hugh," Harriet said. "I think he fancies you."

"He doesn't fancy me," Sarah retorted, and it wasn't that she was lying; it was more that she hoped she was lying. Because she knew that she was falling in love with him, and if he did not feel the same way, she did not know how she could bear it.

"I think you're wrong," Harriet said.

Sarah turned resolutely back to Miss Butterworth's pigeons.

"Do you fancy him?"

Sarah snapped. There was no way she was going to talk to her sister about this. It was too new, and too private, and every time she thought about it she felt as if she might burst out of her skin. "Harriet, I am not having this conversation right now."

Harriet paused to think about this. "Will you have it tomorrow?"

"Harriet!"

"Oh, fine, I won't say another word." Harriet made a big show of turning over in bed, pulling half of Sarah's covers off in the process.

Sarah let out a snort, since an obvious display of irritation was *clearly* called for, then she yanked at the blanket and turned back to her book.

Except she could not concentrate.

Her eyes sat on page thirty-three for what seemed like hours. Beside her, Harriet finally stopped rustling around and fell still, her breathing slowing into light, peaceful snores.

Sarah wondered what Hugh was doing, and if he ever had difficulty falling asleep.

She wondered how much his leg hurt when he went to bed. If it pained him at night, did it still hurt in the morning? Did he ever wake from the pain?

She wondered how he had come to be so talented at mathematics. He'd explained to her once, after she'd begged him to multiply some ridiculously long sums, how he saw the numbers in his head, except he didn't actually *see* them, they just sort of arranged themselves until he knew the answer. She hadn't even tried to pretend that she understood him, but she'd kept asking questions because he was so adorable when he was frustrated.

He smiled when he was with her. She didn't think he'd smiled very often before.

Was it possible to fall in love with someone in

so short a time? Honoria had known Marcus her whole life before she fell in love with him. Daniel had claimed love at first sight with Miss Wynter. Somehow that almost seemed more logical than Sarah's journey.

She supposed she could lie in bed all night and doubt herself, but she was feeling too restless, so she climbed out of bed, walked to the window, and pushed back the curtains. The moon wasn't full, but it was more than halfway there, and the silvery light sparkled on the grass.

Dew, she thought, and she realized she'd already donned her slippers. The house was quiet, and she knew she shouldn't be out of her room, and it wasn't even that the moonlight was calling . . .

It was the breeze. The leaves had long since dropped from the trees, but the tiny points at the ends of the branches were light enough to ruffle and sway. A spot of fresh air, that was all she needed. Fresh air and the wind tickling through her hair. It had been years since she'd been permitted to wear it down outside her bedroom, and she just wanted to go outside and . . .

And be.

The same night
A different room

SLEEP HAD NEVER come easily to Hugh Prentice. When he was a small child, it was because he was listening. He didn't know why the nursery at Ramsgate wasn't off in some far-flung corner like at every other house he'd ever been to, but it wasn't, and it meant that every now and then, and never when they expected it (which was not true; they always expected it), Hugh and Freddie would hear their mother cry out.

The first time Hugh heard it, he jumped out of bed, only to be stopped by Freddie's restraining hand.

"But Mama . . ."

Freddie shook his head.

"And Father . . ." Hugh had heard his father's voice, too. He sounded angry. And then he laughed.

Freddie shook his head again, and the look in his eyes was enough to convince Hugh, who was five years his junior, to crawl back into his bed and cover his ears.

But he didn't close his eyes. If you'd asked him the next day, he would have sworn he had not even blinked. He was six, and he still swore to lots of impossible things.

When he saw his mother that night before supper, she didn't look as if anything was wrong. It really had sounded as if his mother had been hurt, but she didn't have any bruises, and she didn't sound sick. Hugh started to ask her about it, but Freddie stomped on his foot.

Freddie didn't do things like that without a reason; Hugh kept his mouth shut.

For the next few months Hugh watched his parents carefully. It was only then that he realized that he almost never saw them together in the same room. If they ate supper together in the dining room, he would not know; the children dined in the nursery.

When he did see them at the same time it was very difficult to determine what their feelings toward the other might be; it wasn't as if they spoke to each other. Months would pass, and Hugh could almost imagine that everything was perfectly fine.

And then they would hear it again. And he knew that everything was not perfectly fine. And that there was nothing he could do about it.

When Hugh was ten, his mother succumbed to a fever brought on by a dog bite (and a small bite at that, but it had turned ugly very quickly). Hugh grieved for her as much as he might grieve for anyone he saw for twenty minutes each evening, and he finally stopped listening each night as he tried to fall asleep.

But by this point it did not matter. Hugh could no longer fall asleep because he was thinking. He lay in his bed, and his mind buzzed and raced and flipped and generally did everything except calm itself down. Freddie told him that he needed to imagine his mind as a blank page, which actually made Hugh laugh, because if there was one thing his mind would never be able to duplicate, it was a blank page. Hugh saw numbers and patterns all day long, in the petals of a flower, in the cadence of a horse's hooves on the ground. Some of these patterns caught his immediate attention, but the rest lingered at the back of his mind until he was quiet and in bed. That was when they crept back, and suddenly everything was adding and subtracting and rearranging, and did Freddie *really* think he could sleep through that?

(Freddie did not, as a matter of fact. After Hugh told him what went on in his head when he was trying to fall asleep, Freddie never mentioned the blank page again.)

Now there were many reasons he did not drift easily into sleep. Sometimes it was his leg, with its nagging clench of muscle. Sometimes it was his suspicious nature, forcing him to keep one metaphorical eye on his father, whom Hugh would never trust completely, despite his current upper hand in their battles. And sometimes it was that same old thing—his mind humming with numbers and patterns, unable to shut itself off.

But Hugh had a new hypothesis: he could not sleep because he had simply got used to this particular brand of frustration. Somehow he had trained his body to think that he was supposed to lie there like a log for hours before finally giving up and resting. He'd had plenty of nights with no reasonable explanation for his insomnia. His leg might feel almost normal, and his father not even a dot in his mind, and still sleep would elude him.

Lately, however, it had been different.

He still wasn't finding it easy to fall asleep. He probably never would. But the reason why . . .

That was the difference.

In the years since his injury, there had been plenty of nights that had found him awake and wishing for a woman. He was a man, and except for his stupid left thigh, all parts of him were in working order. There was nothing unnatural about it, just a lot that was uncomfortable.

But now that woman had a face, and a name, and even though Hugh behaved with perfect propriety throughout the day, when he was lying in his bed at night, his breathing would grow ragged and his body burned. For the first time in his life, he longed for the numbers and patterns that plagued his mind. Instead all he could think about was that moment a few days earlier, when Sarah tripped over the rug in the library and he'd caught her before she fell. For one ecstatic moment, his fingers had brushed against the side of her breast. She'd been wearing velvet, and God knows what else underneath, but he'd felt the curve of her, the soft tenderness, and the ache that had been growing inside of him turned rampant.

And so he wasn't particularly surprised when he rolled over fitfully in his bed, picked up his pocket watch, and saw that it was half three in the morning. He'd tried reading, as that sometimes nodded him off, but it hadn't worked. He'd spent an hour doing really boring equations in his head, but that hadn't done the trick, either. Finally, he admitted defeat and walked to the window. If he could not sleep, at least he could look at something other than the insides of his eyelids.

And there she was.

He was stunned, and yet not surprised at all. Sarah Pleinsworth had been haunting his dreams for more than a week; of course she'd be out on the lawn in the middle of the night the one time he stood at his window. There was some sort of insane logic to it.

Then he blinked himself out of his stupor, because *what the hell was she doing*? It was half three in the morning, and if he could see her from his window, at least two dozen others could, too. Hugh let out a string of expletives that would have done any sailor proud as he strode to the wardrobe and yanked out a pair of trousers.

And yes, he could stride when absolutely necessary. It wasn't pretty, and he'd feel it later, but it did the trick. A few moments later he was more or less dressed (and the parts that were "less" were covered by his coat), and he was moving through the halls of Whipple Hill as quickly as he could without waking up the entire house.

He paused briefly just outside the rear door. His leg was nearly in spasms, and he knew that if he didn't stop and shake it out, it would collapse beneath him. The delay gave him time to sweep his gaze across the lawn, looking for her. She'd been wearing a coat, but it hadn't completely covered her white gown, so she should be easy to spot . . .

He saw her. Sitting on the grass, so still she might have been a statue. She was hugging her knees to her chest, gazing up at the night sky with an expression of serenity that would have taken his breath away if he weren't already so wrecked by fear and fury, and now by relief.

Hugh made his way slowly, favoring his leg now that speed was no longer of the essence. She must have been lost in her thoughts, for she did not seem to hear him. At about eight steps away, however, he heard her sharply indrawn breath, and she turned.

"Hugh?"

He didn't say anything, just kept walking toward her.

"What are you doing here?" she asked, scrambling to her feet.

"I might ask the same thing of you," he snapped.

She drew back in surprise at his display of anger. "I couldn't sleep, and I—"

"So you thought you would wander outside at half three in the morning?"

"I know it seems silly—"

"Silly?" he demanded. "Silly? Are you bloody well kidding me?"

"Hugh." She reached out to place her hand on his arm, but he shook her off.

"What if I hadn't seen you?" he demanded. "What if someone else had seen you?"

"I would have gone inside," she said, her eyes searching his with an expression of such perplexity that he nearly flinched. She could not possibly be so naïve. He had raced through the house—he, who on some days could barely walk, had raced through this bloody monster of a house, unable to beat away the memory of his mother's cry.

"Do you think that every single person in the world has your best interest at heart?" he demanded.

"No, but I think every person *here* does, and—"

"There are men in this world who hurt people, Sarah. There are men who hurt *women*."

Her face went slack, and she didn't say anything.

And Hugh tried so very hard not to remember. "I looked out my window," he choked out. "I looked out my window at half bloody three in the morning, and there you were, gliding across the grass like some sort of erotic specter."

Her eyes grew wide, and they might have filled with alarm, but he was too far gone to notice.

"And what if it hadn't been me?" He grabbed her arms, both of them, his fingers biting into her flesh. "What if someone else had seen you, and what if someone else had come down here, with different intentions . . ."

His father had never been one to ask permission of the women in his life.

"Hugh," Sarah whispered. She was staring at his mouth. Good God, she was staring at his mouth, and his body felt as if it had been set afire.

"What . . . What if . . ." His tongue felt thick, and his breath was no longer even, and he wasn't even sure he knew what he was saying.

And then she caught her lower lip between her teeth, and he could practically feel the soft scrape of it across his own lips, and then . . .

He was gone.

He crushed her to him, his mouth taking hers with no subtlety, no finesse, nothing but raw passion and need. One of his hands tangled itself in her hair, and the other roamed down her back, finding the lush curve of her bottom, pulling her close.

"Sarah," he moaned, and some part of him realized that she was touching him, too. Her small hands were behind his head, holding him against her, and her lips had softened and opened, and she was making little sounds that shot through him like lightning.

Never once breaking the kiss, he shrugged off his coat and let it fall to the ground. They sank to their knees, and then she was on her back, and he was over her, and he was still kissing her, hard and deep, as if he could remain in this moment forever, just so long as his lips never left hers. Her nightgown was white cotton, designed for sleep, not temptation, but it left the flat plane of her chest bare, and soon he was trailing his lips across her creamy skin, wondering how close he could get to those perfect breasts without taking the edge of her bodice in his teeth and tearing the bloody thing off her completely.

Her hips shifted, and he groaned her name again as he found himself settling between her legs. He was straining against his trousers, and he had no idea if she knew what that meant, but he was not capable of cautious questions. He arched himself against her, knowing full well that even through their clothes, she would feel him at her core.

She let out a little gasp at the pressure, and her hands grew fierce against him, sinking into his hair before sliding down his back and under his untucked shirt.

"Hugh," she whispered, and he felt one finger along the line of his spine. "Hugh."

With fortitude he had no idea he possessed, he pulled back, just far enough so that he could look in her eyes. "I will not— I won't—" Dear God, it was hard to wrench out even a single word. His heart was pounding, and his insides were twisting, and half the time he wasn't even sure he was still breathing.

"Sarah," he began again, "I won't take you. Not now, I promise. But I have to know." He didn't mean to kiss her again, but when she looked up at him, she arched her neck, and it was as if he'd become possessed. His tongue found the hollow of her collarbone, and it was there that he finally got the words out. "I have to know," he repeated, and he tore himself away to once again see her face. "Do you want this?"

She looked at him in confusion. Her desire was written all over her, but he needed to hear her say it.

"Do you want this?" he asked, his voice down to a hoarse plea. "Do you want me?"

Her lips parted, and she nodded. And she whispered, "Yes."

Hugh let the breath leave his body in one ragged exhale. The magnitude of her gift suddenly hit him. She was opening herself to him . . . and trusting him. He'd told her he would not claim her virtue, and he wouldn't, at least not tonight. But he wanted this woman more than he'd ever wanted anything else in his life, and he was not enough of a gentleman to button her back up and send her to her room.

He reached down with one hand until he found the hem of her nightgown. She gasped as his finger slid underneath, but the sound was lost under his own moan as he ran his hand along the warm skin of her leg.

No one had ever touched her there. No one had ever dragged their hand up and up until it was above her knee. That spot was his now.

"Do you like that?" he whispered, lightly squeezing.

She nodded.

He moved a little higher, still far from her center, but he shifted his grip a little so that his thumb stroked the tender skin of the inside of her leg.

"Do you like *that*?"

"Yes." It was barely a sound, but he heard it.

"What about this?" His other hand, the one that had been toying with her hair, cupped her breast through her nightgown.

"Oh my— Oh, Hugh."

He kissed her slowly, deeply. "Was that a yes?"

"Yes."

"I want to see you," he said, dragging his lips to her ear. "I want to see every inch of you, and I know I'm not going to, not right now, but I want some of you. Do you understand?"

She shook her head.

"Do you trust me?"

She waited until their eyes met. "With my life."

For a moment he could not even move. Her words reached into him, grabbed his heart, and squeezed. And when they were done with that, they moved lower. He'd thought he'd wanted her before, but that was nothing compared to the primal lust that washed over him with her three softly spoken words.

Mine, he thought. *She's mine.*

With trembling fingers, he untied the little bow that kept her neckline modest, and he wondered what foolish, foolish person thought to put such a thing on a nightgown that was not meant to tempt. It was a bow, and he got to unwrap her.

With one little tug of his fingers, he was opening his gift, and with one more little nudge, her gown was sliding down, baring one perfect breast. Her neckline had not loosened enough to show them both, but there was something intensely erotic about having just the one.

He licked his lips and slowly pulled his gaze back to her eyes. He did not say a word, and he did not look away from her face as he took one hand and lightly skimmed his palm over her nipple.

He didn't ask her if she liked it. He didn't need to. She whispered his name, and before he could say a word, she nodded.

Mine, he thought again, and it was the most incredible thing, because until recently, he'd assumed—no, he'd known—that he would not find someone, that there would never be a woman he would call his own.

Softly, he kissed her lips. Then her nose, then each of her eyes in turn. It was bursting out of him that he was falling in love with her, but he had never been a man to speak of his feelings, and the words choked in his throat. So he kissed her one last time, truly and deeply, hoping she recognized it for what it was, an offering of his very soul.

Yours, he thought. *I am yours.*

Chapter Fifteen

Sarah was aware that she shouldn't have gone outside in the middle of the night. She wasn't allowed to step outside her house in London without a chaperone; she knew very well that a post-midnight jaunt in Berkshire was equally verboten.

But she had been so restless, so . . . itchy. She'd felt wrong in her own skin, and when she had climbed out of bed and touched her feet to the carpet, her room had felt too small. The *house* had felt too small. She'd needed to move, to feel the night air on her skin.

She had never felt this way before, and truly, she had no explanation for it. Or rather, she hadn't.

Now she did.

She'd needed him. Hugh.

She just hadn't known it.

At some point between the carriage ride and the cake and the crazy waltzing on the lawn, Sarah Pleinsworth had fallen in love with the very last man she should ever have wanted.

And when he kissed her . . .

All she wanted was more.

"You are so beautiful," he murmured, and for the first time in her life, Sarah truly believed that she was.

She touched his cheek. "So are you."

Hugh smiled down at her, a silly half grin that told her he did not believe her for one second.

"You are," she insisted. She tried to make her face stern, but nothing could dampen her smile. "You shall have to take my word for it."

Still, he did not speak. He gazed down at her as if she were something precious, and he made her *feel* precious, and in that moment, all she wanted in the world was for him to feel the same thing.

Because he didn't. She knew that he didn't.

He had said things . . . little things, really, just an odd comment here and there that he surely did not expect to stick in anyone's memory. But Sarah listened. And she remembered. And she knew . . . Hugh Prentice was not happy. Worse, he did not think he deserved to be.

He was not the kind of man who sought large crowds. He did not wish to be a leader among men. But Sarah also knew that Hugh did not wish to be a follower. His was a fiercely independent nature, and he did not mind being alone.

But he had been more than alone these past few years. He had been alone with only his crushing sense of guilt to keep him company. She did not know what Hugh had done to convince his father to allow Daniel to return to England in peace, and she could not begin to imagine how difficult it had been for Hugh to travel to Italy to find Daniel and bring him back.

But he had done all that. Hugh Prentice had done everything humanly possible to make things right, and still he was not at peace.

He was such a *good* man. He defended young girls and unicorns. He waltzed with a cane. He did not deserve to have his life defined by a single mistake.

Sarah Pleinsworth had never done anything by half measures, and she knew that if she loved this man, that meant that she would devote her life to making him understand one simple fact.

He was precious. And he deserved every drop of happiness that came his way.

She reached up and touched her finger to his lips. They were soft, and wondrous, and she felt honored just to feel his breath on her skin. "Sometimes at breakfast," she whispered, "I can't stop looking at your mouth."

He trembled. She loved that she could make him tremble.

"And your eyes . . . ," she continued, emboldened by his reaction. "Women would kill for eyes that color, did you know?"

He shook his head, and something about his expression—so baffled, so overcome—made her smile with pure joy. "I think you're beautiful," she whispered, "and I think . . ." Her heart skipped a beat, and she caught her lower lip between her teeth. "I *hope* that mine is the only opinion that matters."

He leaned down and lightly touched his lips to hers. He kissed her nose, then her brow, and then, after one long moment when his eyes held hers, he kissed her again, this time holding nothing back.

Sarah let out a moan, the husky sound becoming trapped in his mouth. His kiss was hungry, ravenous, and for the first time in her life, she understood passion.

No, this was more than passion.

This was need.

He needed her. She could feel it in his every movement. She could hear it in the harsh rasp of his breath. And with every touch of hand, every flick of his tongue, he was stoking that same need in her. She had not known it was possible to crave another human being with such intensity.

Her fingers found the untucked hem of his shirt, and she slid her hand under the edge, skimming lightly over his skin. His muscles jumped beneath her touch, and he drew a sharp breath, the air whispering past her cheek like a kiss.

"You don't know," he rasped. "You don't know what you do to me."

She could see the passion in his eyes; it made her feel womanly and strong. "Tell me," she whispered, and she arched her neck to bring herself up to his lips for a soft, fleeting kiss.

For a moment she thought he might. But he just shook his head and murmured, "It would be the death of me." Then he kissed her again, and she didn't care what she did to him, just so long as he kept doing the same thing to her.

"Sarah," he said, lifting his lips from hers for just long enough to whisper her name.

"Hugh," she whispered back, and she could hear her grin in her own voice.

He drew back. "You're smiling."

"I can't stop," she admitted.

He touched her cheek, gazing down at her with such emotion that for a moment she forgot to breathe. Was it love she saw in his eyes? It felt like love, even if he had not said the words.

"We have to stop," he said, and he gently tugged her nightgown back to its proper place.

Sarah knew he was right, but still she whispered, "I wish we could stay."

Hugh let out a hoarse chuckle, almost as if he was in pain. "Oh, you have no idea how much I wish the same thing."

"It's hours yet until dawn," she said softly.

"I won't ruin your reputation," he said, bringing her hand to his lips. "Not like this."

A bubble of mirth floated inside her. "Does that mean you intend to ruin me some other way?"

His smile turned hot as he stood and pulled her to her feet. "I would very much like to. But I shouldn't call it ruining. Ruin is what happens to a reputation, not what happens between a man and a woman. Or at least," he added, his voice dropping sensually, "not what happens between us."

Sarah shivered with delight. Her body felt

so alive; *she* felt so alive. She did not know how she managed to walk back to the house. Her feet wanted to run, and her arms wanted to wrap themselves around the man next to her, and her voice wanted to laugh, and deep inside . . .

Deep inside . . .

She was giddy. Giddy with love.

He walked her to her door. No one was up and about; as long as they were quiet, they had nothing to fear.

"I will see you tomorrow," Hugh said, lifting her hand to his lips.

She nodded but said nothing. She could not think of a word big enough to capture everything that was in her heart.

She was in love. Lady Sarah Pleinsworth was in love.

And it was grand.

The following morning

"SOMETHING IS WRONG with you."

Sarah blinked the sleep out of her eyes and looked at Harriet, who was perched on the edge of their four-poster bed, watching her with considerable suspicion.

"What are you talking about?" Sarah grumbled. "Nothing is wrong with me."

"You're smiling."

This caught her off guard. "I can't smile?"

"Not first thing in the morning."

Sarah decided there could not possibly be an

appropriate response and went back to her morning routine. Harriet, however, was in full curiosity mode and followed her to the washbasin, eyes narrowed, head tilted, and letting out dubious little "hmmms" at irregular intervals.

"Is something amiss?" Sarah inquired.

"Is there?"

Good heavens, and people called *her* dramatic. "I'm trying to wash my face," Sarah said.

"By all means, you should do so."

Sarah dipped her hands in the basin, but before she could do anything with the water, Harriet poked her own face even closer, scooting right between Sarah's hands and nose.

"Harriet, what is wrong with you?"

"What is wrong with *you*?" Harriet countered.

Sarah let the water drain through her fingers. "I have no idea what you're talking about."

"You're smiling," Harriet accused.

"What sort of person do you think I am that I'm not allowed to wake up in a pleasant mood?"

"Oh, you're allowed to. I just don't believe that you're constitutionally able."

It was true that Sarah was not known to be a morning person.

"And you're flushed," Harriet added.

Sarah resisted the urge to flick water on her sister's face and instead splashed some on her own. She dried herself off with a small white towel, then said, "Perhaps it is because I have been forced to exert myself arguing with you."

"No, I don't think that's it," Harriet said, ignoring her sarcasm completely.

Sarah brushed past her. If her face hadn't been flushed before, it certainly was now.

"Something is wrong with you," Harriet called, hurrying after her.

Sarah paused but did not turn around. "Are you following me to the chamber pot?"

There was a very satisfying beat of silence. Followed by: "Er, no."

Shoulders high, Sarah marched into the small bathing room and shut the door.

And locked it. Really, she wouldn't put it past Harriet to count to ten, decide that Sarah had had more than enough time to complete her business, and barge right in.

The moment the door was safely barred from invasion, Sarah turned, leaned back against it, and let out a long sigh.

Oh dear heavens.

Oh dear heavens.

Was she really so fundamentally different after last night that her younger sister could see it on her *face*?

And if she looked that different after a night of stolen kisses, what would happen when . . .

Well, she supposed technically it was "if."

But her heart told her it would be "when." She was going to spend the rest of her life with Lord Hugh Prentice. There was simply no way she would allow anything else to come to pass.

By the time Sarah made it down to breakfast (Harriet hot on her heels and questioning every smile), it was clear that the weather had turned.

The sun, which had spent the last week resting amiably in the sky, had retreated behind ominous pewter clouds, and the wind whistled with the threat of an oncoming storm.

The gentlemen's excursion (a horseback journey south to the River Kennet) was canceled, and Whipple Hill buzzed with the unspent energy of bored aristocrats. Sarah had become used to having much of the house to herself during the day, and to her surprise, she found herself resentful of what felt like an intrusion.

To complicate matters, Harriet had apparently decided that her mission for the day was to shadow—and question—Sarah's every move. Whipple Hill was large, but not large enough when one's younger sister was curious, determined, and, perhaps most importantly, aware of every nook and cranny in the house.

Hugh had been at breakfast, like always, but it had been impossible for Sarah to speak with him without Harriet inserting herself in the conversation. When Sarah went to the little drawing room to read her novel (as she had casually mentioned she planned to do at breakfast), there was Harriet at the writing desk, the pages of her current work-in-progress spread before her.

"Sarah," Harriet said brightly, "fancy meeting you here."

"Fancy that," Sarah said, with no inflection whatsoever. Her sister had never been skilled in the art of subterfuge.

"Are you going to read?" Harriet inquired.

Sarah glanced down at the novel in her hand.

"You said you were going to read," Harriet reminded her. "At breakfast."

Sarah looked back toward the door, considering what her other options for the morning might be.

"Frances is looking for someone with whom to play Oranges and Unicorns," Harriet said.

That clinched it. Sarah sat right down on the sofa and opened *Miss Butterworth*. She flipped a few pages, looking for where she'd left off, then frowned. "Is that even a game?" she asked. "Oranges and Unicorns?"

"She says it's a version of Oranges and Lemons," Harriet told her.

"How does one substitute unicorns for lemons?"

Harriet shrugged. "It's not as if one needs actual lemons to play."

"Still, it does ruin the rhyme." Sarah shook her head, summoning the childhood poem from her memory. "Oranges and unicorns say the bells of St. . . ." She looked to Harriet for inspiration.

"Clunicorns?"

"Somehow I don't think so."

"Moonicorns."

Sarah cocked her head to the side. "Better," she judged.

"Spoonicorns? Zoomicorns."

And . . . that was enough. Sarah turned back to her book. "We're done now, Harriet."

"Parunicorns."

Sarah couldn't even imagine where that one had come from. But still, she found herself humming as she read.

Oranges and lemons say the bells of St. Clements.

Meanwhile, Harriet was muttering to herself at the desk. "Pontoonicorns xyloonicorns . . ."

You owe me five farthings say the bells of St. Martins.

"Oh, oh, oh, I have it! Hughnicorns!"

Sarah froze. This she could not ignore. With great deliberation, she placed her index finger in her book to mark her place and looked up. "What did you just say?"

"Hughnicorns," Harriet replied, as if nothing could have been more ordinary. She gave Sarah a sly look. "Named for Lord Hugh, of course. He does seem to be a frequent topic of conversation."

"Not for me," Sarah immediately said. Lord Hugh Prentice might currently occupy her every thought, but she could not recall even once initiating a discussion about him with her sister.

"Perhaps what I *meant* to say," Harriet wheedled, "is that he is a frequent subject of your conversations."

"Isn't that the same thing?"

"He is a frequent *participant* in your conversations," Harriet corrected without missing a beat.

"I enjoy talking with him," Sarah said, because no good could come of denying this. Harriet knew better.

"Indeed," Harriet said, eyes narrowed like a sleuth. "It leads one to wonder if he is also the source of your uncharacteristic good cheer."

Sarah gave a little huff. "I am beginning to take offense, Harriet. Since when have I been known for a lack of good cheer?"

"Every single morning of your life."

"That is quite unfair," Sarah said, since she was fairly certain that no good could come of denying this, either.

In general, it was never good to deny something that was indisputably true. Not with Harriet.

"*I* think you fancy Lord Hugh," Harriet declared.

And because Sarah was reading *Miss Butterworth and the Mad Baron*, in which barons (mad or otherwise) always appeared in doorways the moment someone uttered their name, she looked up.

Nothing.

"That's a refreshing change," she muttered.

Harriet glanced her way. "Did you say something?"

"I was just marveling on the fact that Lord Hugh did not appear in the doorway the moment you said his name."

"You're not that lucky," Harriet said with a smirk.

Sarah rolled her eyes.

"And just to be precise, I believe I said that you *fancy* Lord Hugh."

Sarah turned to the doorway. Because really, she would never be *that* lucky twice.

Still no Hugh.

Well. This was new and different.

She tapped her fingers against her book for a moment, then said under her breath, "Oh, how I wish I could find a gentleman who will look past my three vexing sisters and my"—*why not?*—"vestigial toe."

She looked to the doorway.

And there he was.

She grinned. But all things considered, she ought to stop with the vestigial toe business. It would be just her luck if she ended up giving birth to a baby with an extra digit.

"Am I interrupting?" Hugh asked.

"Of course not," Harriet said with great enthusiasm. "Sarah is reading, and I am writing."

"So I *am* interrupting."

"No," Harriet blurted out. She looked to Sarah for help, but Sarah saw no reason to intercede.

"I don't need quiet to write," Harriet explained.

His brows rose in question. "Didn't you ask your sisters not to chatter in the carriage?"

"Oh, that's different." And then, before anyone might inquire *how*, Harriet turned to Hugh and asked, "Won't you sit down and join us?"

He gave a polite nod and came into the room. Sarah watched as he made his way around a wingback chair. He was depending on his cane more heavily than usual; she could see it in his gait. She frowned, then remembered that he had rushed all the way down from his room the night before. Without his cane.

She waited until he took a seat at the other side of the sofa, then quietly asked, "Is your leg bothering you?"

"Just a little." He set his cane down and idly rubbed the muscle. Sarah wondered if he even noticed when he did that.

Harriet suddenly shot to her feet. "I just remembered something," she blurted out.

"What?" Sarah asked.

"It's . . . ehrm . . . something about . . . Frances!"

"What about Frances?"

"Oh, nothing much, really, just . . ." She shuffled her papers together and grabbed the whole sheaf, folding a few sheets in the process.

"Careful there," Hugh warned.

Harriet looked at him blankly.

"You're crumpling," he said, motioning to the paper.

"Oh! Right. All the more reason I should leave." She took a sideways step to the door, and then another. "So I'll be on my way . . ."

Sarah and Hugh both turned to watch her depart, but despite all of her protestations, she seemed to be hovering by the door.

"Did you need to find Frances?" Sarah asked.

"Yes." Harriet rolled to her toes, came back down again, and said, "Right. Good-bye, then." And she finally left.

Sarah and Hugh looked at each other for several seconds before chuckling.

"What was that ab—," he started to say.

"Sorry!" Harriet called out, dashing back into the room. "I forgot one thing." She ran over to the desk, picked up absolutely nothing that Sarah could see (although to be fair, Sarah did not have a clean line of sight), and hurried out, closing the door behind her.

Sarah's mouth fell open.

"What is it?"

"That little minx. She just pretended to have

forgotten something so she could shut the door."

Hugh quirked a brow. "This bothers you?"

"No, of course not. I just never thought she could be so devious." Sarah paused to reconsider this. "Never mind, what was I saying? Of course she's that devious."

"What I find interesting," Hugh said, "is that your sister is so determined that we should be left alone together. With the door shut," he added meaningfully.

"She did accuse me of fancying you."

"Oh, she did, did she? What was your reply?"

"I believe I avoided making one."

"Well played, Lady Sarah, but I am not so easily subdued."

Sarah inched a little closer to his side of the sofa. "Is that so?"

"Oh, no," he replied, reaching out to take her hand in his. "If *I* were to ask if you fancied me, I can assure you that you would not escape so easily."

"If *you* were to ask if I fancied you," Sarah said, allowing him to tug her closer, "I might not wish to escape."

"Might?" he echoed, his voice dropping to a husky murmur.

"Well, I might need a little convincing . . ."

"Just a little?"

"A little might be all I *need*," she said, letting out a little gasp when her body came into contact with his, "but I might actually *want* quite a lot."

His lips brushed hers. "I can see that I have my work cut out for me."

"Lucky for me, you never struck me as the kind of man who shies away from hard work."

He smiled wolfishly. "I can assure you, Lady Sarah, that I will work very hard to ensure your pleasure."

Sarah thought that sounded very nice, indeed.

Chapter Sixteen

Sarah wasn't sure how long they kissed. It might have been five minutes, it might have been ten. All she knew was that Hugh's mouth was very wicked, and even though he had not removed or even rearranged a single item of her clothing, his hands were cunning and bold.

He made her feel things, naughty things that started in her belly and oozed through her like molten flame. When his lips were on her neck she wanted to stretch like a cat, arching until every muscle in her body was warm and supple. She wanted to kick off her slippers and run her toes along his calves. She wanted to curve her back and press her hips against his, then allow her legs to grow soft and pliant so that he could settle between them.

He made her want to do things no lady would

ever talk about, things no lady should even think about.

And she loved it. She had not acted on any of these urges, but she loved that she wanted to. She loved this sense of abandon, this insane desire to draw him closer and closer until they merged. She had never wanted to even kiss a man before, and now all she could think of was how perfect his hands had felt on her bare skin the night before.

"Oh, Hugh," she sighed as his fingers found the curve of her thigh and squeezed through the soft muslin of her dress. He rubbed his thumb in lazy circles, each motion bringing him closer to her most private area.

Dear God, if he could make her feel like this through her dress, what would happen when he actually touched her skin?

Sarah shivered at the thought, stunned by how excited she was just from *thinking* about it.

"You have no idea," Hugh murmured between kisses, "how very much I wish we were anywhere but this room."

"Anywhere?" she asked teasingly. She ruffled one of her hands through his tawny hair, delighting in how easy it was to muss.

"Somewhere with a bed." He kissed her cheek, then her neck, then the tender skin at the base of her throat. "And a locked door."

Sarah's heart leapt at his words, but at the same time, his comment awakened a sliver of common sense. The door to the little drawing room was shut, but it wasn't locked. Sarah didn't even think it could be locked, and more to the point, she knew that it *shouldn't* be locked. Anyone who tried the door and found it barred would immediately want to know what was going on inside, which meant that unless one of them wanted to brave the twelve-foot drop out the window, there would be just as much scandal as if someone had simply walked through the unlocked door.

And while Sarah had every intention of marrying Lord Hugh Prentice (once he asked, which he would, and if he didn't, she would make him), she didn't much fancy a marriage-inducing scandal mere days before her cousin's wedding.

"We have to stop," she said, without much conviction.

"I know." But he didn't stop kissing her. He might have slowed a bit, but he didn't stop.

"Hugh . . ."

"I know," he said again, but before he pulled away, the door handle turned decisively, and Daniel strode briskly in, saying something about looking for Anne.

Sarah gasped, but there was no way she could right the situation in time. Hugh was more than half on top of her, there were at least three hairpins on the floor, and—

And, well, Hugh was *more than half on top of her.*

"What the devil?" Daniel stared with frozen shock before his natural quick thinking set in and he kicked the door shut behind him.

Hugh got to his feet with more speed than Sarah would have thought possible under the circumstances. Freed of his weight, she sat up, instinctively covering her breasts with her arms, even though her frock had not even a single button undone.

But she felt exposed. She could still feel the heat of Hugh's body against hers, and now Daniel was staring at her with an expression of such fury and disappointment that she could not meet his eyes.

"I trusted you, Prentice," Daniel said in a low, menacing voice.

"Not in this," Hugh replied, and even Sarah was surprised at the lack of gravity in his tone.

Daniel started to lunge at him.

Sarah shot to her feet. "Stop! It's not what you think!"

It was what they always said in novels, after all.

"Very well," she said, taking in the incredulous expressions on both men, "it is what you think. But you can't hit him."

Daniel growled. "Oh, can't I?"

Sarah planted her hand on his chest. "No," she said firmly, then turned to Hugh with a pointed finger. "And you can't either."

Hugh shrugged. "I wasn't trying to."

Sarah blinked. He did look astonishingly casual, all things considered.

She turned back to Daniel. "This is none of your affair."

Daniel's body went rigid with fury, and he could barely control his voice when he said, "Go to your room, Sarah."

"You are not my father," she shot back.

"I'm bloody well *in loco parentis* until he arrives," Daniel nearly spat.

"Oh, *you're* one to talk," she scoffed. Daniel's fiancée used to live with the Pleinsworths, after all. Sarah knew quite well that his romantic pursuit of her had not been entirely chaste.

Daniel crossed his arms. "This isn't about me."

"It *wasn't* until you barged into the room."

"If it makes you feel better," Hugh said, "I was planning to ask Lord Pleinsworth for her hand just as soon as he arrives."

Sarah snapped her head back around. "*That's* my proposal?"

"Blame him," Hugh replied, with a nod toward Daniel.

But then Daniel did something unexpected. He took a step toward Hugh, leveled a hard stare at his face, and said, "You will not ask Lord Pleinsworth for her hand. You will not say even a word to him until you tell her the truth."

The truth? Sarah looked from Daniel to Hugh and back again. Several times. But she might not have even been there, for all they noticed her. And for once in her life, she kept her mouth shut.

"What," Hugh bit off, his temper finally ignited, "do you mean by that?"

"You know very well," Daniel seethed. "I trust you have not forgotten the devil's bargain you made."

"You mean the one that saved your life?" Hugh countered.

Sarah took a step back in alarm. She did not know what was going on, but it terrified her.

"Yes," Daniel confirmed in a silky voice. "That one. Wouldn't you think that a woman ought to *know* before she accepts your offer?"

"Know what?" Sarah asked uneasily. "What

are you talking about?" But neither man so much as spared her a glance.

"Marriage is a lifetime commitment," Daniel said in an awful voice. "A *lifetime*."

Hugh's jaw went rigid. "This is not the time, Winstead."

"Not the time?" Daniel echoed. "Not the time? When the bloody hell else would be the time?"

"Watch your language," Hugh snapped.

"She's my cousin."

"She's a *lady*."

"She's right here," Sarah said weakly, lifting a hand.

Daniel whipped around to face her. "Have I offended you?"

"Ever?" Sarah asked, desperate to break the tension in the room.

Daniel scowled at her pathetic attempt at humor and turned back to Hugh. "Will you tell her?" he asked. "Or shall I?"

No one said a word.

Several seconds went by, then Daniel snapped toward Sarah with a suddenness that almost made her dizzy. "Do you recall," he said in an awful tone of voice, "how furious Lord Hugh's father was after the duel?"

Sarah nodded, even though she was not sure he expected an answer. She had not been out in society at the time of the duel, but she'd heard her mother whispering about it with her aunts. Lord Ramsgate had gone mad, they'd said. He was positively unhinged.

"Did you ever wonder," Daniel continued, still

in that terrible tone she now realized was for Hugh even as his words were directed toward her, "how Lord Hugh managed to convince his father to leave me alone?"

"No," Sarah said slowly, and it was the truth. Or at least it had been until a few weeks ago. "I assumed . . . I don't know. You came back, and that was all that mattered."

She felt like an idiot. Why *hadn't* she wondered what Hugh had done to retrieve Daniel? Should she have done?

"Have you ever met Lord Ramsgate?" Daniel asked her.

"I'm sure I have, at some point," Sarah said, her eyes flicking nervously from Hugh to Daniel. "But I—"

"He's a rat bastard," Daniel snarled.

"Daniel!" Sarah had never heard him use such words. Or such a tone. She looked to Hugh, but he only shrugged and said, "I have no objection to such a characterization."

"But . . ." Sarah fought for words. She didn't see her own father very often; he rarely left Devon, and more often than not Sarah found herself toted around the south of England by her mother, in the endless pursuit of a suitable husband. But he was her *father*, and she loved him, and she couldn't imagine standing by while someone called him such awful names.

"We don't all have genial and benign fifty-three-hound fathers," Hugh said.

Sarah hoped she was misinterpreting the note of condescension that sat upon his words.

"What does that have to do with anything?" she asked testily.

"It means that my father is an ass. It means he is a sick son of a bitch who hurts people and rather enjoys doing so. It means"—Hugh stepped closer, his voice growing cold with fury—"that he is stark raving mad no matter what sort of face he puts on for the rest of humanity, and there is no, I repeat, *no* reasoning with him when he's got his teeth stuck into something."

"Into me," Daniel clarified.

"Into anything," Hugh snapped, "but yes, you're included. You, on the other hand," he said to Sarah, his voice turning uncomfortably normal, "he'd like."

She felt sick.

"Your family's title dates to the Tudors, and you probably have a decent dowry." Hugh leaned one hip against the arm of the sofa and extended his injured leg in front of him. "But more to the point, you're in good health and of childbearing age."

Sarah could only stare.

"My father will adore you," he finished with a shrug.

"Hugh," Sarah began. "I don't . . ." But she didn't know how to finish her statement. She didn't recognize this man. He was hard, and brittle, and the way he described her left her feeling soiled and wrung dry.

"I'm not even his heir," Hugh said, and Sarah could hear something stirring in his voice. Something angry, something ready to strike.

"He shouldn't even care if my bride can reproduce

properly," Hugh went on, each syllable more clipped than the last. "He's got Freddie. He should be pinning his hopes there, and I keep telling him—"

He turned suddenly away, but not before Sarah heard him curse under his breath.

"I've never met your brother," Daniel said, after nearly a minute of silence strangled the room.

Sarah looked at him. His brow was knitted, and she realized that Daniel was more curious than he was surprised.

Hugh did not turn around. But he did say, in a strange monotone, "He does not move in the same circles that you do."

"Is-is there something wrong with him?" Sarah asked hesitantly.

"No!" Hugh thundered, whipping around so quickly that he lost his footing and nearly tumbled to the floor. Sarah shot forward to steady him, but Hugh thrust out his arm to push her away. "I'm fine," he grunted.

But he wasn't. She could see that he wasn't.

"There is nothing wrong with my brother," Hugh said, his voice low and precise, even as he caught his breath from his near fall. "He is perfectly healthy, perfectly able to sire a child. But"—his eyes flicked meaningfully toward Daniel—"he is not likely to marry."

Daniel's eyes clouded, and he gave a nod of understanding.

But not Sarah. "What does that mean?" she burst out, because bloody hell, it was like they were talking in a different language.

"It's not for your ears," Daniel said swiftly.

"Oh, is that so?" she demanded. "And 'rat bastard, sick son of a bitch' *is*?"

If she hadn't been so furious, she would have taken some satisfaction in the way both men flinched.

"He prefers men," Hugh said curtly.

"I don't even know what that means," Sarah snapped.

Daniel let off a bitter curse. "Oh, for the love of Christ, Prentice, she is a gentlewoman. And my *cousin*."

Sarah couldn't imagine what that had to with anything, but before she could ask, Daniel took a step toward Hugh and growled, "If you say another word, I swear I will have you drawn and quartered."

Hugh ignored him, his eyes never leaving Sarah's. "The way I prefer you," he said with slow deliberation, "my brother prefers men."

She stared at him, uncomprehending, and then: "*Oh*." She looked to Daniel, although she had no idea why. "Is that even possible?"

He looked away, his cheeks burning red.

"I do not profess to understand Freddie," Hugh said, each word deliberately chosen, "or why he is as he is. But he is my brother, and I love him."

Sarah wasn't sure how to respond. She looked to Daniel for guidance, but he was facing away.

"Freddie is a good man," Hugh continued, "and he was—"

Sarah turned back to him. His throat was working convulsively, and she did not think she'd ever seen him so undone.

"He was the only reason I survived my childhood." Hugh blinked, and then he actually smiled wistfully. "Although I imagine he would say the same thing about me."

Dear God, Sarah thought, what sort of man *was* their father?

"He's . . . not as I am," Hugh said with a swallow, "but he is a good man, as honorable and kind as you will ever know."

"All right," Sarah said slowly, trying to take this all in. "If you say he is good, and that I should love him as a brother, I will. But what does this have to do with . . . with anything?"

"It was why my father was so hell-bent on revenge against your cousin," Hugh replied, motioning with his head toward Daniel. "It is why he still is."

"But you said—"

"I can hold him in check," Hugh cut in. "I cannot change his mind." He shifted his weight, and Sarah thought she saw a spark of pain flash through his eyes. She followed his gaze to his cane, lying on the carpet near the sofa. He took a step toward it, but before he could do anything more, she rushed to retrieve it for him.

The expression on his face when she handed it to him was not one of gratitude. But whatever he wanted to say to her, he swallowed it bitterly down and said instead, to the room at large, "I'm told that the day of the duel, it was not known whether I would survive."

Sarah looked at Daniel. He gave a grim nod.

"My father is of the belief, and . . ." Hugh stopped

speaking, and he let out a weary, resigned breath. "And he may be right," he finally continued, as if he was only just accepting it himself, "that Freddie will never marry. I'd always thought he might, even though . . ." Again, his words trailed off.

"Hugh?" Sarah said softly, after nearly a minute had passed.

He turned and looked at her, then his expression hardened. "It doesn't matter what I thought," he said dismissively. "All that matters is what my father thought, and that he is convinced that I must be the one to provide an heir for the next generation. When Winstead nearly killed me . . ." He shrugged, letting Sarah and Daniel come to their own conclusions.

"But he didn't kill you," Sarah said. "So you can still . . ."

No one spoke.

"Er, you can, can't you?" she finally asked. This was no time to be missish and demure.

He chuckled grimly. "I have no reason to suppose otherwise, although I will confess to not having assured my father to that fact."

"Well, don't you think you should have done?" she demanded. "He would have let Daniel alone, and—"

"My father," Hugh cut in sharply, "does not easily let go of vengeance."

"Indeed," Daniel said.

"I still don't understand," Sarah said. What did any of this have to do with how Hugh brought Daniel back from Italy?

"If you want to marry him," Daniel said to her,

"I will not stand in your way. I like Hugh. I have always liked Hugh, even when we met on that damned dueling field. But I will not permit you to marry him without knowing the truth."

"What truth?" Sarah demanded. She was so bloody sick of them talking around the issue when she didn't even know what the issue *was*.

Daniel stared at her for a long moment, then turned his attention to Hugh. "Tell her how you convinced your father," he said in a clipped voice.

She looked at Hugh. He was staring at some point over her shoulder. It was like she wasn't even there.

"*Tell her.*"

"My father loves nothing so much as the Ramsgate title," Hugh said in a strange monotone. "I am nothing but a means to an end, but he believes I am his only means, and thus I am invaluable."

"What does that *mean*?" she asked.

He turned back to her, blinking as if he was bringing her into focus. "Don't you understand?" he said softly. "When it comes to my father, the only thing with which I have to bargain is myself."

Sarah's uneasiness began to grow.

"I drew up a contract," Hugh said to her, "explaining exactly what would happen if your cousin met with any harm."

Sarah's gaze slid to Daniel, then back to Hugh. "What?" she said, the dread in her voice threatening to drag the very breath from her body. "What will happen?"

Hugh shrugged. "I kill myself."

Chapter Seventeen

"No, really," Sarah said. Her voice was forced; her eyes were wary. "What did you say would happen?"

Hugh fought the urge to dig his thumbs into his temples. His head had begun to pound, and he was fairly certain the only remedy would be the cheerful strangulation of Daniel Smythe-Smith. For once, everything in Hugh's life was looking up—looking bloody *perfect*—and Daniel had to butt his head in where it was not wanted. Where it was not *needed*.

This was not how Hugh had meant to have this conversation.

Or maybe he hadn't meant to have it at all, a small voice within tried to say. He hadn't so much as thought about it. He'd been so infatuated with Lady Sarah, so utterly entranced by the bliss of falling in love that he hadn't given a thought to his "agreement" with his father.

But surely—surely she could see that he'd had no other option.

"Is this a joke?" Sarah demanded. "Because if it is, it's not funny. What did you really say would happen?"

"He's not lying," Daniel said.

"No." Sarah shook her head, aghast. "That can't be true. It's preposterous. It's mad, it's—"

"The only thing that could ever convince my father to leave him alone," Hugh said sharply.

"But you didn't mean it," she said, desperation in her voice. "Because you lied to him, didn't you? It was just a threat. An empty threat."

Hugh didn't answer. He had no idea if he'd meant it. He'd had a problem—no, he'd been *battered* by a problem—and he had finally seen a way to solve it. In all honesty, he'd been *pleased* with himself. He'd thought his plan was brilliant.

His father would never risk losing Hugh before Hugh could see to it that a new generation of Prentice men roamed the land. Although once that happened, Hugh mused, all bets were off. If the marquess had a healthy grandson or two under his power, he likely wouldn't blink if Hugh went and offed himself.

Well, he might blink once, if only for the sake of appearances. But after that Hugh would be just so much water under the bridge.

Oh, it had been *grand* when he'd presented his father with that contract. Maybe he was a sick son of a bitch, but the sight of his father so poleaxed, so utterly without recourse or retort . . .

It had been magnificent.

There were advantages to being thought such a loose cannon, Hugh had realized. His father had ranted and railed and upset the tea tray, and all the while Hugh had just watched him with that detached, almost clinical, amusement that never failed to infuriate the marquess.

And then, after Lord Ramsgate declared that Hugh would never go through with such an absurd threat, he'd finally looked at his son. He'd really, truly looked at him for the first time in Hugh's memory. He'd seen the insolent, empty smile, the steely resolve in the set of his chin, and the marquess had gone so white that his eyes seemed to shrivel in their sockets.

He'd signed the contract.

After that, Hugh hadn't given the matter much thought. He might make the occasional inappropriate joke (he always did have a dark sense of humor), but as far as he was concerned, he and his father were at a stable impasse of mutually assured destruction.

In other words, there was nothing to worry about. And he did not understand why no one else seemed to realize that.

Of course the only ones who knew about the contract were Daniel and Sarah, but they were intelligent people, rarely illogical in their decisions.

"Why aren't you answering me?" Sarah asked, her voice rising with panic. "Hugh? Tell me you didn't mean it."

Hugh stared at her. He'd been thinking, remembering, and it was almost as if a part of him had left the room, found some quiet corner in which to ponder the sad state of his world.

He was going to lose her. She was not going to understand. Hugh could see that now, in her frantic eyes and trembling hands. Why couldn't she see that he had made a hero's choice? He was sacrificing himself—or at least threatening to—for the sake of her beloved cousin. Shouldn't that count for something?

He had brought Daniel back to England, he had ensured his safety; for this he would be punished?

"Say something, Hugh," Sarah begged. She looked to Daniel, then back to Hugh, her head moving in awkward jerks. "I don't understand why you won't say something."

"He signed a contract," Daniel said quietly. "I have a copy."

"You gave him a *copy*?"

Hugh wasn't sure how that changed anything, but Sarah looked horrified. The color had drained from her skin, and her hands, which she was trying so hard to keep still at her sides, were shaking. "You have to tear it up," she said to Daniel. "Right this moment. You have to tear it up."

"It doesn't—"

"Is it back in London?" she cut in. "Because if it is, I leave right now. I don't care if I miss your wedding, it's not a problem. I can just go back, and I'll get it, and—"

"Sarah!" Daniel practically yelled. When he had her attention, he said, "It wouldn't make a difference. It's not the only copy. And if he's right"—he motioned to Hugh—"it's the only thing keeping me safe."

"But it might *kill* him," she cried.

Daniel crossed his arms. "That is entirely up to Lord Hugh."

"Actually, my father," Hugh said. Because really, that was where the chain of madness began.

Sarah's body went still, but her head was shaking, almost as if she were trying to jog her brain into understanding. "Why would you *do* this?" she asked, even though Hugh felt he had made his reasons perfectly clear. "It's wrong. I-i-it's *unnatural*."

"It's logical," Hugh said.

"Logical? *Logical?* Are you insane? It's the most illogical, irresponsible, selfish—"

"Sarah, stop," Daniel said, putting a hand on her shoulder. "You're overset."

But she just shook him off. "Don't patronize me," she snapped. She turned back to Hugh. He wished he knew what to say. He'd thought he had said the right thing. It was what would have convinced him had their positions been reversed.

"Were you thinking of anyone but yourself?" she demanded.

"I was thinking of your cousin," Hugh said quietly.

"But it is different now," she cried out. "When you made that threat, it was just you. But now it's—"

Hugh waited, but she did not finish the sentence. She did not say, *It's not.* She didn't say, *It's us.*

"Well, you don't have to do it," she announced, as if she'd just solved all of their problems. "If something happened to Daniel, you wouldn't have to actually go through with it. No one would hold you to such a contract, no one. Certainly not your father, and Daniel would be *dead*."

The room went still until Sarah clapped a horrified hand over her mouth. "I'm sorry," she said, turning frantic eyes to her cousin. "I'm so sorry. Oh, my God, I'm sorry."

"We're done," Daniel bit off, shooting a look of near hatred at Hugh. He put his arm around Sarah and murmured something in her ear. Hugh could not hear what he said, but it did nothing to stem the flow of tears that were now pouring down her face.

"I will pack my things," Hugh said.

No one told him not to do so.

SARAH ALLOWED DANIEL to lead her from the room, protesting only when he offered to carry her up the stairs.

"Please, no," she said in a choked voice. "I don't want everyone to realize how upset I am."

Upset. What a pathetic excuse for a word. She wasn't upset, she was wrecked.

Shattered.

"Let me take you back to your room," he said.

She nodded, then blurted, "No! Harriet might be there. I don't want her asking questions, and you know she will."

In the end, Daniel took her back to his own bedchamber, reasoning that it was one of the only rooms in the house in which she could be guaranteed privacy. He asked her one last time if she wanted her mother, or Honoria, or anyone, but Sarah shook her head and curled up in a ball atop his quilts. Daniel found a blanket and laid it over her, and then, once he was assured that she did indeed wish to be left alone, he exited the room and quietly closed his door behind him.

Ten minutes later Honoria arrived.

"Daniel told me you said you wanted to be alone," Honoria said before Sarah could do more than look at her with an exhausted expression, "but we think you're wrong."

The very definition of family. The people who got to decide when you were wrong. Sarah supposed she was as guilty of this as anyone. Probably more so.

Honoria sat next to her on the bed and gently brushed Sarah's hair from her face. "How can I help you?"

Sarah did not lift her head from her pillow. Nor did she turn to face her cousin. "You can't."

"There must be something we can do," Honoria said. "I refuse to believe that all is lost."

Sarah sat up a little and looked at her in disbelief. "Did Daniel tell you *nothing*?"

"He told me some," Honoria replied, showing no reaction to Sarah's unkind tone.

"Then how can you say all is not lost? I thought I loved him. I thought he loved me. And now, I find out—" Sarah felt her face contorting with anger that Honoria did not deserve, but she could not control herself. "Don't tell me all is not lost!"

Honoria caught her lower lip between her teeth. "Perhaps if you talked to him."

"I did! How do you think I ended up like this?" Sarah waved her arm in front of her as if to say—

As if to say, *I'm angry and I'm hurt and I don't know what to do.*

As if to say, *There's nothing I can do except wave my stupid arm.*

As if to say, *Help me because I don't know how to ask.*

"I'm not entirely certain I got the whole story," Honoria said in a careful voice. "Daniel was very upset, and he said you were crying, and then I rushed off . . ."

"What did he tell you?" Sarah asked in a monotone.

"He explained that Lord Hugh . . ." Honoria grimaced, as if she couldn't quite believe what she was saying. "Well, he told me how Lord Hugh was able to finally convince his father to leave Daniel alone. It's . . ." Once again, Honoria's face found at least three different expressions of incredulity before she was able to continue. "I thought it was rather clever of him, actually, although certainly somewhat . . ."

"*Mad?*"

"Well, no," Honoria said slowly. "It would only be mad if there was no reasoning behind it, and I don't think Lord Hugh does anything without reasoning it through."

"He said he would *kill* himself, Honoria. I'm sorry, I cannot— Good God, and people call *me* dramatic!"

Honoria bit back a tiny smile. "It is . . . somewhat . . . ironic."

Sarah gave her a look.

"Not that I'm saying it's funny," Honoria said, very quickly.

"I thought I loved him," Sarah said in a small voice.

"Thought?"

"I don't know if I still do." Sarah turned away, letting her head fall back against the bed. It hurt to look at her cousin. Honoria was so happy, and she *deserved* to be happy, but Sarah would never be pure enough of heart not to hate her just a little bit. Just for this moment.

Honoria held silent for a few seconds, then quietly asked, "Can you fall out of love so quickly?"

"I fell into it quickly." Sarah swallowed uncomfortably. "Maybe it was never really true. Maybe I just wanted it to be true. All these weddings and you and Marcus and Daniel and Anne and everyone looking so happy, and I just *want* that. Maybe that's all it was."

"Do you really think so?"

"How could I be in love with someone who would threaten such a thing?" Sarah asked in a broken voice.

"He did it to ensure the happiness of another person," Honoria reminded her. "My brother."

"I know," Sarah answered, "and I could admire him for that, honestly I could, but when I asked him if it was just an empty threat, he didn't say that it was." She swallowed convulsively, trying to calm her breathing. "He did not say to me that if . . . if it were *necessary*"—she choked on the word—"he would not go through with it. I asked him straight to his face, and he did not answer."

"Sarah," Honoria began, "you need to—"

"Do you even understand how awful this conversation is?" Sarah cried. "We are discussing something that would only come to pass if your brother was *murdered*. As if . . . as if then . . . whatever Hugh did would be *worse*?"

Honoria laid a gentle hand on Sarah's shoulder.

"I know," Sarah choked out, as if Honoria's gesture had been a question. "You're going to tell me I need to ask him again. But what if I do and he says that he does mean it, and that if his father changes his mind and does something to Daniel he's going to take a pistol and put it in his stupid *mouth*?"

There was a terrible moment of silence, then Sarah jammed her hand over her mouth, physically trying to hold in a sob.

"Take a deep breath," Honoria said soothingly, but her eyes were horrified.

"How can I even talk about it?" Sarah cried. "How awful I would feel about Hugh and how angry I would be at him when obviously that would mean Daniel is already dead, and shouldn't *that* be what crushes me and— God above, Honoria, it is against the very nature of man. I can't— I can't—"

She fell into her cousin's arms, gasping through her tears. "It isn't fair," she sobbed into Honoria's shoulder. "It just isn't fair."

"No. It's not."

"I love him."

Honoria did not stop rubbing her back. "I know that you do."

"And I feel like a monster, being upset that he said—" Sarah gasped, her lungs pulling in an unexpected gulp of air. "That he said that he would kill himself, and then I begged him to tell me that he wouldn't do it, when shouldn't I really be upset that all this would mean that something had happened to Daniel?"

"But you can see why Lord Hugh made that bargain in the first place," Honoria said. "Can't you?"

Sarah nodded against her. Her lungs hurt. Her whole body hurt. "But it should be different now," she whispered. "He should feel differently now. *I* should mean something."

"And you *do*," Honoria said reassuringly. "I know that you do. I've seen the way you look at each other when you think no one is watching."

Sarah pulled back just far enough to look at her cousin's face. Honoria was gazing down at her with the tiniest of smiles, and her eyes—her amazing lavender eyes that Sarah had always envied—were clear and serene.

Was that the difference between the two of them? Sarah wondered. Honoria approached each day as if the world were made of greenglass seas and soft ocean breezes. Sarah's world was one storm after another. She'd never had a serene day in her life.

"I've watched the way he looks at *you*," Honoria said. "He is in love with you."

"He has not said it."

"Have you?"

Sarah let her silence be her reply.

Honoria reached out and took her hand. "You might have to be the brave one and say it first."

"That's easy for you to say," Sarah said, thinking of Marcus, always so honorable and reserved. "You fell in love with the easiest, loveliest, least complicated man in England."

Honoria gave a sympathetic shrug. "We can't help with whom we fall in love. And you're not the easiest, least complicated woman in England, you know."

Sarah gave her a sideways look. "You left out loveliest."

"Well, you might be the loveliest," Honoria said with a crooked smile. Then she nudged Sarah with her elbow. "I daresay Lord Hugh thinks you're the loveliest."

Sarah buried her face in her hands. "What am I going to do?"

"I think you're going to have to talk to him."

Sarah knew Honoria was right, but she could not stop her mind from racing through all of the eventualities such a conversation might bring. "What if he says he will hold to the bargain?" she finally asked, her voice small and scared.

Several seconds went by, and Honoria said, "Then at least you will know. But if you don't ask him, you will never know what he might have said. Just think if Romeo and Juliet had actually *talked* to each other."

Sarah looked up, momentarily flabbergasted. "That's a *terrible* comparison."

"Sorry, yes, you're right." Honoria looked abashed, then changed her mind and pointed at Sarah with a jaunty finger. "But it made you stop crying."

"If only to scold you."

"You may scold me all you wish if it brings a smile back to your face. But you must promise me that you will talk to him. You don't want some big, awful misunderstanding to ruin your chance at happiness."

"What you're saying is, if my life is to be ruined, I need to do it myself?" Sarah asked in a dry voice.

"It's not quite how I would have put it, but yes."

Sarah was quiet for a long moment, and then she asked, almost absentmindedly, "Did you know he can multiply large sums in his head?"

Honoria smiled indulgently. "No, but it does not surprise me."

"It takes him only an instant. He tried to explain it once, what it looks like in his head when he does it, but I couldn't follow a thing he was saying."

"Arithmetic works in mysterious ways."

Sarah rolled her eyes. "As opposed to love?"

"Love is entirely incomprehensible," Honoria said. "Arithmetic is merely mysterious." She shrugged, stood up, and held out a hand to Sarah. "Or maybe it's the other way around. Shall we go find out?"

"You're coming with me?"

"Just to help you locate him." She gave a little one-shouldered shrug. "It's a large house."

Sarah quirked a suspicious brow. "You're afraid I will lose my nerve."

"Without a doubt," Honoria confirmed.

"I won't," Sarah said, and despite the butterflies in her stomach and dread in her heart, she knew it was true. She was not one to back down from her fears. And she would never be able to live with herself if she did not do everything in her power to ensure her own happiness.

And Hugh's. Because if anyone in this world deserved a happy ending, it was he.

"But not right away," Sarah said. "I need to tidy up. I don't want to go to him looking as if I've been crying."

"He should know he made you cry."

"Why, Honoria Smythe-Smith, that might be the most hard-hearted thing I have ever heard you say."

"It's Honoria Holroyd now," Honoria said pertly, "and it's true. The only thing worse than a man who makes a woman cry is a man who makes a woman cry and then doesn't feel guilty about it."

Sarah looked at her with a new sort of respect. "Married life agrees with you."

Honoria's smile was a touch smug. "It does, doesn't it?"

Sarah scooted herself to the edge of the bed and slid off. Her legs were stiff, and she stretched each one in turn, bending and straightening at the knee. "He already knows he made me cry."

"Good."

Sarah leaned against the side of the bed and looked down at her hands. Her fingers were swollen. How did *that* happen? Who got sausage fingers from crying?

"Is something wrong?" Honoria asked.

Sarah gave her a rueful look. "I believe I would rather Lord Hugh think I'm the sort of woman who looks gorgeous while she cries, eyes all glistening and such."

"As opposed to red-rimmed and puffy?"

"Is that your way of telling me I look a mess?"

"You'll want to redo your hair," Honoria said, ever the epitome of tact.

Sarah nodded. "Do you know where Harriet is? We're sharing a room, and I don't want her seeing me like this."

"She would never judge," Honoria assured her.

"I know. But I'm not up to her questions. And you know she'll have questions."

Honoria bit back a grin. She knew Harriet. "I'll tell you what," she said, "I will make sure that Harriet is distracted, and you can go to your room to . . ." She fluttered her hands near her face, the universal signal for fixing one's appearance.

Sarah gave a nod. "Thank you. And Honoria . . ." Sarah waited until her cousin had turned back around to face her. "I love you."

Honoria gave a wobbly smile. "I love you, too, Sarah." She brushed a nonexistent tear from her eye, then asked, "Would you like me to send word to Lord Hugh, asking him to meet with you in thirty minutes?"

"Perhaps an hour?" Sarah was brave, but not that brave. She needed more time to bolster her confidence.

"In the conservatory?" Honoria suggested, walking toward the door. "You'll have privacy. I don't think anyone's used the room all week. I imagine they're all afraid they might stumble upon us practicing for a musicale."

Sarah smiled despite herself. "All right. The conservatory in an hour. I shall—"

She was interrupted by a sharp rap on the door.

"That's odd," Honoria said. "Daniel knows we—" She shrugged, not bothering to finish her statement. "Enter!"

The door opened, and one of the footmen stepped in. "My lady," he said to Honoria, blinking with surprise. "I was looking for his lordship."

"He very kindly allowed us the use of his room," Honoria said. "Is there a problem?"

"No, but I have a message from the stables."

"From the stables?" Honoria echoed. "That's very strange." She looked over at Sarah, who had been waiting patiently through the exchange. "Whatever could be so important that they told George to come find Daniel in his bedchamber?"

Sarah shrugged, figuring George was the footman. Honoria had grown up at Whipple Hill; of course she'd know his name.

"Very well," Honoria said, turning back to the footman. She held out her hand. "If you give the message to me, I will make sure that Lord Winstead receives it."

"Begging your pardon, ma'am. It's not written down. I was asked just to tell him."

"I will relay it," Honoria said.

The footman looked undecided, but only for a

moment. "Thank you, ma'am. I was asked to tell his lordship that Lord Hugh took one of the carriages to Thatcham."

Sarah snapped to attention. "Lord Hugh?"

"Er, yes," George confirmed. "He's the gentleman who limps, isn't he?"

"Why would he go to Thatcham?"

"Sarah," Honoria said, "I'm sure George doesn't know—"

"No," George interrupted. "That is, I'm sorry, my lady. I didn't mean to cut in."

"Please, go ahead," Sarah said urgently.

"I was told that he went to the White Hart to see his father."

"His *father*?"

George didn't quite flinch, but it was close.

"Why would he go see his father?" Sarah demanded.

"I-I-I don't know, my lady." He threw a rather desperate glance over at Honoria.

"I don't like this," Sarah said.

George looked pained.

"You may go, George," Honoria said. He gave a quick bow and fled.

"Why is his father in Thatcham?" Sarah asked the moment they were alone again.

"I don't know," Honoria replied, sounding as baffled as Sarah felt. "He certainly wasn't invited to the wedding."

"This can't be good." Sarah turned to the window. The rain was still coming down in sheets. "I need to go to the village."

"You can't go in this weather."

"Hugh did."

"That's entirely different. He was going to his father."

"Who wants to *kill* Daniel!"

"Oh, dear God," Honoria said, giving her head a shake. "This is all such madness."

Sarah ignored her, instead dashing out into the hall and yelling for George, who thankfully had not yet headed downstairs. "I need a carriage brought 'round," she said. "Immediately."

As soon as he was gone, she turned back to Honoria, who was standing in the doorway. "I will meet you in the drive," Honoria said. "I'm going with you."

"No, you can't," Sarah said immediately. "Marcus would never forgive me."

"Then we'll bring him, too. And Daniel."

"No!" Sarah grabbed Honoria's hand and yanked her back even though she hadn't taken more than a step. "Under no circumstances may Daniel go see Lord Ramsgate."

"You cannot leave him out of this," Honoria insisted. "He is as deeply involved as—"

"Fine," Sarah said, just to cut her off. "Get Daniel. I don't care."

But she did care. And the moment Honoria dashed off to fetch the two gentlemen, Sarah yanked on her coat and raced to the stables. She could ride to the village faster than any carriage could be driven, even in—no, *especially* in this rain.

Daniel, Marcus, and Honoria would follow her to the White Hart; Sarah knew that they would.

But if she got there far enough ahead of them, she could— Well, to be quite honest, she wasn't sure what she could do, just that she could do something. She would find a way to placate Lord Ramsgate before Daniel showed up, irate and itching for a fight.

She might not be able to engineer a happy ending for all; in fact, she was fairly certain she could not do so. More than three years of hatred and bitterness could not be swept away in a single day. But if Sarah could somehow keep tempers from rising, and fists from flying, and—good heavens—anyone from getting killed . . .

It might not be a happy ending, but by God, it would have to be happy enough.

Chapter Eighteen

An hour prior
Whipple Hill
A different room

IF HUGH EVENTUALLY did become the Marquess of Ramsgate, the first thing he was going to do was change the family motto. He could do that, couldn't he? Because *With Pride Comes Valor* made no sense in the context of the current generations of Prentice men. No, if Hugh had any say in the matter, he was changing the whole bloody thing to *Things Can Always Get Worse*.

Case in point: the short missive that had been delivered to his room at Whipple Hill while he was off in the little drawing room, breaking Sarah's heart, making her cry, and apparently being a terrible person.

The card was from his father.

His father.

It had been bad enough to have to look upon his familiar sharp handwriting. Then he read the words and realized that Lord Ramsgate was here. In Berkshire, practically down the road from Whipple Hill at the White Hart, the most fashionable of the local inns.

How the marquess had got a room when all of the inns were full of wedding guests, Hugh could not imagine. But his father had always had a way of bludgeoning through life. If he wanted a room, he'd get one, and Hugh could only pity the cascade of guests who would be moved to the next-nicest room until some poor bloke found himself out in the barn.

What his father's note had not indicated, however, was *why* he'd traveled to Berkshire. Hugh was not particularly surprised by this omission; his father had never believed in explaining himself. He was at the White Hart, he wanted to speak to Hugh, and he wanted to do so immediately.

That was all he wrote.

Hugh generally went out of his way to avoid interaction with his father, but he was not so stupid as to ignore a direct summons. He told his valet to pack up his things and await further instructions, and then he set off for the village. He wasn't sure that Daniel would look kindly upon his using one of the Winstead carriages, but as the rain was still beating mercilessly against the earth, and Hugh was a man with a cane . . . He really didn't see how he had much choice in the matter.

Not to mention that this was his *father* he'd been forced to go see. No matter how furious Daniel was with Hugh—and Hugh suspected he was irreversibly furious—he would understand the necessity of meeting with the marquess.

"God, I hate this," Hugh said to himself as he climbed awkwardly into the carriage. And then he wondered if some of Sarah's propensity toward drama was rubbing off on him, because all he could think was—

I'm off to meet my doom.

The White Hart Inn
Thatcham
Berkshire

"WHAT ARE YOU doing here?" Hugh demanded, the words spitting from his mouth before he had taken more than two steps into one of the White Hart's private dining rooms.

"No greeting?" his father said, not bothering to rise from his seat. "No 'Father, what brings you to Berkshire this fine day?' "

"It's raining."

"And the earth is renewed," Lord Ramsgate said in a jolly voice.

Hugh gave him a cold stare. He hated when his father pretended to be paternal.

His father motioned to the chair across the table. "Sit."

Hugh might have preferred to stand, if only to countermand him, but his leg ached, and his desire to thwart his father was not great enough for him to sacrifice his own comfort. He sat.

"Wine?" his father asked.

"No."

"It's not very good, anyway," his father said, tossing back the remains of his glass. "I really ought to bring my own when I travel."

Hugh sat in stony silence, waiting for his father to get to the point.

"The cheese is tolerable," the marquess said. He reached out for a slice of bread from the cheese-board on the table. "Bread? They can't really muck up a loaf of—"

"What the devil is this about?" Hugh finally exploded.

His father had been clearly waiting for this moment. His face stretched into a smug smile, and he leaned back in his chair. "You can't guess?"

"I wouldn't dare try."

"I'm here to congratulate you."

Hugh stared at him with unconcealed suspicion. "On what?"

His father wagged a finger at him. "Don't be coy. I heard a rumor you were to be engaged."

"From whom?" Hugh had only just kissed Sarah for the first time the night before. How in God's name did his father know he'd been planning to ask her to marry him?

Lord Ramsgate flicked his hand. "I have spies everywhere."

This Hugh did not doubt. But still . . . His eyes narrowed. "Who were you spying upon?" he asked. "Winstead or me?"

His father shrugged. "Does it matter?"

"Intensely."

"Both, I suppose. You make it so easy to kill two birds with one stone."

"You'd do well not to use such metaphors in my presence," Hugh said with a raised eyebrow.

"Always so literal," Lord Ramsgate said with a *tsk-tsk* sound. "You never could take a joke."

Hugh gaped at him. His *father* accusing *him* of being without humor? It was staggering.

"I am not engaged to be married," Hugh said to him, each word a crisp and precise dart from his lips. "And I won't be anytime in the foreseeable future. So you can pack your things and go back to whatever hell you crawled out of."

His father chuckled at the insult, which Hugh found unnerving. Lord Ramsgate never brushed off insults. He fisted them up into tight little balls, filled them with nettles and nails, and hurled them back at the sender.

And then laughed.

"Are we done?" Hugh asked coldly.

"Why such a rush?"

Hugh gave a sick smile. "Because I detest you."

Again, his father chuckled. "Oh, Hugh, when will you ever learn?"

Hugh said nothing.

"It doesn't matter if you detest me. It will never matter. I'm your father." He leaned forward with an oily grin. "You can't be rid of me."

"No," Hugh said. He leveled a frank stare across the table. "But you can be rid of me."

Lord Ramsgate's jaw twitched. "I assume you refer to that unholy document you forced me to sign."

"No one forced you," Hugh said with an insolent shrug.

"You really believe that?"

"Did I place the pen in your hand?" Hugh countered. "The contract was a formality. You know that as well as I do."

"I know no such—"

"I told you what would happen if you harm Lord Winstead," Hugh said with deadly calm, "and that stands whether it is in writing or not."

It was true; Hugh had had the contract drawn up and placed before his father and his solicitor because he'd wanted them to know he was serious. He'd wanted his father to sign his name—his full name and the title that meant so much to him—acknowledging all he would lose if he did not let go of his vendetta against Daniel.

"I have kept my end of the bargain," Lord Ramsgate snarled.

"Insofar as Lord Winstead is still alive, yes."

"I—"

"I must say," Hugh interrupted, taking great pleasure in cutting his father off at the very first pronoun, "that I'm not asking much of you. Most people would find it rather easy to conduct their lives without killing another human being."

"He made you a cripple," his father hissed.

"No," Hugh said softly, remembering that magical night on the lawn at Whipple Hill. He had waltzed. For the first time since Daniel's bullet had torn apart his thigh, Hugh had held a woman in his arms, and he had danced.

Sarah had refused to allow him to call himself a cripple. Was that the moment he had fallen in love with her? Or was it one of a hundred moments?

"I prefer to call myself lame," Hugh murmured. With a smile.

"What the devil is the difference?"

"If I'm a cripple, then that's all I—" Hugh looked up. His father's face was red, the kind of veiny, mottled red that came from too much anger, or too much drink.

"Never mind," Hugh said. "You'd never understand." But Hugh hadn't understood, either. It had taken Lady Sarah Pleinsworth to make him understand the difference.

Sarah. That was who she was now. Not Lady Sarah Pleinsworth or even Lady Sarah. Just Sarah. She'd been his, and he'd lost her. And he still didn't quite understand why.

"You underestimate yourself, son," Lord Ramsgate said.

"You just called me a cripple," Hugh said, "and you're accusing *me* of underestimating?"

"I do not refer to your athletic ability," his father said, "although it is true that a lady will want a husband who can ride and fence and hunt."

"Because you're so good at all those things," Hugh said, dropping his gaze to his father's paunchy middle.

"I *was*," his father replied, apparently taking no offense at the insult, "and I had my pick of the litter when I decided to marry."

Of the litter. Was that really how his father saw women?

Of course it was.

"Two daughters of dukes, three of marquesses, and one of an earl. I could have had any of them."

"Lucky Mother," Hugh said flatly.

"Indeed," Lord Ramsgate said, missing the sarcasm entirely. "Her father may have been the Duke of Farringdon, but she was one of six daughters, and her dowry was not large."

"Larger than the other duke's daughter, I assume?" Hugh drawled.

"No. But the Farringdons descend from the Barons de Veuveclos, the first of whom, as you know—"

Oh, he knew. Lord, but he knew.

"—fought alongside William the Conqueror."

Hugh had been forced to memorize the family trees at the age of six. Luckily, he had a talent for such things. Freddie had not been nearly so lucky. His hands had been swollen for weeks from the caning.

"The other dukedom," the marquess finished with disdain, "was of a relatively new creation."

Hugh could only shake his head. "You really do take snobbism to new levels."

His father ignored him. "As I was saying, I believe you underestimate yourself. You may be a cripple, but you have your charms."

Hugh practically choked. "My charms?"

"A euphemism for your last name."

"Of course." How could it be anything but?

"You may not be first in line for the title, but much as it disgusts me, anyone who bothers to do a bit of digging will realize that even if you never become the Marquess of Ramsgate, your son will."

"Freddie is more discreet than you think," Hugh felt compelled to point out.

Lord Ramsgate snorted. "I was able to find out that you're panting after Pleinsworth's daughter. Do you think her father won't discover the truth about Freddie?"

As Lord Pleinsworth was buried in Devon with fifty-three hounds, Hugh thought not, but he did see his father's point.

"I would not go so far as to say that you could have any woman you wanted," Lord Ramsgate continued, "but I see no reason you could not snag the Pleinsworth chit. Especially after spending the entire week mooning over each other at breakfast."

Hugh bit his cheek to keep from responding.

"I notice you do not contradict."

"Your spies, as always, are excellent," Hugh said.

His father sat back in his chair and tapped his fingertips together. "Lady Sarah Pleinsworth," he said with admiration in his voice. "I must congratulate you."

"Don't."

"Oh, dear. Are we being shy?"

Hugh gripped the edge of the table. What exactly *would* happen if he leapt across the table and gripped his father by the throat? Surely no one would mourn the old man.

"I've met her, you know," his father continued. "Nothing much, of course, just an introduction at a ball a few years ago. But her father is an earl. Our paths cross from time to time."

"Don't talk about her," Hugh warned.

"She's quite pretty in an unconventional way. The curl of her hair, that lovely wide mouth . . ." Lord Ramsgate looked up and wagged his brows. "A man could get used to such a face on the pillow next to his."

Hugh felt his blood growing hot in his veins. "Shut up. *Now.*"

His father made a show of conceding. "I can see that you don't wish to discuss your personal affairs."

"I'm trying to recall when that has stopped you before."

"Ah, but if you were to marry, then your choice of bride would be very much my affair, too."

Hugh shot to his feet. "You sick son of a—"

"Oh, stop," his father said, laughing. "I'm not talking about *that*, although now that I think of it, it might have been a way around Freddie's problem."

Oh, dear God. Hugh felt ill. He wouldn't put it past his father to force Freddie to marry and then rape his wife.

All in the name of dynasty.

No, it wouldn't work. Freddie, for all his quiet ways, would never allow himself to be forced into a marriage under such pretenses. And even if somehow . . .

Well, Hugh could always put a stop to it. All

he had to do was get married himself. Give his father a reason to expect that a Ramsgate heir was forthcoming.

Which he was finally happy to do.

With a woman who would not have him.

Because of his father.

The irony of it all was just killing him.

"Her dowry is respectable," the marquess said, continuing as if Hugh hadn't been on his feet with a murderous look in his eyes. "Please, sit. It's difficult to have a rational discussion with you listing to one side like that."

Hugh took a breath, trying to steady himself. He was favoring his leg. He hadn't even realized. Slowly, he sat.

"As I was saying," his father continued, "I had my solicitor look into it, and it is much the same situation I saw with your mother. The Pleinsworth dowries are not large, but they are large enough, considering Lady Sarah's bloodlines and connections."

"She's not a horse."

His father quirked a smile. "Isn't she?"

"I'm going to kill you," Hugh growled.

"No, you're not." Lord Ramsgate reached for another slice of bread. "And you really should have something to eat. There's more than I—"

"Will you stop with the food?" Hugh roared.

"You *are* in poor temper today."

Hugh forced his voice back to a normal register. "Conversations with my father generally have that effect upon me."

"I suppose I walked into that one."

Again, Hugh stared at his father in shock. He was admitting that Hugh had got the best of him? He never did that, even with something so small as a conversational parry.

"From your comments," Lord Ramsgate continued, "I can only deduce that you have not, in fact, proposed to Lady Sarah."

Hugh said nothing.

"My spies—as we seem to enjoy calling them—assure me that she would appear to be amenable to such a prospect."

Hugh still said nothing.

"The question is"—Lord Ramsgate shifted forward, leaning his elbows on the table—"what can I do to aid you in your suit?"

"Stay out of my life."

"Ah, but I can't."

Hugh let out an exhausted sigh. He hated showing weakness in front of his father, but he was so bloody tired. "Why won't you leave me alone?"

"You have to ask me that?" his father retorted, even though Hugh had clearly been talking to himself.

Hugh put one hand to his forehead and pinched at his temples. "Freddie might still marry," he said, but by now it was more out of habit than anything else.

"Oh, *stop*," his father said. "He wouldn't know what to do with a woman if she pulled his cock out and—"

"Stop!" Hugh roared, nearly upsetting the table as he lurched back to his feet. "Shut up! Just shut your bloody mouth!"

His father looked almost baffled at the outburst. "It's the truth. The tested truth, I might add. Do you know how many whores I—"

"Yes," Hugh snapped. "I know exactly how many whores you locked in the room with him. It's that bloody brain of mine. I can't stop counting, remember?"

His father exploded with laughter. Hugh stared at him, wondering what the hell could be so funny at such a moment.

"I counted, too," Lord Ramsgate gasped, nearly doubled over with mirth.

"I know," Hugh said without emotion. His room had always been next to Freddie's. He'd heard everything. When Lord Ramsgate brought the prostitutes to Freddie, he'd stayed to watch.

"Fat lot of good it did," Lord Ramsgate continued. "I thought it might help. Set a rhythm, you know."

"Oh, God," Hugh nearly groaned. "Stop." He could still hear it. Most of the time it had just been his father, but every now and then one of the women would get into the spirit of it and join in.

Lord Ramsgate was still chuckling as he stood back up. "One . . . ," he said, making a lewd gesture to go along with the count. "Two . . ."

Hugh recoiled. A memory flashed through his brain.

"Three . . ."

The duel. The count. He'd been trying not to remember. He'd been trying so hard to blot out the memory of his father's voice that he'd flinched.

And he'd pulled the trigger.

He'd never meant to shoot Daniel. He'd been aiming to the side. But then someone had started counting, and suddenly Hugh was a boy again, huddled in his bed while he heard Freddie pleading with his father to leave him alone.

Freddie, who had taught Hugh never to interfere.

The counting hadn't just been for the prostitutes. Lord Ramsgate was very fond of his beautifully polished, mahogany cane. And he saw no reason to spare it when his sons displeased him.

Freddie always displeased him. Lord Ramsgate liked to count the blows.

Hugh stared at his father. "I hate you."

His father stared back. "I know."

"I'm leaving."

His father shook his head. "No, you're not."

Hugh stiffened. "I beg your—"

"I didn't want to have to do this," his father said, almost apologetically.

Almost.

Then he slammed his booted foot into Hugh's bad leg.

Hugh howled in agony as he went down. He felt his body curling up, trying to contain the pain. "Bloody hell," he gasped. "Why would you *do* that?"

Lord Ramsgate knelt by his side. "I needed you not to leave."

"I'm going to kill you," Hugh ground out, still panting against the pain. "I'm going to bloody well—"

"No," his father said, pressing a damp, sweet-smelling cloth against his face, "you're not."

Chapter Nineteen

The Duke of York Suite
The White Hart Inn

WHEN HUGH OPENED his eyes, he was in a bed. And his leg hurt like the devil. "What on earth?" he groaned, reaching over to massage the screaming muscle. Except—

Bloody hell! The bastard had tied him down.

"Oh, you're awake." His father's voice. Mild and slightly . . . bored?

"I'm going to kill you," Hugh growled. He twisted against his bindings until he saw his father sitting in a chair in the corner, watching him over a newspaper.

"It's possible," Lord Ramsgate said, "but not today."

Hugh yanked again. And again, but all he got

for his trouble was a chafed wrist and a serious case of vertigo. He shut his eyes for a moment, trying to regain his equilibrium. "What the hell is this about?"

Lord Ramsgate pretended to consider this. "I'm concerned," he finally said.

"About what?" Hugh ground out.

"I fear that you are taking too long with the lovely Lady Sarah. Who knows when we shall next find a woman willing to overlook"—Lord Ramsgate's face wrinkled with distaste—"you."

This insult did not register. Hugh was well used to such barbs and at some point had begun to take pride in them. But his father's comment about taking "too long" left him profoundly uneasy. "I have known Lady Sarah"—*in this incarnation, at least,* he added silently—"for barely two weeks."

"Is that all? It feels like quite a bit longer. A watched pot and all that, I suppose."

Hugh slumped. The world had clearly been turned inside out. His father, who usually ranted and raved while Hugh maintained an aloof disdain, was regarding him with nothing more than raised brows.

Hugh, on the other hand, was ready to spit nails.

"I'd hoped you'd be further along with your courtship by now," Lord Ramsgate said, pausing to turn a page in his newspaper. "When did it all start, again? Oh, yes, that night at Fensmore. With Lady Danbury. God, she's an old bat."

Hugh felt ill. "How do you know this?"

Lord Ramsgate held up his hand and rubbed

his fingers together. "I have people in my employ."

"Who?"

Lord Ramsgate cocked his head, as if he was debating the wisdom of revealing this information. Then he shrugged and said, "Your valet. Might as well tell you. You would have figured it out."

Hugh stared at the ceiling in queasy shock. "He's been with me for two years."

"Anyone can be bribed." The marquess lowered the newspaper and peered over the top. "Have I taught you nothing?"

Hugh took a breath and tried to remain calm. "You need to untie me right now."

"Not yet." Lord Ramsgate picked up the newspaper again. "Oh, bloody hell, this wasn't ironed." He set the paper back down and irritably inspected his hands, now streaked with black ink. "I hate travel."

"I must return to Whipple Hill," Hugh said in as reasonable a voice as he could muster.

"Really?" The marquess smiled blandly. "Because I heard you were leaving."

Hugh's fingers curled into claws. His father was disturbingly well informed.

"I received a note from your valet while you were indisposed," Lord Ramsgate continued. "He wrote that you'd told him to pack your things. This concerns me, I must say."

Hugh yanked against his bonds, but they did not slip even a hairsbreadth. His father clearly knew his knots.

"I hope it won't be much longer." Lord Ramsgate stood, walked over to a small basin, and dunked his hands. He picked up a small white cloth, then looked over his shoulder at Hugh to say, "We're just waiting for the lovely Lady Sarah to arrive."

Hugh gaped at him. "What did you say?"

His father dried his hands with meticulous precision, then pulled out his pocket watch and snapped it open. "Soon, I should think." He glanced over at Hugh with an unnervingly mild expression. "Your man will have informed her by now of your whereabouts."

"Why the bloody hell are you so certain she will come here?" Hugh snarled. But he sounded desperate. He could hear it in his own voice, and it terrified him.

"I'm not," his father replied. "But I'm hopeful." He glanced over at Hugh. "You should be, too. God only knows how long you'll be stuck in that bed if she doesn't."

Hugh shut his eyes and groaned. How on earth had he let his father get the best of him? "What was on that cloth?" he demanded. He still felt dizzy. And tired, as if he'd just run a mile at top speed. No, not that. He wasn't breathless, just—

His lungs felt shallow. Deflated. He didn't know how else to explain it.

Hugh repeated his question, his voice rising with impatience. "What was on that cloth?"

"Eh? Oh, that. Oil of sweet vitriol. Clever stuff, isn't it?"

Hugh blinked against the dots still swimming before his eyes. *Clever* was not quite the word he would have chosen.

"She's not going to come to the White Hart," Hugh said, trying to keep his voice dismissive. Derisive. Anything that might lead his father to doubt the efficacy of his plan.

"Of course she will," Lord Ramsgate said. "She loves you, although God only knows why."

"Your paternal tenderness never ceases to amaze me." Hugh gave his bindings a little yank to further illustrate the point.

"Wouldn't you go to her if she'd run off to an inn?"

"That's completely different," Hugh snapped.

Lord Ramsgate just smiled.

"You do realize that there are countless reasons why this will not work," Hugh said, trying to sound reasonable.

His father glanced over at him.

"It's pouring, for one," Hugh improvised, trying to motion to the window with his head. "She'd have to be mad to go out in this."

"You did."

"You didn't leave me much choice," Hugh said in a tight voice. "And furthermore, Lady Sarah has no reason to worry over my coming here to see you."

"Oh, come now," his father scoffed. "Our mutual distaste is no secret. I daresay everyone knows of it by now."

"Our mutual distaste, yes," Hugh said, aware that his words were spilling too quickly from his lips. "But she does not know how deep the enmity goes."

"You did not tell Lady Sarah of our"—Lord Ramsgate sneered—"contract?"

"Of course not," Hugh lied. "Do you think she'd accept my suit if she knew?"

His father considered that for a moment, then said, "All the more reason to carry out my plan."

"Which is?"

"Ensuring your marriage, of course."

"By tying me to a *bed*?"

His father smiled smugly. "And allowing her to be the one to release you."

"You are mad," Hugh whispered, but to his horror, he felt something stirring in his loins. The thought of Sarah, bending over him, crawling over him to reach the knot around the bedpost . . .

He clamped his eyes shut, trying to think of tortoises, and fisheyes, and the fat vicar in the village where he'd grown up. Anything but Sarah. *Anything* but Sarah.

"I should think you would be grateful," Lord Ramsgate said. "Isn't she what you wanted?"

"Not like this," Hugh ground out.

"I'll have the two of you locked up tight in here for at least an hour," his father continued. "She'll be compromised in full whether you do the deed or not." Lord Ramsgate leaned over and leered. "All will be well. You will get what you want, and I will get what I want."

"What about what *she* wants?"

Lord Ramsgate quirked a brow, then cocked his head to the side, then shrugged. Apparently that would be all the thought he would give to Sarah's hopes and dreams. "She will be grateful," he decided. He started to say something more, but then stopped, tilting his head to better aim his ear toward the door. "I do believe she's arrived," he murmured.

Hugh didn't hear anything, but sure enough, a moment later an insistent knock sounded at the door.

Hugh pulled furiously against his bonds. He wanted Sarah Pleinsworth; dear Lord, he wanted her with everything that he was. He wanted to stand up with her before God and man, slide his ring onto her finger, and pledge his eternal devotion. He wanted to take her to bed and with his body show her everything that was in his heart, and he wanted to cherish her as she grew heavy with their child.

But he would not steal these things from her. She had to want them, as well.

"This is so exciting," Lord Ramsgate said, his mocking tone perfectly calibrated to make Hugh's nerves stand on end. "Dear me, I feel like a school-girl."

"Don't touch her," Hugh snarled. "By God, if you lay a hand on her . . ."

"Now, now," his father said. "Lady Sarah is going to be the mother of my grandsons. I would never dream of causing her injury."

"Don't do this," Hugh said, his voice choking before he could add, *please*. He did not want to beg. He had not thought he could stomach doing so, but in this, *for Sarah*, he would do it. She did not wish to marry him; this much was clear after all that had transpired with Daniel earlier that morning. If she entered the room, Lord Ramsgate would lock her in and seal her fate. Hugh would gain the hand of the woman he loved, but at what cost?

"Father," Hugh said, and their eyes met in shock. Neither could recall the last time Hugh had addressed him as anything other than *"sir."* "I implore you, *do not do this.*"

But Lord Ramsgate just rubbed his hands together with glee and walked to the door. "Who's there?" he called.

Sarah's voice came through the door.

Hugh closed his eyes in anguish. This was going to happen. He couldn't stop it.

"Lady Sarah," Lord Ramsgate said the moment he opened the door. "We've been expecting you."

Hugh turned and forced himself to look at the doorway, but his father was still blocking his view.

"I'm here to see Lord Hugh," Sarah said in as cold a voice as he'd ever heard. "Your son."

"Don't come in, Sarah!" Hugh yelled.

"Hugh?" Her voice rang with panic.

Hugh thrashed against his bindings. He knew he wouldn't break free, but he couldn't just lie there like a bloody lump.

"Oh my God, what have you done to him?" Sarah shrieked, and she pushed past Lord Ramsgate with enough force to knock him into the door frame. She was dripping wet, her hair plastered to her face, the hem of her gown muddied and torn.

"Just getting him ready for you, my dear girl," Lord Ramsgate said with a laugh. And then, before Sarah could utter a word, he stepped out of the room and slammed the door behind him.

"Hugh, what happened?" Sarah asked, rushing to his side. "Oh my God, he tied you to the bed. Why would he do such a thing?"

"The door," Hugh practically barked, jerking his head to the side. "Check the door."

"The door? But—"

"*Do it.*"

Her eyes grew wide, but she did as he asked. "It's locked," she said, twisting back to face him.

Hugh swore viciously under his breath.

"What is going on?" She hurried back to the bed, immediately going to the bindings on one of his ankles. "Why did he tie you to the bed? Why would you come here to see him?"

"When my father issues a summons," Hugh said in a tight voice, "I do not ignore it."

"But you—"

"Especially on the eve of your cousin's wedding."

Her eyes flared with understanding. "Of course."

"As for the bindings," Hugh added in a voice full of loathing, "they were for your benefit."

"What?" she asked, mouth agape. Then: "Oh, drat, ouch!" She stuck her index finger in her mouth. "Bent back my nail," she grumbled. "These knots are monsters. How did he get them so tight?"

"I was not able to struggle," Hugh said, unable to keep the self-loathing from his voice.

Her eyes flew to his face.

But he turned away, unable to look at her when he said, "He did it while I was unconscious."

Her lips formed a whisper, but whether she made actual words or mere sound, he did not know.

"Oil of sweet vitriol," he said in a flat voice.

She shook her head. "I don't know . . ."

"Soaked into a cloth and pressed against a face, it can render a person unconscious," Hugh explained. "I've read about it, but this is the first time I've had the pleasure."

Her head shook; he didn't think she was even aware of the movement. "But why would he *do* such a thing?"

It would have been a sensible question had they been talking about anyone other than Hugh's father. Hugh closed his eyes for a moment, utterly mortified by what he was forced to say. "My father believes that if we are locked in the room together, you will be compromised."

She didn't say a word.

"And thus forced to marry me," Hugh added, not that he thought this had been unclear.

She froze, her eyes never leaving the knot she'd been so diligently trying to release. Hugh felt something heavy and dark settle around his heart.

"I'm not sure why," she finally said. Her voice was slow, and very careful, as if she was worried that the wrong word might set off an avalanche of distasteful events.

Hugh had no idea how to respond to that. They both knew the rules that bound their society. They would be discovered together, in a room with a bed, and Sarah would be presented with two choices: marriage or ruin. And despite everything she had learned about him that morning, Hugh had to think that of the two, he was still the better choice.

"It's not as if you could compromise me while you're tied to a bed," she said, still not looking at him.

Hugh swallowed. His tastes had never run toward such things, but now it was impossible not to think of all the ways one could be compromised while tied to a bed.

She caught her lower lip between her teeth. "Maybe I should just leave you like this," she said.

"Leave me . . . like this?" he choked out.

"Well, yes." She frowned, bringing one hand to her mouth in a worried gesture. "That way when someone arrives, and someone will—Daniel can't have been too far behind me—he will see that nothing could possibly have happened."

"Your cousin knows you're here?"

She nodded. "Honoria insisted upon telling him. But I thought— Your father— I didn't want—" She pushed her wet hair from her eyes. "I thought if I could get here first, I might be able to— I don't know, calm everything down."

Hugh groaned.

"I know," she said, the expression in her eyes matching his grim chuckle precisely. "I wasn't expecting . . ."

" . . . this?" he finished for her, and he would have motioned to himself with a derisive wave of his hand . . . if said hands hadn't been bloody well tied to the bedposts.

"It's going to be ugly when Daniel gets here," Sarah whispered.

Hugh didn't bother to confirm. She knew it was true.

"I know you said that your father will not hurt him, but—" She turned abruptly, her eyes alight with thought. "Would it do any good if I pounded on the door? I could scream for help. If someone arrived before Daniel . . ."

He shook his head. "That will give him precisely what he wants. A witness to your alleged destruction."

"But you're tied to the bed!"

"I don't suppose it has occurred to you that someone might think that *you* tied me."

She gasped.

"Precisely."

She jumped away from the bed as if burned. "But that's— That's—"

He decided *not* to finish her sentence this time.

"Oh, my God."

Hugh tried not to notice the horror in her expression. Bloody hell, if she had not been completely revolted by him after the revelations of that morning, she certainly was now. He let out an uneven breath. "I'll find some way," he said, even though he had no idea how he might keep such a promise. "You won't have to . . . I'll find a way."

Sarah looked up. Her eyes were fixed on the wall, and he could see her face in three-quarter profile. Her expression was stiff, uncomfortable. "If we explain to Daniel . . ." She swallowed, and Hugh followed the slight motion down the soft length of her neck. He'd kissed her there once. More than once. She had tasted of lemons and salt and she had smelled like woman, and he had been so bloody hard for her he'd thought he would embarrass himself.

And now here he was, with his every dream being handed to him on the proverbial platter, and all he could think was that he needed to find a way to prevent it. He could not live with himself if she was forced into marriage, even if it was his most desperate desire.

"I think he will understand," Sarah said haltingly. "And he will not force the issue. I don't want . . ." She looked away, completely now, and he could not see her face. "I don't want anyone to feel obliged . . ."

She did not finish. Hugh nodded, deciding how best to interpret her words. He'd been planning to ask her to marry him; she knew that. Was this her way of hinting that he should not ask? After all this, she still sought to spare him the humiliation.

"Of course not," he finally said. Three meaningless words, spoken just to fill the silence. He had no idea what he was about any longer.

She chewed on her lip again, and he could only stare as her tongue flicked gently out to moisten the spot where her teeth had just been. And just like that, his body was set aflame. It was the most inappropriate reaction imaginable, but he could not stop thinking about taking his tongue and sliding it along her lip, across the spot she was worrying and over to the corner. Then he'd move lower, to the curve of her neck, and—

"Please untie me," he practically croaked.

"But—"

"I can't feel my hands," he said, seizing on the first excuse he could think of. It wasn't remotely true, but his body was leaping to life, and if he did not get free soon, there would be no way to hide his desire.

Sarah hesitated, but only for a moment. She moved toward the head of the bed and got to work on the knot at his right wrist. "Do you think he's right outside the door?" she whispered.

"Undoubtedly."

Her face twisted with disgust. "That's . . ."

"Sick?" he finished for her. "Welcome to my childhood."

He regretted the words the moment he said them. Her eyes filled with pity, and he felt bile rising up his throat. He didn't want her pity, not for his leg, or his childhood, or any of the sodding ways he could not hope to protect her. He just wanted to be a *man*, and he wanted her to know that, to *feel* it. He wanted to hover over her in bed, nothing between them but heat, and he wanted her to know that she had been claimed, that she was his, and no other man would ever know the warm silk of her skin.

But he was a fool. She deserved someone who could protect her, not a cripple who had been so easily bested. Kicked, drugged, and tied to a bed—how could she possibly respect him after this?

"I think I've got this one," she said, yanking hard at the rope. "Hold on, hold on . . . There!"

"One quarter of the way," he said, trying to sound jolly and failing wretchedly.

"Hugh," she said, and he could not tell if this was the precursor to a statement or a question.

And he never found out. There was a terrific commotion in the hall, followed by a grunt of pain and a loud string of expletives.

"Daniel," Sarah said, wincing slightly.

And here I am, Hugh thought miserably, *still tied to the damned bed.*

Chapter Twenty

SARAH BARELY HAD time to look up before the door flew open and the air was rent by the sound of wood ripping and splintering around the useless lock. "Daniel!" she shrieked, and for the life of her, she did not know why she sounded surprised.

"What the *hell*—"

But Daniel's shout was cut off by the Marquess of Ramsgate, who ran in from the hall, hurling himself through the doorway and onto Daniel's back.

"Get off me, you bloody—"

Sarah tried to jump into the fray, but Hugh yanked her back with the hand she had so recently freed. She shook him loose and ran toward her cousin, only to be knocked down by Lord Ramsgate's shoulder as Daniel spun him around, trying to dislodge him from his back.

"Sarah!" Hugh cried out. He was pulling so hard at his remaining bindings that the bed started scooting across the floor.

Sarah scrambled to her feet, but Hugh swung his arm out in a wild arc and caught a fistful of her sodden skirt.

"Let go of me," she ground out, tumbling back onto the bed.

He wrapped his arm around her, his fingers still holding her skirt in a death grip. "Not on your bloody life."

Daniel, meanwhile, had been unable to get Lord Ramsgate off his back and was now slamming him into the wall. "You bloody madman," he grunted. "Get off me."

Sarah grabbed a chunk of her skirt and started pulling in the opposite direction. "He's going to kill your father."

Hugh's eyes met hers with steely disdain. "Let him."

"Oh, you'd like that, wouldn't you? He'd be hanged!"

"Not with only us as witnesses," Hugh shot back.

Sarah gasped and gave her skirt another yank, but Hugh had her in an astonishingly firm grip. She tried to twist out of his grasp, and that was when she saw Daniel's face going terrifyingly periwinkle. "He's choking him!" she screamed, and Hugh must have looked up, because he let go of her skirt so abruptly that Sarah went skidding across the room, barely able to maintain her balance.

"Get off him!" she yelled, grabbing at Lord Ramsgate's shirt. She looked around for something—anything—with which to bash him over the head. The only chair was far too heavy to lift, so with a quick prayer, she balled her hand into a fist and swung hard.

"Ow!" She howled in pain and shook out her fist. No one had told her that punching a man in the face *hurt*.

"Jesus Christ, Sarah!" It was Daniel, gasping for breath and clutching his eye.

She'd punched the wrong man.

"Oh, I'm sorry!" she yelped. But at least she'd set the human tower off balance. Lord Ramsgate had been forced to let go of Daniel's neck as both men tumbled to the floor.

"I'll kill you," Lord Ramsgate growled, scrambling back over to Daniel, who was in no condition to defend himself.

"Stop it," Sarah snapped, stepping hard on Lord Ramsgate's hand. "If you kill him, you kill Hugh."

Lord Ramsgate looked up at her, and she couldn't tell if he was confused or furious.

"I lied," came Hugh's voice from over on the bed. "I did tell her about our bargain."

"Did you stop to think about that?" Sarah demanded. Because she had *had it* with these men. "Did you?" she fairly screamed.

Lord Ramsgate held up his hand—the one that she was not crunching under her boot—in supplication. Slowly, Sarah lifted her weight, not taking her eyes off him until he'd scooted several feet away from Daniel.

"Are you all right?" she asked Daniel perfunctorily. The skin under his eye was turning purple. He was not going to look pretty for his wedding.

He grunted in response.

"Good," she said, deciding that his grunt had sounded healthy enough. And then it occurred to her. "Where are Marcus and Honoria?"

"Somewhere behind me in a carriage," he said furiously. "I rode."

Of course, Sarah thought. She didn't know why it had not occurred to her that he would insist upon riding after her once it was discovered that she'd departed without them.

"I think you broke my hand," Lord Ramsgate whined.

"It's not broken," Sarah said testily. "I would have heard it snap."

From over on the bed, Hugh let out a choke of laughter. Sarah shot him a scowl. This wasn't funny. None of this was funny. And if he couldn't see that, he was not the man she thought he was. Gallows humor only counted when one wasn't *at* actual gallows.

Swiftly, she turned to her cousin. "Do you have a knife?"

Daniel's eyes widened.

"For his *bindings*."

"Oh." Daniel reached into his boot and pulled out a small dagger. She took it with some surprise; she hadn't really thought she'd meet with success.

"I acquired the habit of carrying a weapon in Italy," Daniel said in a flat voice.

Sarah nodded. Of course he would have done.

That was when Lord Ramsgate had had trained assassins hunting him down. "Don't move," she snapped at the marquess, and she stalked across the room to Hugh.

"I would recommend that you not move, either," she said, and she walked around to the far side of the bed to saw through the rope that immobilized his left hand. She was about halfway through the fibers when she saw Lord Ramsgate begin to rise to his feet. "Eh eh eh!" she screeched, pointing the knife in his direction. "Back on the floor."

He complied.

"You're terrifying me," Hugh murmured. But it sounded like a compliment.

"You could have been killed," she hissed.

"No," he told her, his eyes serious. "I'm the only one he would never touch, remember?"

Her lips parted, but whatever she was going to say evaporated as her mind began to spin.

"Sarah?" Hugh sounded concerned.

He wasn't the only one, she realized. *He wasn't the only one.*

The last bit of rope snapped, and Hugh pulled his arm to his side, groaning as he massaged his overstretched shoulder.

"You can do your ankles," Sarah said, just barely remembering to turn the handle out as she gave him the knife. She marched back over to Lord Ramsgate. "Stand up," she ordered.

"You just told me to sit down," he drawled.

Her voice fell to a menacing growl. "You do not want to argue with me right now."

"Sarah," Hugh ventured.

"Quiet," she snapped, not even bothering to turn around. Lord Ramsgate rose to his feet, and Sarah stepped forward until he was backed against the wall. "I want you to listen to me very closely, Lord Ramsgate, because I am only going to say this once. I will marry your son, and in return, you will swear to me that you will leave my cousin alone."

Lord Ramsgate opened his mouth to speak, but Sarah was not yet done. "Furthermore," she said before he could make more than a syllable of sound, "you will not attempt to contact me or any member of my family, and that includes Lord Hugh and any children we might have."

"Now see here—"

"*Do* you want me to marry him?" Sarah cut in loudly.

Lord Ramsgate's face went red with rage. "Who do you think—"

"Hugh?" she said, holding her hand behind her. "The knife?"

He must have freed his feet, because when he spoke, he was a lot closer than the bed. She turned to look; he was standing a few feet behind her. He said, "I'm not sure that's a good idea, Sarah."

He was probably right, blast him. She had no idea what devil had overtaken her, but she was so bloody angry right now that she had half a mind to strangle Lord Ramsgate with her bare hands.

"You wanted an heir?" Sarah growled at the marquess. "Fine. I'll give you one or I'll die trying."

Hugh cleared his throat, presumably trying to

remind her that this whole cockup of a day had started with *his* predicted demise.

"Not a word out of you, either," she said furiously, swinging around with an irately pointed finger. He was standing just a few feet away, his cane lightly gripped in his hand. "I am sick of you and you and him"—she jerked her head toward Daniel, who was still sitting against the wall, clutching his rapidly blackening eye—"trying to solve things. You're useless, the lot of you. It's been over three years, and the only way *you've* managed to keep peace is by threatening to kill yourself." She swung back around to face Hugh, and her eyes narrowed dangerously. "Which you will not do."

Hugh stared at her until he realized he was supposed to speak. "I will not," he said.

"Lady Sarah," Lord Ramsgate said, "I must tell you—"

"Shut up," she snapped. "I have been told, Lord Ramsgate, that you are desirous of an heir. Or should I say an heir beyond the two you already possess."

The marquess gave a terse nod.

"And, in fact, you are so desirous of this heir that Lord Hugh was able to bargain for my cousin's safety with his own life."

"It was an unholy bargain," Lord Ramsgate spat.

"In that we are in agreement," Sarah said, "but I believe you have forgotten an important detail. If, indeed, all you care about is procreation, Lord Hugh's life is worthless without mine."

"Oh, so now you're going to tell me that you are also going to threaten suicide."

"Nothing of the sort," Sarah said with a derisive snort. "But think for a moment, Lord Ramsgate. The only way you can get your precious grandchild is if your son and I remain in good health and happiness. And let me tell you, if you make me unhappy in any manner, I will bar him from my bed."

There was a highly satisfying lurch of silence.

Lord Ramsgate scoffed. "He will be your lord and master. You can't bar him from anywhere."

Hugh cleared his throat. "I wouldn't dream of violating her wishes," he murmured.

"You worthless excuse—"

"You're making me unhappy, Lord Ramsgate," Sarah warned.

Lord Ramsgate let out a furious breath, and Sarah knew she had bested him. "If any permanent harm should ever come to my cousin," she warned, "I swear I will hunt you down and rip you apart with my bare hands."

"I would take her at her word," Daniel said, still gently palpating the skin around his eye.

Sarah crossed her arms. "Do we all understand these terms?"

"I certainly do," Daniel mumbled.

Sarah ignored him, instead stepping closer to Lord Ramsgate. "I am certain you will see that it is a most beneficial solution for all involved parties. You will get what you want—an eventual heir for Ramsgate—and I will get what I want: peace for my family. And Hugh—" Her words came to an abrupt halt as she forced down the bile that threatened her throat. "Well, Hugh doesn't have to kill himself."

Lord Ramsgate held himself preternaturally still. Finally, he said, "If you agree to marry my son and you do not bar him from your bed—and I hope you will trust me when I tell you that I will have spies in your household and I *will* know if you are not fulfilling your end of the bargain—then I will leave your cousin alone."

"Forever," Sarah added.

Lord Ramsgate gave a quick, bitter nod.

"And you will not attempt to contact my children."

"I cannot agree to that."

"Very well," she acquiesced, since she never expected to win on that point, "I will allow you to see them, but only in my or their father's presence, and at a time and place of our choosing."

Lord Ramsgate shook with rage, but he said, "You have my word."

Sarah turned and looked to Hugh for confirmation.

"On this you can trust him," Hugh said quietly. "For all his cruelty, he does not break his promises."

Then Daniel said, "I have not known him to lie."

Sarah gaped at him.

"He said he was going to try to kill me and he did," Daniel said. "Try, that is."

Sarah's mouth fell open. "This is your endorsement?"

Daniel shrugged. "Then he said he *wouldn't* try to kill me, and as far as I know, he didn't."

"How hard did you hit him?" Hugh asked.

Sarah looked down at her hand. Her knuckles were turning purple. Good Lord, and his wedding was in two days. Anne would never forgive her.

"It was worth it," Daniel said, one of his hands making a loopy wave near his face. His head tilted drunkenly to the side as he quirked a brow toward Hugh. "She did it," he said. "What you and I were never able to manage."

"And all she had to do was sacrifice herself," Lord Ramsgate said with an oily smile.

"I'm going to kill you," Hugh growled, and Sarah had to step in front of him and forcibly hold him back.

"Go back to London," Sarah ordered the marquess. "I will see you at the christening of our first child, and not a moment before."

Lord Ramsgate just chuckled.

"Are we clear?" she demanded.

"As water, my dear lady." Lord Ramsgate walked to the door, then turned around. "If you had been born sooner," he said with an intense stare, "I would have married you."

"You *bastard*!"

Sarah was pushed to the side as Hugh launched himself toward his father. Fist met flesh with a horrible crack. "You are not fit to speak her name," Hugh hissed, looming menacingly over his father, who had fallen to the floor, his nose bloodied and almost certainly broken.

"And you're the better of the two," Lord Ramsgate said with a little shiver of revulsion. "God above, I do not know what I did to deserve such sons."

"Nor do I," Hugh bit off.

"Hugh," Sarah said, laying her hand on his upper arm. "Get off. He's not worth it."

But Hugh was not himself. He did not pull his arm away, nor did he give any indication that he'd heard her. He leaned down and retrieved his cane, which had clattered to the floor in the fracas, never once taking his eyes from his father's face.

"If you touch her," Hugh said, his voice terrifyingly clipped and even, "I will kill you. If you speak one untoward word, I will kill you. If you so much as *breathe* in the wrong direction, I—"

"Will kill me," his father said scornfully. He jerked his head toward Hugh's bad leg. "You just go on thinking you're able, you stupid little cr—"

Hugh moved like lightning, his cane arcing before him like a sword. He was beautiful in motion, Sarah thought. Was this what he had been like . . . before?

"Would you care to repeat that?" Hugh said, pressing the tip of his cane against his father's throat.

Sarah stopped breathing.

"Please," Hugh said, in a tone that was all the more devastating for its calm. "Say more." He moved the cane along Lord Ramsgate's windpipe, easing the pressure without breaking contact. "Anything?" he murmured.

Sarah wet her lips, watching him warily. She

could not tell if he was the epitome of control or whether he was one breath away from snapping. She watched his chest rise and fall with his heartbeat, and she was mesmerized. Hugh Prentice was more than a man in that moment; he was a force of nature.

"Let him go," Daniel said in a weary voice, finally rising to his feet. "He is not worth a trip to the gallows."

Sarah stared at the tip of the cane, still flush with Lord Ramsgate's throat. It seemed to press forward, and she thought, *No, he wouldn't* . . . and then, quick as mercury, the cane flew away, leaving Hugh's grip for a split second before he caught it again and stepped away. He was favoring his injured leg, but there was something dashing about his uneven gait, something almost graceful.

He was still beautiful in motion. One had only to look.

Sarah felt herself exhale. She wasn't certain when she had last drawn breath. She watched in silence as Lord Ramsgate pulled himself to his feet and left the room. And then she stared at the open doorway, half expecting him to return.

"Sarah?"

Dimly, she registered Hugh's voice. But she couldn't tear her eyes from the doorway, and she was shaking . . . her hands were shaking, and maybe her whole body was shaking.

"Sarah, are you all right?"

No. She wasn't.

"Let me help you."

She felt Hugh's arm on her shoulder, and suddenly the shaking intensified, and her legs . . . What was happening to her legs? There was an awful, wrenching noise, and when she gasped for breath, she realized that it had come from her, and then suddenly she was in his arms, and he was carrying her to the bed.

"It's all right," he said. "Everything will be all right."

But Sarah was no fool. And she didn't feel all right.

Chapter Twenty-one

Whipple Hill
Later that evening

Hugh's hand hovered in the air for a long moment before connecting with the door in a crisp knock. He wasn't sure what sort of shuffle had taken place among the guests, but Sarah had been moved to a room of her own upon their return to Whipple Hill. Honoria, who had arrived at the White Hart with Marcus shortly after Lord Ramsgate had departed, had set it about that Sarah had reinjured her ankle and needed to rest. If anyone was curious as to why she could not do so in the room she'd been sharing with Harriet, they had not said anything. Probably no one had even noticed.

Hugh had no idea how Daniel was explaining the black eye.

"Enter!" It was Honoria's voice. This was not a surprise; she had not left Sarah's side since they'd returned.

"Am I interrupting?" Hugh asked, taking just two steps into the room.

"No," Honoria said, but he did not see her turn to face him. He could only stare at Sarah, who was sitting up in bed, a mountain of pillows propped behind her back. She was wearing the same white nightgown as—dear God, could that have been just the night before?

"You shouldn't be here," Honoria said.

"I know." But he made no move to leave.

Sarah's tongue darted out to moisten her lips. "We are betrothed now, Honoria."

Honoria's brows rose. "I know as well as anyone that that does not mean he should be in your bedroom."

Hugh held Sarah's gaze. This would have to be her decision. He would not force it.

"It has been a most uncommon day," Sarah said quietly. "This would hardly be the most scandalous moment of it."

She sounded exhausted. Hugh had held her the entire ride home, until her sobs had given way to a gut-wrenching stillness. When he'd looked into her eyes, they had been blank.

Shock. He knew it well.

But she looked more like herself now. If not better, then at least improved.

"Please," he said, directing the single word to her cousin.

Honoria hesitated for a moment, then stood.

"Very well," she acquiesced, "but I will return in ten minutes."

"An hour," Sarah said.

"But—"

"What is the worst that could happen?" Sarah asked with an incredulous expression. "We could be forced to marry? That's already been taken care of."

"That's not the point."

"Then what is the point?"

Honoria's mouth opened and closed as she looked from Sarah to Hugh and back. "I'm supposed to be your chaperone."

"I don't believe that exact word crossed my mother's lips when she was here earlier."

"Where *is* your mother?" Hugh asked. Not that he was planning to make any untoward advances, but as long as he was going to be alone with Sarah for the next hour, it did seem a good fact to know.

"Supper," Sarah replied.

Hugh pinched the bridge of his nose. "Lud, is it that late?"

"Daniel told us that you took a nap, too," Honoria said with gentle smile.

Hugh gave a tiny nod. Or maybe it was a shake. Or an eye roll. He was turned so inside out he couldn't even be sure. He had wanted to stay with Sarah when they'd got back to Whipple Hill, but even he had known that such a liberty would not be tolerated by her cousins. And more to the point, he had been so exhausted himself that it had been all he could do to climb the stairs and crawl into his own bed.

"They're not expecting you," Honoria added. "Daniel said ... er, I don't know what he said, but he's always been good at credible excuses for such things."

"And his eye?" Hugh asked.

"He said that he had a blackened eye when he met Anne, so it was only fitting that he'd have one when he married her."

Hugh blinked. "And Anne was all right with this?"

"I can honestly say that I have no idea," Honoria said in a prim voice.

Sarah snorted and rolled her eyes.

"But," Honoria continued, her smile sneaking back onto her face as she rose to her feet, "I can also honestly say that I am very glad I was not present when she saw him."

Hugh moved to the side as Honoria made her way to the door. "One hour," she said. She paused before stepping into the hall. "You should lock the door."

Hugh started in surprise. "I beg your pardon?"

Honoria swallowed uncomfortably, and her cheeks took on a telltale blush. "It will be assumed that Sarah is resting and does not wish to be disturbed."

Hugh could only stare at her in shock. Was she giving him permission to ravish her cousin?

It took but a moment for Honoria to realize where his thoughts had led him. "I did not mean— Oh, for heaven's sake. It's not as if either of you is in a state to *do* anything."

Hugh glanced over at Sarah. Her mouth was hanging open.

"You don't want anyone walking in while you're alone," Honoria said, her skin now on hue with a slightly unripe strawberry. She narrowed her eyes at Hugh. "You'll just be sitting in the chair, but still."

Hugh cleared his throat. "Still."

"It would be highly improper," she said, followed by: "I'm leaving now." She hurried from the room.

Hugh turned back to Sarah. "That was awkward."

"You'd best lock the door," Sarah said. "After all that."

He reached out and turned the key. "Indeed."

With Honoria gone, however, they had no buffer upon which to rely for a sense of normalcy, and Hugh found himself standing near the door like a badly posed statue, unable to decide where to take his feet.

"What did you mean," Sarah blurted out, "when you said 'there are men who hurt women'?"

He felt his brow furrow. "I'm sorry. I don't know—"

"Last night," she interrupted, "when you found me, you were so upset, and you said something about men who hurt people, men who hurt *women*."

His lips parted and his throat closed, choking any words that might have formed there. How could she not have understood his meaning? Surely she wasn't *so* innocent. She had led a sheltered life, but she had to know what went on between a man and a woman.

"Sometimes"—he began slowly, for this was not a conversation he'd ever anticipated—"a man can—"

"Please," she cut in. "I know that men hurt women; they do it every day."

Hugh wanted to flinch. He wished that her statement had been shocking, but it wasn't. It was merely the truth.

"You were not speaking generally," she said. "You may have thought you were, but you weren't. Who were you talking about?"

Hugh went very still, and when he finally spoke, he did not look at Sarah. "It was my mother," he said, very quietly. "Surely you have realized that my father is not a kind man."

"I'm sorry," she said.

"He hurt her in *bed*," Hugh said, and suddenly he did not feel quite right. His neck cricked, and he jerked it to one side, trying to shake off the weight of his memories. "He never hurt her out of bed. Only in." He swallowed. Took a breath. "At night I could hear her cries."

Sarah didn't speak. He was very grateful for that.

"I never saw anything," Hugh said. "If he marked her, he was always careful to do it where it would not show. She never limped, she never bruised. But"—he looked up at Sarah; he finally looked up at Sarah—"I could see it in her eyes."

"I'm sorry," Sarah said again, but there was something wary in her expression, and after a moment she looked away.

Hugh watched as she tucked her chin against

her shoulder, shadows flickering across her throat as she swallowed. He'd never seen her so uncomfortable, so ill-at-ease.

"Sarah," he began, and then he cursed himself for an idiot, because she looked up, expecting more, and he had no idea what he ought to say. His mouth hung wordlessly slack, and she let her eyes fall back down to her lap, where her hands were nervously picking at her bedsheets.

"Sarah, I would—" he blurted out. And what? *What?* Why couldn't he finish a bloody sentence?

She looked up, again waiting for him to continue.

"I would never . . . do that." The words choked forth from his throat, but he had to say it. He had to make sure she understood. He was not his father. He would never be that man.

She shook her head, the motion so tiny he nearly missed it.

"Hurt you," he said. "I would never hurt you. I could never—"

"I know," she said, blessedly cutting off his awkward avowals. "You would never . . . You don't even need to say it."

He nodded, turning sharply away when he heard himself draw a short, tortured breath. It was the sort of sound one made right before losing oneself completely, and he couldn't—after everything that had happened that day—

He could not go there. Not now. So he shrugged, as if an insouciant motion could flick it all away. But all it seemed to do was intensify the silence. And Hugh found himself in the same position he'd been in before she had asked about his mother, frozen near the door, not knowing what to do with himself.

"Did you sleep?" Sarah finally asked.

He nodded and found the momentum to move forward and settle into the chair Honoria had vacated. He hooked his cane over the arm and turned to look at her. "And you?"

"I did. I was overset. No, I was overcome." She tried to smile, and he could see that she was embarrassed.

"It's all right," he started to say.

"No," she blurted out, "it's not, really. I mean, it will be, but—" She blinked like a cornered rabbit, then said, "I was so tired. I don't think I've ever been so tired."

"It's understandable."

She stared for a long moment, then said, "I don't know what came over me."

"I don't either," he admitted, "but I'm glad it did."

She did not speak for several seconds. "You have to marry me now."

"I had been planning to ask," he reminded her.

"I know"—she picked at the hem of her bedsheet—"but no one likes to be forced."

He reached out and grasped her hand. "I know."

"I—"

"*You* were forced," he said vehemently. "It is not fair, and if you wish to withdraw—"

"No!" She drew back, looking surprised by her outburst. "That is to say, no, I don't wish to withdraw. I can't really."

"You can't," he echoed, his voice dull.

"Well, *no*," she said, eyes flashing with impatience. "Were you even listening today?"

"What I heard," he said with what he hoped was adequate patience, "was a woman sacrificing herself."

"And that's not what you did?" she shot back. "When you went to your father and threatened to kill yourself?"

"You can't compare the two. I caused this whole bloody mess. It is incumbent upon me to fix it."

"You're angry because you've been *usurped*?"

"No! For the love of—" He raked his hand through his hair. "Don't put words in my mouth."

"I would not dream of it. You're doing quite a job of it on your own."

"You should not have come to the White Hart," he said in a very low voice.

"I'm not even going to dignify that with a reply."

"You did not know what sort of dangers awaited you."

She snorted. "Apparently neither did you!"

"My God, woman, must you be so stubborn? Don't you understand? I cannot protect you!"

"I didn't ask you to."

"I am to be your husband," he said, each word slicing his throat on the way to his lips. "It is my duty."

Her teeth were clenched so tightly that her chin was shaking. "Do you know," she ground out, "that since this afternoon, no one—not you, not your father, not even my cousin—has *thanked* me?"

Hugh's eyes flew to hers.

"No, don't say it now," she snapped. "Do you think I could possibly believe you? I went to the inn because I was so scared, because you and Daniel had painted a picture of a madman, and all I could think was that he was going to hurt you—"

"But—"

"*Don't* say that he would never hurt you. That man is stark raving mad. He would cut off your arm as long as he was assured you could still sire children."

Hugh blanched. He knew it was true, but he hated that she even had to think about it. "Sarah, I—"

"No." She jabbed her index finger toward him. "This is my turn. I'm speaking. *You're* being quiet."

"Forgive me," he said, so softly the words were but a whisper on his lips.

"No," she said, shaking her head as if she'd just seen a ghost. "You don't get to be nice now. You can't beg my forgiveness and expect me to . . . to . . ." Her throat convulsed with a choking sob. "Do you understand what you've put me through? In one single day?"

The tears were running freely down her cheeks, and it took all of Hugh's strength not to lean forward and kiss them away. He wanted to beg her not to cry, to apologize for this moment, and for the future, because he knew it would happen again. He could devote his life to one of her smiles, but at some point he would fail, and he would make her cry again, and it would wreck him.

He took her hand and pressed it to his lips. "Please don't cry," he begged.

"I'm not," she gasped, swiping away her tears with her sleeve.

"Sarah . . ."

"I'm not crying!" she sobbed.

He didn't argue. Instead, he sat beside her on the bed, and he held her and stroked her hair, and murmured nonsensical sounds of comfort until she sagged next to him, utterly spent.

"I can't imagine what you think of me," she finally whispered.

"I think," he said with every ounce of his soul, "that you are magnificent."

And that he did not deserve her.

She had come and saved the day; she had bloody well done what he and Daniel had not managed in nearly four years, and she'd done it while Hugh had been tied to a damned bed. Perhaps not at the exact moment of her triumph, but if he'd been freed, it was only because *she* had been the one to do it.

She had saved *him*. And while he understood that the circumstances of this particular situation were unique, it clawed at him that he would never be able to protect her as a husband was meant to protect his wife.

This was where any man worth his salt would step aside and allow her to marry someone else, someone better.

Someone whole.

Except that any man worth his salt wouldn't have been in this situation to begin with. Hugh had caused this debacle. He had been the one to get drunk and challenge an innocent man to a duel. He was the one with a bat-crazy father who required a threat of suicide to get him to leave Daniel alone. But Sarah was the one who was paying the price. And Hugh—even if he was that man worth his salt—couldn't possibly step aside. Because to do so would be to put Daniel in peril. And Sarah would be mortified.

And Hugh loved her too much to ever let her go.

I'm a selfish bastard.

"What?" Sarah murmured, not moving her head from the cradle of his chest.

Had he said that aloud?

"Hugh?" She shifted her position, her chin rising so that she could see his face.

"I can't let you go," he whispered.

"What are you talking about?" She moved again, pulling away, just enough so that she could look into his eyes.

She was frowning. He did not want to make her frown.

"I can't let you go," he said again, shaking his head in a slow, tiny motion.

"We're getting married," she said. Cautiously, like she wasn't sure why she was saying it. "You don't have to let me go."

"I should. I can't be the man you need."

She touched his cheek. "Isn't that for me to decide?"

He took a deep, shuddering breath, closing his eyes against the awfulness of memory. "I hate that you had to see my father today."

"I hate it, too, but it's done."

He stared at her in amazement. When had she become so calm? Not five minutes earlier, she had been sobbing and he had been soothing her, and now she was clear-eyed, watching him with such peace and wisdom he could almost believe that their future was bright and uncomplicated.

"Thank you," he said.

She tilted her head to the side.

"For today. For so much more than today, but for now I'll stick with today."

"I—" Her mouth hung open in an indecisive oval, and then she said, "It seems a very strange thing about which to say, *You're welcome.*"

He searched her face, although for what he was not certain. Perhaps he just wanted to look at her, at the deep chocolate warmth of her eyes and her wide, lush mouth that understood so well how to smile. He looked at her in amazement, and in wonder, as he recalled the fierce warrior of that afternoon. If she defended him so well, he could not imagine how she might be as a mother, with her own flesh and blood to protect.

"I love you," he said, the words tumbling from his lips. He was not sure he'd meant to say them, but now he could not stop. "I don't deserve you, but I love you, and I know you never thought to marry someone under such circumstances, but I vow that I will devote the rest of my life toward your happiness."

He took her hands to his lips and kissed them fervently, nearly undone by the force of his emotions. "Sarah Pleinsworth," he said, "will you marry me?"

Tears glistened on her lashes, and her lips quivered as she said, "We already—"

"But I did not ask you," he cut in. "You deserve to be asked. I don't have a ring, but I can get one later, and—"

"I don't need a ring," she blurted out. "I just need you."

He touched her cheek, his hand softly caressing her skin, and then—

He kissed her. It came without thought—this urge, this hunger. His hand sank into the thick tumble of her hair as his lips devoured hers.

"Wait!" she gasped.

He pulled back, but just an inch.

"I love you, too," she whispered. "You didn't give me a chance to say it."

If he had had any hope of controlling his desire, it was lost in that moment. He kissed her mouth, her ear, her throat, and when she was on her back and he was over her, he took the delicate tie that held her gown together between his teeth and pulled open the knot.

She laughed, a throaty, wonderful sound that nevertheless startled him in so heated a moment.

"It was so easily undone," she said with a helpless smile. "I could not help but compare it to your father's knots this morning. And we're in bed, too!"

He couldn't help but grin, even though bed was the last place he ever wanted to think about his father.

"I'm sorry," she said with a giggle. "I couldn't help it."

"I wouldn't love you so well if you could," he teased.

"What does that mean?"

"Just that you have a marvelous ability to find humor in the most unexpected of places."

She touched his nose. "I found humor in *you*."

"Precisely."

Her lips came together in a rather satisfied smile. "I think— Oh!"

Clearly, she had just noticed his hand sliding up her leg.

"You were saying?" he murmured.

She made a delightful little noise when he found the soft flesh of her thigh, then said in a breathy voice, "I was going to say that I think we should not have a lengthy engagement."

His hand crept higher. "Really?"

"For the sake of . . . Daniel . . . of course, and— Hugh!"

"Definitely for my sake," he said, taking her earlobe lightly between his teeth. But he rather thought her exclamation had a bit more to do with the soft heat he had just discovered between her legs.

"We need to show that we mean to keep our side of the bargain," she said, her words punctuated by soft squeals and moans.

"Mmmm-hmmm." He let his lips trail softly down her neck as he pondered the wisdom of sliding one finger into her. He had just enough presence of mind to estimate that they had about thirty minutes before her cousin returned, certainly not enough time to properly make love to her.

But it was more than enough time to give her pleasure.

"Sarah?" he murmured.

"Yes?"

He touched his fingers to her core.

"Hugh!"

He smiled against her skin as he slid one finger into her heat. Her body jerked, but not away from him, and even as he began to move within her, his thumb found her most sensitive spot, pressing lightly on the nub before beginning a slow spiral of pressure.

"What is this . . . I didn't . . ."

She wasn't making any sense, and he didn't want her to. He just wanted her to feel the pleasure of his touch, to know that he *worshipped* her. "Relax," he murmured.

"Impossible."

He chuckled. He had no idea how he was keeping his own urges in check. He was rock hard but still in control. Maybe it was because his breeches were doing a fine job of holding him back; maybe it was because he knew that this was not the time or the place.

But he thought . . . No, he knew it was because he just wanted to please *her*.

Sarah.

His Sarah.

He wanted to watch her face when she climaxed. He wanted to hold her as she came shuddering down from heaven. Anything he desired could wait. This was for her.

But when it happened, and he watched her face

and held her while her body sang with bliss, he realized that it had been for him, too.

"Your cousin will be back soon," he said once her breathing had returned to normal.

"But you locked the door," she said, not bothering to open her eyes.

He smiled down at her. She was adorable when she was sleepy. "You know I have to leave."

"I know." She opened one eye. "But I don't have to like it."

"I would be most grievously wounded if you did." He slid from the bed, grateful that he was still fully dressed, and retrieved his cane. "I will see you tomorrow," he said, leaning over to drop one last kiss on her cheek. Then, before he could fall back into temptation, he crossed the room to the door.

"Oh, Hugh?"

He turned to see her smiling like a cat with cream. "Yes, my love?"

"I said I didn't need a ring."

He quirked a brow.

"I do." She wiggled her fingers. "Need a ring. Just so you know."

He threw back his head and laughed.

Chapter Twenty-two

Even later that evening
Technically the next day
But only just

THE HOUSE WAS very quiet as Sarah tiptoed through the night-dark hallways. She had not grown up at Whipple Hill, but if she added all of her visits together, she was certain it would come to more than a year.

It would not be hyperbole to say that she knew the house like the back of her hand.

You could never know a house like the ones you roamed as a child. Hide-and-seek had ensured that she knew every connecting door and every back staircase. But most importantly, it meant that when someone had mentioned to her several days earlier that Lord Hugh Prentice had been given the north green bedroom, she knew precisely what that meant.

And how best to get there.

When Hugh had left her room that evening, just five minutes before Honoria had returned, Sarah had thought that she would fall into a lazy, luxurious sleep. She was not sure she understood what exactly he'd done to her body, but she'd found it quite impossible to lift even a finger for some time after he left. She felt so . . . sated.

But despite her utter physical contentment, she did not sleep. Perhaps it was due to all the napping she'd done earlier, perhaps it was a casualty of an overactive mind (she did have a lot to think about, after all), but by the time her mantel clock read one in the morning, she had to accept that she would not be sleeping that night.

This should have frustrated her—she was not one who did well when overtired—and she did not want to be cranky at breakfast. But instead, all she could think was that this extra period of wakefulness was a gift, or at least she ought to consider it as such.

And gifts should never be squandered.

Which was why, at one-oh-nine in the morning, she wrapped her fingers around the handle of the door to the north green bedroom, carefully applied pressure until she felt the mechanism click, and allowed the door to swing open on its thankfully silent hinges.

With very careful movements, she closed the door behind her, turned the key in the lock, and tiptoed toward the bed. A pale shaft of moonlight striped across the carpet, providing just enough light for her to make out Hugh's sleeping form.

She smiled. It wasn't a large bed, but it was large enough.

He was splayed more toward the right side of the mattress, so she padded around to the left, took a small breath of courage, and climbed in. Slowly, carefully, she inched toward him until she was close enough to feel the heat that rose off his body. She moved even closer, lightly placing her hand on his back, which she was delighted to discover was bare. . . .

He came awake with a start, making such a funny snorting sound that she couldn't help but giggle.

"Sarah?"

She smiled flirtatiously, even though he probably couldn't see her in the darkness. "Good evening."

"What are you doing here?" he asked groggily.

"Are you complaining?"

There was a beat of silence. And then, in a husky timbre she recognized from earlier that evening: "No."

"I missed you," she whispered.

"Apparently."

She poked his chest even though she'd heard the smile in his voice. "You're supposed to say that you missed me, too."

His arms came around her, and before she could say a word, he'd pulled her on top of him, his hands lightly cupping her bottom through her nightgown. "I missed you, too," he said.

Softly, she kissed his lips. "I'm going to marry you," she said with a goofy smile.

He returned the expression, then rolled them both so they were on their sides, facing one another.

"I'm going to marry you," she said again. "I really like saying that, you know."

"I could listen all day."

"But the thing is . . ." She let her head rest on her arm and slowly reached out her foot, letting her toes run lightly along one of his legs, which, she was delighted to note, were also quite bare. "I just can't seem to summon the moral rectitude required of a woman in my position."

"An interesting choice of words, considering your current position in my bed."

"As I was saying, I *am* going to marry you."

His hand found the curve of her hip, and the hem of her nightgown began to travel up her leg as his fingers slowly bunched the fabric.

"It will be a short engagement."

"Very short," he agreed.

"So short, in fact, that—" She gasped; he'd managed to get her nightgown all the way up to her waist, and now his hand was squeezing her bottom in the most delightful manner.

"You were saying?" he murmured, one of his fingers straying wickedly toward the very spot it had pleasured earlier that evening.

"Just that . . . maybe . . ." She tried to breathe, but with everything he was doing to her, she wasn't so sure she remembered how. "It wouldn't be so very naughty if we got a bit ahead of our vows."

He pulled her closer. "Oh, it will be naughty. It will be very naughty."

She smiled. "You're terrible."

"May I remind you that you were the one to sneak into my bed?"

"May I remind you that I'm a monster of *your* making?"

"A monster, eh?"

"An expression of speech." She kissed him, softly, at the corner of his mouth. "I didn't know I could feel this way."

"Neither did I," he admitted.

She stilled. Surely he wasn't saying that he'd never done this before. "Hugh? This isn't . . . Is this your first time?"

He smiled as he drew her into his arms and rolled her onto her back. "No," he said quietly, "but it might as well be. With you, it's all new." And then, while she was still reeling from the beauty of that statement, he kissed her deeply.

"I love you," he said, his words almost lost against her mouth. "I love you so much."

She wanted to return the sentiment, she wanted to whisper her own love against his skin, but her nightgown seemed to have melted away, and the moment his body touched hers, skin to skin in full, she was insensible.

"Can you feel how much I want you?" he said, his lips moving along her cheek to her temple. He pushed his hips against hers, the hard length of him pressing relentlessly against her belly. "Every night," he groaned. "Every night I have dreamed of you, and every night I have been like this, with no release. But tonight"—his mouth made a slow, wicked trail down her neck—"it will be different."

"Yes," she sighed, arching beneath him. He was cupping her breasts, plumping them in his hands. Then he licked his lips . . .

She nearly came off the bed when he took her into his mouth. "Oh my oh my oh my oh my," she gasped, clutching at the sheets beneath her for purchase. She'd barely given thought to this part of her body before. They looked nice in a dress, and she'd been warned that men liked to look at them, but heaven above, no one had told her that her breasts could feel such pleasure.

"I had a feeling you'd like that," he said with a satisfied grin.

"Why do I feel it . . . everywhere?"

"Everywhere?" he murmured. His fingers moved between her legs. "Or here?"

"Everywhere," she said breathlessly, "but there most of all."

"I really can't be sure," he said in a teasing voice. "We shall have to investigate the matter, don't you think?"

"Wait," she said, placing a hand on his arm.

He gazed down at her, his brows rising in question.

"I want to touch you," she said shyly.

She saw the instant he understood what she meant. "Sarah," he said hoarsely, "that might not be such a good idea."

"Please."

He drew a ragged breath as he took her hand and slowly led her down his body. She watched his face as she drifted past his ribs, his abdomen . . . He almost looked as if he was in pain. His eyes closed, and when her fingers reached the smooth, taut skin of his manhood, he groaned audibly, his breath coming in shorter, hotter gasps.

"Am I hurting you?" she whispered. It wasn't at all what she'd expected. She knew what went on between a man and a woman; she had more older cousins than she could count, and several were quite indiscreet. But she had not expected him to be quite so . . . solid. His skin was soft and smooth as velvet, but underneath . . .

She wrapped her hand around him, so intent on her exploration that she did not even notice the indrawn breath that shook his body.

Underneath, he was hard as stone.

"Is it always like this?" she asked. Because it didn't seem comfortable, and she could not imagine how men fit it into their breeches.

"No," he rasped. "It . . . changes. With desire."

She thought about that, her fingers continuing to stroke him until his hand closed over hers and pulled it away.

She looked up at him apprehensively. Had she displeased him in some way?

"It's too much," he said raggedly. "I can't hold out . . ."

"Then don't," she whispered.

He shuddered as his lips rejoined hers, nipping and teasing. His movements, once languid and seductive, grew hot and needy, and she gasped as his hands splayed over her thighs and pushed them apart.

"I can't wait any longer," he growled, and she felt him at her entrance. "Please tell me you're ready."

"I-I think so," she whispered. She knew she wanted something. When he'd pressed his fingers into her earlier, it had been the most amazingly intimate sensation, but his member was so much larger.

His hand snaked between their bodies and touched her the same way he had before, although not as deeply. "My God, you're so wet," he groaned, and then he pulled his hand away, bracing himself above her. "I'll try to be gentle," he promised, and then his manhood was back, slowly pushing forward.

Sarah's breath caught, and she tensed as the friction increased. It hurt. Not a lot, but enough to dampen the fire that had been burning within her.

"Are you all right?" he asked anxiously.

She nodded.

"Don't lie."

"I'm almost all right." She gave him a weak smile. "Really."

He started to withdraw. "We shouldn't have—"

"No!" She wrapped her arms tightly around him. "Don't go."

"But you—"

"Everyone tells me it hurts the first time," she said reassuringly.

"Everyone?" He managed a shaky smile. "Who have you been talking to?"

A nervous bubble of laughter crossed her lips.

"I have a great many cousins. *Not* Honoria," she said quickly, because she could see that was what he was thinking. "Some of the older ones like to talk. Quite a bit."

He braced himself above her, leaning on his forearms so as not to crush her with his weight. But he didn't say anything. From the look of intense concentration on his face, she was not sure that he could.

"But then it gets better," she murmured. "That's what they say. If your husband is kind, it gets much better."

"I'm not your husband," he said in a hoarse voice.

She sank one of her hands in his thick hair and drew his lips down to hers, whispering, "You will be."

It was his undoing. All thought of stopping was swept aside as he captured her in a searing kiss. He moved slowly, but with great deliberation, until somehow—she was not sure how they managed it—their hips met, and he was fully sheathed within her.

"I love you," she said, before he could ask if she was all right. She wanted no more questions, just passion. He began to move again, and they tumbled into a rhythm that brought them to the edge of their precipice.

And then, in a moment of blinding beauty, she quivered and tightened around him. He buried his face in her neck to muffle his shout, and he thrust forward one last time, spilling himself within her.

They breathed. It was all either of them could do. They breathed, and then they slept.

HUGH AWAKENED FIRST, and once he assured himself that they were still several hours from dawn, he allowed himself the simple luxury of lying on his side and watching Sarah sleep. After several minutes, however, he could no longer ignore the cramping in his leg. It had been quite some time since he'd used his muscles in such a manner, but while the exertions were delightful, the aftermath was not.

Moving slowly so as not to wake Sarah, he slid himself into a sitting position, stretching his injured limb before him. Wincing, he dug his fingers into the muscle, kneading through the stiffness. He'd done this countless times; he knew exactly how to locate a knot and jab his thumb into it— *hard*—until the muscle quivered and relaxed. It hurt like the devil, but it was an oddly good sort of pain.

When his fingers grew tired, he switched to the heel of his hand, moving it against his leg in a tight, circular motion. This was followed by a firm, sweeping motion, then—

"Hugh?"

He turned at the sleepy sound of Sarah's voice. "It's all right," he said with a smile. "You can go back to sleep."

"But . . ." She yawned.

"It's hours yet until morning." He leaned down and kissed the top of her head, then returned to his slowly relaxing muscle, going back to using his thumbs against the knots.

"What are you doing?" She yawned again, pulling herself into a slightly more upright position.

"It's nothing."

"Does your leg hurt?"

"Just a bit," he lied. "But it's much improved now." Which wasn't a lie. It was feeling almost well enough for him to consider exercising it in exactly the manner that had got him into this situation.

"May I try?" she asked quietly.

He turned in surprise. It had never occurred to him that she might wish to minister to him in such a manner. His leg was not pretty; between the fracture and the bullet (and the doctor's ungraceful probing to remove the bullet), he'd been left with skin that was puckered and scarred, pulled tight over a muscle that no longer held the long, smooth shape it had been born with.

"I might be able to help you," she said in a soft voice.

His lips parted, but no words emerged. His hands were covering the worst of his scars, and he could not seem to lift them from his leg. It was dark, and he knew she would not be able to see the angry, pinching welts, at least not well.

But they were ugly. And they were an ugly reminder of the most selfish mistake of his life.

"Tell me what to do," she said, placing her hands near his.

He nodded jerkily and covered one of her

hands with his own. "Here," he said, directing her toward the most intransigent of the knots.

She pressed her fingers down but with not nearly enough pressure. "Is that all right?"

He used his hand to push hers down harder. "Like this."

She caught her lower lip between her teeth and tried again, this time reaching that awful spot deep in what was left of his muscle. He groaned, and she immediately let up. "Did I—"

"No," he said, "it's good."

"All right." She gave him a hesitant look and got back to work, pausing every few seconds to stretch her fingers.

"Sometimes I use my elbow," he told her, still feeling somewhat self-conscious.

She looked at him curiously, then gave a little shrug and tried his suggestion.

"Oh, my God," he moaned, falling back against the pillows. Why did this feel so much better when someone else did it?

"I have an idea," she said. "Lie on your side."

Honestly, he didn't think he could move. He managed to lift one hand, but only for a second. He was boneless. There couldn't possibly be another explanation.

She chuckled and rolled him herself, turning him away from her so that his injured leg was on top. "You should stretch it," she said, and she held his knee in place as she bent his leg, bringing his ankle to his buttocks.

Or rather, halfway there.

"Are you all right?" she asked.

He nodded, shaking from the pain. But it was—Well, maybe not a good pain, but a useful one. He could feel something loosening in his flesh, and when he lay again on his back and she gently massaged the aching muscle, it almost felt as if something angry was leaving him, rising through his skin and lifting away from his soul. His leg throbbed, but his heart felt lighter, and for the first time in years, the world seemed to be filled with possibility.

"I love you," he said. And he thought to himself, *That makes five.* Five times he'd said it. It wasn't nearly enough.

"And I love you." She bent down and kissed his leg.

He touched his face and felt tears. He hadn't realized he was crying. "I love you," he said again.

Six.

"I love you."

Seven.

She looked up with a perplexed smile.

He touched her nose. "I love you."

"What are you doing?"

"Eight," he said aloud.

"What?"

"That makes eight times I've said it. I love you."

"You're counting?"

"It's nine now, and"—he shrugged—"I always count. You should know that by now."

"Don't you think you should finish the night with an even ten?"

"It was morning before you got here, but yes, you're right. And I love you."

"You've said it ten times," she said, coming close for a soft, slow kiss. "But what I want to know is—how many times have you *thought* it?"

"Impossible to count," he said against her lips.

"Even for you?"

"Infinite," he murmured, sliding her back down to the mattress. "Or maybe . . ."

Infinity plus one.

Epilogue

Pleinsworth House
London
The following spring

MARRIAGE OR DEATH: the only two ways to avoid conscription into the Smythe-Smith Quartet. Or perhaps more accurately: the only two ways to extricate oneself from its clutches.

Which was why no one could understand (except Iris, but more on that later) how it came to pass that in three hours the Smythe-Smith Quartet would take the "stage" for their annual musicale, and Lady Sarah Prentice, recently married and very much alive, was going to have to sit down at the pianoforte, grit her teeth, and play.

The irony, Honoria had said to Sarah, was exquisite.

No, Sarah had said to Hugh, the irony was not exquisite. The irony should have been beaten with a cricket bat and stamped into the ground.

If irony had a corporeal form, of course. Which it didn't, much to Sarah's disappointment. The urge to swing a cricket bat at something other than a cricket ball was positively life-altering.

But there were no bats available in the Pleinsworth music room, so she had instead appropriated the bow to Harriet's violin and was using it in the way God had surely intended.

To threaten Daisy.

"Sarah!" Daisy shrieked.

Sarah growled. She actually growled.

Daisy ran for cover behind the pianoforte. "Iris, make her stop!"

Iris raised a brow as if to say, *Do you really think I would rise from this chair to help you, my exceedingly annoying younger sister, today of all days?*

And yes, Iris did know how to say all that with a quirk of the brow. It was a remarkable talent, really.

"All I did," Daisy pouted, "was say that she could have a slightly better attitude. I mean, really."

"In retrospect," Iris said in a very dry voice, "that may have not been the best choice of words."

"She's going to make us look bad!"

"*She*," Sarah said menacingly, "is the only reason you have a quartet."

"I still find it difficult to believe that we did not have anyone available to take Sarah's place on the pianoforte," Daisy said.

Iris gaped at her. "You say that as if you suspect Sarah of foul play."

"Oh, she has good reason to suspect foul play," Sarah said, advancing with the bow.

"We're running out of cousins," Harriet said, briefly looking up from her notes. She had spent the entire altercation writing everything down. "After me there is only Elizabeth and Frances before we must turn to a new generation."

Sarah gave Daisy one final glare before returning Harriet's bow. "I'm not doing this again," she warned. "I don't care if you have to shrink to a trio. The only reason I'm playing this year is—"

"Because you felt guilty," Iris said. "Well, you do," she added when her comment was met with nothing but silence. "You still feel guilty about abandoning us last year."

Sarah opened her mouth. It was her natural inclination to argue when accused of something, wrongfully or not. (And in this case, not.) But then she saw her husband, standing in the doorway with a smile on his face and a rose in his hand, and instead she said, "Yes. Yes, I do."

"You do?" Iris asked.

"I do. I'm sorry to you, and you"—she nodded toward Daisy—"and probably to you, too, Harriet."

"She didn't even play last year," Daisy said.

"I'm her older sister. I'm sure I owe her an apology for *some*thing. And if you'll all excuse me, I'm leaving with Hugh."

"But we're practicing!" Daisy protested.

Sarah gave her a jolly wave. "Ta-ta!"

" 'Ta-ta?' " Hugh murmured in her ear as they made their way out of the music room. "You say 'ta-ta'?"

"Only to Daisy."

"You really are a good egg," he said. "You didn't have to play this year."

"No, I think I did." She would never admit it aloud, but when she realized that she was the only person capable of saving the annual musicale . . . Well, she couldn't let it *die*. "Tradition is important," she said, hardly able to believe the words that were coming from her mouth. But she had changed since falling in love. And besides . . .

She took Hugh's hand and placed it on her abdomen. "It could be a girl."

It took him a moment. And then: "Sarah?"

She nodded.

"A baby?"

She nodded again.

"When?"

"November, I should think."

"A baby," he said again, as if he couldn't quite believe it.

"You shouldn't be so surprised," she teased. "After all—"

"She'll need to play an instrument," he interrupted.

"*She* might be a boy."

Hugh looked down at her with dry humor. "That would be most unusual."

She laughed. Only Hugh would make such a joke. "I love you, Hugh Prentice."

"And I love you, Sarah Prentice."

They resumed their walk toward the front door, but after only two steps, Hugh leaned down and murmured in her ear, "Two thousand."

And Sarah, because she was Sarah, chuckled and said, "Is that all?"

Do you love historical fiction?

Want the chance to hear news about your favourite authors (and the chance to win free books)?

Mary Balogh
Charlotte Betts
Jessica Blair
Frances Brody
Gaelen Foley
Elizabeth Hoyt
Eloisa James
Lisa Kleypas
Stephanie Laurens
Claire Lorrimer
Sarah MacLean
Amanda Quick
Julia Quinn

Then visit the Piatkus website and blog
www.piatkus.co.uk | www.piatkusbooks.net

And follow us on Facebook and Twitter
www.facebook.com/piatkusfiction | www.twitter.com/piatkusbooks

piatkus